Red Corona

Red Corona

Red Corona

Tim Glister

W F HOWES LTD

This large print edition published in 2022 by
W F Howes Ltd
Unit 5, St George's House, Rearsby Business Park,
Gaddesby Lane, Rearsby, Leicester LE7 4YH

1 3 5 7 9 10 8 6 4 2

First published in the United Kingdom in 2020
by Point Blank

A CIP catalogue record for this book is available
from the British Library

ISBN 978 1 00409 403 5

Typeset by Palimpsest Book Production Limited,
Falkirk, Stirlingshire

Printed and bound by
T J Books in the UK

PROLOGUE

Everyone on the **Shining Emerald** was bored. The captain of the small Mexican fishing trawler's arms ached from holding the same position off the California coast for the last three hours. The crew hadn't thrown out any nets for days and were stiff from inaction. Even the KGB officer standing alone on the forward deck had grown weary of endlessly searching the sky for a sign of his target.

For the last six months, instead of sailing south out of the Sea of Cortez to the fertile waters of the southern Pacific, every few weeks the **Shining Emerald** had left its home port of La Paz, rounded the Baja peninsula, and headed north. Always to the same spot fifty nautical miles out to sea, and always with a KGB officer aboard.

The Russian held a pair of binoculars to his eyes, scanning the sky. He completed a wide arc, dropped his head a few degrees, and began again. The work wasn't hard, but it was tiring, on his eyes and his mind.

He was anxious. Mexico was supposed to have been an easy posting. America was busy obsessing over the Caribbean turning red and for once its

1

politicians and spies weren't paying attention to its southern neighbour, which meant neither were Russia's. That was until the Cold War turned into a space race.

Arc after arc he saw nothing but bright blue until, on what felt like the hundredth sweep of the sky, he spotted a distant glint. He gently stroked the large dial on the top of the binoculars and slowly, very slowly, it began to change shape and come into focus. Suddenly there it was: a parachute no more than five metres across. Hanging beneath it was a silver cone-shaped canister with the letters **NASA** written in dark red along its side – the payload capsule of a Corona spy satellite.

'Hello, **Falling Star**,' the KGB officer whispered to himself.

The **Shining Emerald**'s crew sensed a change in the Russian, from tense frustration to anticipation, and finally began to prepare their nets. Moments later a familiar droning sound started to fill the air. A US Air Force Hercules C-130 transport plane was rapidly approaching from the California coast.

'**Star Catcher**.' Another nickname.

The Hercules wasn't as large or elegant as its Soviet counterpart, the Tupolev Tu-95 with its swept-back wings and chromed, missile-shaped fuselage, but the Russian had to admit it was an impressive beast.

It had taken the KGB months to find out exactly what Corona was, and where it was operating from, after a Soviet submarine stumbled on a jettisoned test capsule in the Arctic Ocean near Svalbard. Their breakthrough came when an informant at Cooke Air Force Base outside Lompoc, California, reported that one of the Hercules transports stationed there was undergoing a very strange refit.

As the KGB officer watched the American plane fly over the trawler its rear cargo door opened and a large hooped hook extended from it, snaking out into space.

The Hercules had been sent to retrieve the Corona payload as it fell through the sky. It slowed down as it closed on its prey, letting its hook fall beneath it. It swooped mere metres over the parachute, but failed to snag the thin guidelines. The plane banked, lined up again, and missed again.

When the Hercules came back round for a third pass, the crew of the **Shining Emerald** started to smell a catch. And the Russian started to hope. He'd already watched the Americans snatch their capsule out of thin air twice. If he reported a third failed mission to the KGB **residentura** in Mexico City he wasn't sure what would happen to him – a demotion if he was lucky, a trip somewhere far less hospitable than Mexico or Moscow if he wasn't.

The captain swung the wheel and pushed the throttle. If the Hercules missed again and the capsule splashed down, the **Shining Emerald** would only have a few minutes to grab it off the ocean surface before its salt plug dissolved, flooding it and consigning it to the depths.

'Andale! Andale!' the crew chanted as one. In the sudden excitement of the race the KGB officer didn't know if they were begging their captain or the Americans to go faster.

The Hercules had one last chance. It went into a steep dive, racing the capsule and the trawler to the splashdown point. For a terrifying moment, the Russian wondered if the Americans were going to ram the capsule and maybe even the **Shining Emerald,** destroying them both rather than letting the KGB capture the precious secrets the spy satellite had dropped from orbit.

But at the last second the plane flattened out, barely ten metres above the water. Then it pulled up, inclining over the capsule so the parachute grazed and snagged on the underside of the fuselage. The payload smacked against the Hercules until the force of the plane thrusting up into the sky shook the parachute loose and at last it was caught by the hook and swept up behind the plane.

A minute later, the Hercules disappeared back over the horizon towards California, leaving the **Shining Emerald** and the KGB officer sitting alone in the middle of the ocean.

JULY 1961

CHAPTER ONE

The Gresham Arms was not a salubrious establishment.

A casual observer might assume it had seen better days, but it hadn't. Tucked away in a quiet backstreet off Whitehall, it had struggled to deliver its various owners any kind of profit for two hundred years. But, from the height of Empire and through two world wars, its doors had opened at the same time every day, offering the same three things to whoever needed them – time, space, and a drink.

Richard Knox wasn't a regular. In fact, he'd only been to the Gresham Arms once before. But sitting alone at a corner table, two empty pint glasses in front of him and another well on its way at one o'clock in the afternoon, he looked like he belonged. His tie was loose, the top button of his shirt undone. His suit jacket had been discarded on the stool next to him. His face was drawn, and his thick black hair, normally kept in place with a heavy pomade, had fallen over his forehead, concealing the old scar that stuck out from his hairline above his left temple. He looked like someone had recently done a number on him, because they had.

Two weeks ago Knox had been the darling of MI5. The officer who had broken the Calder Hall Spy Ring, a network of Soviet sympathisers who had been passing classified information about the nuclear plant at Sellafield in Cumbria to the KGB. Two hours ago he had been summarily suspended from the Service, escorted from its headquarters in Leconfield House in Mayfair, and found himself walking the short distance to the Gresham Arms. It was a sunny morning, but he'd felt very much out in the cold.

The breaking of the Calder Hall network – made up of Nigel Slaughter, a security guard at the nuclear plant, Patrick Montcalm, a travelling salesman, and Sandra and Peter Horne, a retired couple in Richmond with a house full of radio equipment and one-time code pads – had been a major triumph for Knox.

Rumours had lingered about Soviet infiltration of MI6 ever since Guy Burgess and Donald Maclean had disappeared from a trip on the cross-Channel ferry SS *Falaise* and popped up in Moscow a decade ago. Then those same quiet voices had started talking about moles in MI5. It was Knox's job to find any leaks and, if they existed, stop them.

Both Knox and James Holland, the director general of MI5, were convinced that groups like Calder Hall couldn't flourish without someone inside the intelligence community supporting them, and that breaking the network would be a crucial step in discovering whoever this invisible someone was. But three days ago, on the night of Sunday 9 July, Holland had been found unconscious and unresponsive on the floor of the living room in his Highgate home by his wife, Sarah. His personal diary showed that he was supposed to be having dinner with Knox, his loyal deputy, but Knox hadn't appeared.

For two days Knox was grilled by interrogators in Leconfield House, and, he assumed, shadowed by Watchers, the Service's leg men, whose job it was to keep an eye on persons of interest. Knox refused again and again to admit where he'd been on Sunday night, claiming that Holland himself had sworn him to secrecy. Eventually, the interrogators gave up, and a summary review board was convened. Knox didn't expect to emerge unscathed, and he didn't.

He took another swig of his beer. It was warm and flat. He needed another one.

'Well, that didn't take long,' a voice above him said.

Knox looked up from his glass at Nicholas Peterson.

'Come to rub it in, Nicholas?'

'The DG wants to see you,' Peterson replied. His voice was a clipped, officious staccato.

Peterson was the right-hand man of Gordon Manning, the newly installed acting director

9

general. His garish Prince of Wales check suit, currently in fashion among a certain type of civil servant, looked very out of place in the middle of the Gresham Arms. Peterson was, according to Knox, a subservient, bureaucratic yes-man who had no business being anywhere near MI5. They did not get on.

'You just suspended me.'

'The Service suspended you.'

'Of course.' Knox reached out to finish the dregs of his beer, but thought better of it. 'What do you want?' he asked.

'I don't want anything,' Peterson replied, 'Manning does.'

'Well, he knows where to find me.'

'Don't be tedious, Richard. He's offering you a way back in.'

'Really? Thanks, but I think I'm done.'

'You're done when the Service says you're done. You're suspended, not fired,' Peterson said. 'And when you are fired, you'll have a résumé almost entirely covered by the Official Secrets Act.'

Knox caved. He knew Peterson was right. He couldn't just walk away from MI5 after fifteen years, and deep down he didn't want to.

'Where?' he asked.

'Deptford.'

'Jesus,' Knox said, smoothing back his hair and picking up his jacket. 'It must be serious.'

CHAPTER TWO

The further east they went, the worse the city looked. From the alabaster facades of Mayfair and Westminster to the shuttered shops and Blitz bomb craters of Lewisham, Knox watched the city decline through the window of Peterson's MI5 standard-issue Ford Consul as he did his best to sober up.

'We've never had it so good,' he said to himself, parroting Harold Macmillan's favourite slogan as he watched an old, broken-backed woman lean over to brush her cracked and pitted front step. Peterson ignored him.

Half an hour after leaving Whitehall the car pulled into a narrow turning off Deptford High Street and stopped outside a low-rise tenement block.

Knox and Peterson made their way up the dim staircase to the top floor. Peterson watched his step as they plunged into darkness between landings, making sure he never came close to touching the walls, the banister, or the half-hidden bits of detritus littering the stairs.

The higher they got, the more stale and warm

the air became. At first, Knox thought this was just a lack of airflow in the old building conspiring with the summer afternoon heat. But, as they walked down the short corridor to the only open door, he began to suspect otherwise. And, as Peterson stepped into the flat ahead of him and doubled over, retching, his suspicion was confirmed.

In the hallway of the flat were two bodies. The odour was now pungent, acrid, familiar. Knox had seen, and smelled, death enough during the war to not be shocked by it now. Apparently Peterson hadn't. Whoever these people were, they'd been lying there for a while.

Knox was curious about what two dead bodies might have to do with him. He was also curious about why there were no police officers or forensics team present but the acting director general of MI5 was. Gordon Manning emerged from a door at the end of the hallway that ran the length of the flat. He stopped for a moment on the other side of the bodies, looking at Knox and Peterson, then beckoned them to follow him as he ducked back into the room he'd just stepped out of.

Manning was a tall man. Too tall, and thin. He'd never carried either well. The three-piece grey worsted suits he insisted on wearing whatever the weather always hung off his skeletal frame, their jacket pockets bagging slightly from his habit of planting his long, bony hands in them.

Knox looked down at the corpses as he stepped around them. The bodies were neat, lying next to each other, their legs straight and arms by their sides. The men's clothes were plain, dark, normal. They looked like the type of people you'd pass on the street without noticing, except that their mouths and noses were wet with some kind of liquid and they both had thick marks across their necks.

'Thank you for coming, Richard,' Manning said, as Knox stepped into the small room. 'Though I suspect you're wondering why you're here.'

'Actually, I'm wondering why you're here, sir,' Knox replied.

'Those men out there,' Manning said. 'I want to know who killed them.'

'Why?' No *sir* this time.

'They were troublemakers, Italians,' he said, as if that was explanation enough. 'Camillo Bianchi and Piero Moretti. Liked breaking into electronic systems, then holding people to ransom to find out how they'd done it. Five has been keeping an eye for some time.'

Manning slowly circled the room, as if showing it off to Knox. It had been set up as an office. A small desk strewn with a mess of papers, a few boxes stacked in a corner, and an empty bookcase.

'They'd been pitching themselves all over,' Manning continued. 'National Provincial Bank, British Petroleum, even tried to get a meeting at the Ministry of Defence. After they briefly interrupted a BBC Overseas Service broadcast, the director of radio passed on their information to us.'

Knox took another look at what potential evidence the room had to offer. There wasn't much.

'They sound like chancers,' he said. 'With a couple of clever tricks.'

'Perhaps, but those tricks were making them rather well known in some circles. People were starting to pay attention to them. Serious people. Then they seemed to drop off the face of the earth. Now we know why.'

'The coroner estimates they've been dead between forty-eight and seventy-two hours,' said Peterson, stepping through the door, face still as grey as the dead men's. 'But he can't be more precise about time, or cause, until he's done an autopsy.'

'Can't the Watchers give you a smaller window?' Knox asked.

'They were on light surveillance. Weekly check-ins only.'

'Sounds like they weren't much of a priority.'

'They weren't,' Peterson said, the colour slowly returning to his face.

'So, my original question,' Knox said, turning to Manning. 'Why are you here?'

Manning slid his hands into his pockets. 'I'm here because of you,' he said. 'I need to know what happened to these men, and I need to know quickly. Five is stretched preparing for the OECD conference, but you aren't.'

In less than a week's time, London would be

hosting the inaugural conference of the Organisation for Economic Co-Operation and Development. It was a major political event, bringing leaders from nineteen of the world's most powerful nations together in one city, and the primary reason Whitehall had been so fast to put someone else at the top of MI5. Manning was one of the Service's longest-serving officers. Like Holland, he'd worked for MI5 through the war and ever since. He'd also gone to Eton and Oxford with most of the cabinet. He was the obvious choice.

'You also have a personal interest in finding the solution to this little puzzle,' Manning said.

'I do?' Knox asked.

'I know you think I'm working for the Russians.'

Knox didn't rise to Manning's bait. But he also didn't deny his accusation. Knox had a short list of possible moles operating at the highest level of MI5 – people who would have enough access to sensitive information to compromise the Service, and enough power to act without scrutiny and cover their tracks – and Manning was at the top of it.

'It's a natural conclusion to reach,' Manning continued. 'Particularly with my rather unconventional elevation to DG.'

'It's one possible conclusion,' Knox replied, eliciting a thin smile from Manning.

'And this,' Manning said, gesturing around him, 'bears all the marks of a KGB hit squad.'

Knox had to concede that what he'd seen so far

– the lack of forced entry or disturbance, and the neatness of the bodies – fitted the Soviet security agency's modus operandi.

'For all we know,' Manning continued, 'they're quietly up to things like this all over the city. Lord knows they're enjoying keeping us on our toes at the moment, sending that cosmonaut of theirs to take photos with the PM.'

While Knox was being questioned about Holland in Leconfield House, Major Yuri Gagarin, the first human to slip the surly bonds of Earth and successfully orbit the planet in the Russian *Vostok 3KA* space capsule, was being entertained by Macmillan at the end of a highly publicised trip to London. It had been a coup for Russia, and a very large headache for MI5 and the Metropolitan Police.

Manning pulled his hands out of his pockets and made a brief, ineffective show of patting them back into place.

'The point is,' he said, 'if it is the Russians behind all this, you'll do your damnedest to find a connection to me, and when you can't this mole hunt can be put to bed and we'll all be able to get on with our jobs.'

And with that, Manning made his way out of the flat, trailed by Peterson. He paused briefly at the front door, turning back and looking at Knox across the bodies.

'I'm throwing you a bone, Richard,' he said. 'Possibly your last one.'

CHAPTER THREE

Irina Valera was running late. She knew she was late because by the time she reached the gates of her son Ledjo's school, he was the only child left waiting to be collected.

When Ledjo saw his mother finally arrive, he quietly walked across the small concrete playground to her and, saying nothing, held out his hand for her to take. It might have looked like the six-year-old was so angry he was giving his mother the silent treatment. But he wasn't. He was just obeying one of the many rules of life in Povenets B.

Valera and Ledjo walked in shared silence, hand in hand, down the wide tarmac strip that doubled as road and pavement, and stretched from the centre of town to the small bungalow they called home. The buildings changed the closer they got, becoming more uniform until each one was identical to the last. The outskirts of Povenets B were made up of row after row of single-storey homes, with clapboard walls, flat shingle roofs, and five metres of empty scrub between them. Beyond the outermost row of bungalows stood two three-metre high fences, topped with barbed wire and

17

patrolled day and night to stop anyone from entering or leaving.

Nestled in thick forest at the top of Lake Onega in the semi-autonomous region of Karelia near the Finnish border, Povenets B wasn't on any maps. It was so secret it hadn't even been found by the stray street dogs that were a permanent feature of towns and villages all over Russia. And if Povenets B looked like an internment camp, it was because that's exactly what it had been. And in Valera's mind it still was.

Povenets B had started life as a prison, a remote set of grey huts where members of the Karelian population who hadn't sufficiently demonstrated their commitment to the Soviet cause were indefinitely interred. Since then it had grown in fits and starts. Larger, equally grey slabs of buildings were hastily erected; drab, prefabricated housing extended the original grid of prison blocks; basic roads were laid. Then the fence had gone up.

Povenets B was now a *naukograd*, a science city closed off from the outside world and administered by the GRU, the Soviet Union's foreign military intelligence directorate.

As World War Two had given way to the Cold War, all sensitive state-sponsored operations like advanced scientific research, nuclear development, and weapons testing had been moved to secure locations across the Soviet Union. Some closed cities were little more than a factory with a few cabins for housing workers; others were entire

18

cities, either built almost from scratch, like Povenets B, or simply redesignated, like Perm or Vladivostok, with fences and sentry posts surrounding them seemingly overnight.

Three years ago a member of the GRU had approached Valera outside Andrei Zhdanov University in Leningrad and made her the same offer that had been extended to a select group of academics across the country – to leave her low salary and cold apartment for the higher standards of living and unlimited research budgets of a *naukograd*. Facing another bitter winter in a draughty, underheated two-room home at the top of a housing block that somehow managed to bear the brunt of winds from the Baltic and the Arctic, Valera decided she couldn't refuse. Along with fifty other families, she and Ledjo moved to Povenets B. She soon regretted her decision.

A quarter of the homes in Povenets B were old prison barracks, and the rest had been built in the same utilitarian style. Valera and Ledjo's bungalow was one of the prefabricated additions. It had looked solid enough when they'd first arrived, but a few Karelian winters had revealed just how fragile it was. The walls were paper-thin, wind crept between the door and windows, and the water pipes that had been left running along the outside of it were bent and rusted from exposure.

There was a school for Ledjo, but so few teachers that all the children were taught together. There was no hospital, and only one food shop, which, depending on the day, might or might not be stocked.

All *naukograds* were expected to generate their own energy, a necessity both for security and because they tended to be built away from established supply lines. Povenets B's power plant was by far its largest building. It was three storeys of dark concrete, patterned by stains from months of sun and more of ice; black, painted pipes that were big enough for a full-grown man to walk through and which seemed to knot through each other; and a tall, stretched-out cooling tower that for much of the day cast a deep shadow on the smaller structures next to it, including the school.

Valera had never understood why Povenets B's planners had put these two buildings next to each other. There was some kind of minor emergency at the plant every day, and power cuts were a regular occurrence. But whenever she voiced her concerns she was informed that infrastructure policy was none of her concern.

Major Yuri Zukolev, the GRU administrator in charge of Povenets B, treated the city like a medieval fiefdom, and its scientists and their families as his personal serfs. Povenets B was a long way from Moscow and the prying eyes of Zukolev's superiors, and as long as he kept the peace, didn't ask for too much money, and delivered regular, positive progress reports, he was mostly left to run the *naukograd* as he saw fit. His chosen methods involved regimenting daily life down to half-hour intervals, restricting the supply of food to encourage obedience, and constantly demanding that the scientists under his care produced more results with fewer resources.

One of the sirens that marked the passing of another half-hour blasted from a tower next to the power plant as Valera and Ledjo stepped through the door into their modest little home. As the door shut behind them they both let out a high-pitched scream, shook their bodies, and gave each other a big hug.

'Hello, Pikku,' Valera said, using her pet name for her son.

'Hello, Mama,' Ledjo replied, squeezing her waist tight.

Valera helped Ledjo take off his worn school shoes, which were at least a size too small, then followed him into their spartan living room, waiting for him to climb onto their sofa – the one seat in the room – before jumping on top of him. They both giggled together. Valera pretended she couldn't feel her son's ribs pressing into her as she tickled him.

'Mama,' Ledjo said, when Valera had stopped gently attacking his sides. 'Teacher told us today that we have conquered space and all the stars are ours. Is that true?'

Valera grinned, leaned in close to Ledjo, and whispered 'no' in his ear. She could never have said anything as inflammatory as that single word outside, but in the privacy of her own home she was free to rebel a little.

21

Ledjo's face turned into a thoughtful frown.

'That must be why we have to hide under our desks every day,' he said. 'Because of the Mercan bombs.'

She wanted to tell him it wasn't the American bombs he should be worried about, but some trigger-happy major accidentally launching one of theirs. But there'd be hell to pay if he accidentally repeated something so un-Soviet in the playground or classroom.

It was now past the *naukograd*'s unofficial curfew. They had nowhere to go, but for the rest of the day they were safe from prying eyes and ears. Valera would make them a stew on their single-flame stove with whatever food they had in the kitchen, and they would play games they made up or tell each other stories, pretending to paint them on the living room's bare white walls until it was time for Ledjo to go to bed.

For Valera and Ledjo's first six months in Povenets B life had been very different. Zukolev had gone out of his way to make things pleasant for them. They were his favourites. They were invited to events at his home – the only two-storey house in the *naukograd* – with senior scientists. Ledjo was allowed to play in the major's immaculately kept garden. They were even occasionally given extra meat from the monthly supply delivery. Karelia itself even wanted them to feel welcome, stretching out the warm autumn.

But one morning at the school gates, just as the winter chill was starting to bite, Valera noticed the same look on the faces of several of the other mothers – a mix of pity and disgust. Valera was the only woman in Povenets B who wasn't just a wife or mother, and she had no friends among the other women to ask what the look meant. But one of them was kind enough to whisper 'whore' as she walked past Valera two mornings later.

Valera had brought a lie with her when she'd come to Povenets B, and she'd trapped herself in it. Ledjo had been the result of a brief affair with a young Red Army officer. The relationship had been intense, but when Valera told her lover she was pregnant and wanted to get married, he told her to get rid of the baby and then left himself. Valera didn't want an abortion, but she also didn't want a child who would have to grow up with the stigma of being a bastard. So, she invented another end to the story of the Red Army officer, which involved him dying tragically in service of Soviet glory.

She'd forgotten that the role of the mourning, withdrawn widow was one she was supposed to play for the rest of her life, until the stranger at the school gates had reminded her. They'd also made her realise that she wasn't Zukolev's favourite at all. She was his prey. She was the only single woman and only single parent in Povenets B, and she'd let herself be manoeuvred into a position that made both her and Ledjo extremely vulnerable.

Finally seeing the real agenda beneath Zukolev's kindness, Valera refused his next invitation to dinner, and sent away the man who appeared at her door with two plucked chickens the following night.

Zukolev's behaviour changed instantly. He became as cold as the winter wind that rattled through Valera's bungalow and chattered Ledjo's milk teeth. For the next eighteen months he delighted in making her life difficult, reminding her at every opportunity that he had the power to make it – and Ledjo's – even worse whenever he wanted. He would sporadically summon her to his office to tell her that her research was too slow, too expensive, or just outright useless. It didn't matter that he had no comprehension of the particular area of radio wave physics to which Valera had dedicated every last bit of her energy and life that wasn't already given to Ledjo.

Over the last year their run-ins had become more frequent, and they now averaged one a week. Moscow had started to put pressure on Zukolev, so he was heaping it on her. Even locked away in the depths of Karelia, news from the outside world filtered through. Valera knew that America's desire to win the space race was as strong as Russia's. And she guessed scientists somewhere in the West were working on the same problems she'd been tasked with solving to help their side achieve a final, insurmountable victory.

'What shall we have for supper, Pikku?' Valera

asked Ledjo as she untangled herself from his arms.

'Caviar!' Ledjo cried. 'Goose!'

'Of course, Pikku. Anything for you.'

Valera left Ledjo to lose himself his imagination, and scoured the dark kitchen cupboards for any potatoes or grains that might have magically appeared in them.

Years surviving on a subsistence diet had taken its toll on Valera. She was thin, and her skin was pale. The almond eyes that her mother had told her were so beautiful when she was young now looked like they belonged to someone far older. And her hair, which had never been thick but once upon a time had shone with life, hung dull and limp around her shoulders.

Other women in Povenets B tried to disguise their deterioration, tying their brittle hair into elaborate plaits or squirrelling away their meagre supplies of butter and oil to give their faces an unnatural sheen. Valera did neither. She had no interest in pretending life in the *naukograd* was any better than it was.

She also didn't want anyone paying attention to her – especially Zukolev. But, as she took a blunt knife to halve an old beetroot she'd been saving to make a thin borscht, she realised it was ten days since she'd last had to face the commandant of this prison she was locked away in, and she was overdue a visit.

CHAPTER FOUR

After Manning had left Bianchi and Moretti's flat with Peterson at his heels, several MI5 officers arrived to pack up the scene and arrange transport of the bodies to a secure morgue.

Knox made his own way back into town. There were no black cabs on Deptford High Street, so he caught a train to London Bridge, then walked over the river to Bank and took the Central Line to Oxford Circus.

The Central Line in July was one of the least pleasant places to be in the whole of London. It was hot, pungent with the smell of stale bodies and cigarette smoke, and, somehow, always crowded. But it was also the fastest way across the city.

Less than an hour after leaving Deptford, he was walking the short distance from Oxford Circus to Berwick Street and Kemp House, the eighteen-storey high-rise block that towered over the centre of Soho.

The building had only been complete for a few months and Knox had been its first resident. When he'd seen the announcement by Westminster

Council about the block in the *Evening Standard* over a year ago he knew he had to live there, and he'd used some contacts to pull a few strings and cut a deal with the council to buy a flat on the top floor off the architect's plans.

His flat was made up of a single large living area wrapped by windows, which served as his kitchen, dining, and living room. The space looked austere but considered. There was nothing extraneous, and everything served a purpose. On one side of the room was a free-standing granite kitchen counter. On the other was a large marble dining table and chairs. Along the wall halfway between them a well-stocked drinks trolley sat next to a black leather and rosewood Eames lounger. Behind the open plan was an equally minimalist bedroom and en suite.

Of all the absences from the flat, one was particularly noticeable: a television. In less than a decade they'd become a feature of almost every British home, but Knox had never seen the appeal. He understood the excitement a little window on the world might offer people locked away in semi-detached houses up and down the country, but he saw more than his fair share of life on a daily basis.

Knox always said he liked living in Kemp House because it made him feel connected to the heart of the city. Holland had countered that he'd chosen it so he could see his enemies coming from a long way off. Knox admitted it was a little bit of both.

Ten minutes after arriving home and making himself a stiff gin and tonic to take the edge off the afternoon, there was a knock at his front door.

Knox didn't receive many visitors, which was another part of the attraction of living at the top of a high-rise. He valued his privacy, and still hadn't introduced himself to the building's few other residents. And should any of them want to learn more about him, all they'd find in any public records would be his name and job title at Avalon Logistics, one of the more prosaic cover company names used by members of MI5.

He checked his watch – a 1956 Omega with a silver body, clear face, and tan leather strap he'd treated himself to when Holland had been made director general and promoted him three years ago – and took a guess about who was calling on him at four in the afternoon.

He opened his door and proved himself right. A Watcher was standing in the hallway, holding a small crate.

'Is this everything?' Knox asked, fairly sure it wasn't.

'It's what I was told to bring. So it's what I brought.' The Watcher thrust the crate into Knox's hands and turned back to the lift without saying anything else. Knox let him go.

Back inside his flat, Knox emptied the crate onto the dining table and spread out the contents. He picked up the slim MI5 file on Bianchi and Moretti. It was scant. Copies of their passports, a few details about their daily routines, a police report for a night Moretti had spent in a cell for being drunk and disorderly a few months ago, and not much else.

Then, the rest of the crate: business cards for both men, an address book, and several bundles of paper, which Knox assumed must have been the ones scattered across the desk in their makeshift office.

Knox's instincts told him he'd been given the edited lowlights. Nothing jumped out to him that justified Manning's interest in their deaths, or even MI5's surveillance of them, as light as it might have been. Manning was already tying his hands behind his back. It was frustrating. But it was all Knox had to work with, so it was where he had to start.

The business cards were elegant, but didn't give away anything other than the Italians' names and their address, which Knox already knew. There was no company or mysterious foreign phone number to call. The address book contained the details of several high-profile organisations, but they all matched the list Manning had reeled off in their makeshift study. There were no curious omissions or additions.

Of the four bundles of papers, three of them were written entirely in Italian, which Knox had never learned. The fourth appeared to be a series of mathematical equations, advanced enough to use symbols rather than letters or numbers –

another language Knox couldn't read. It wouldn't have taken much to get the Italian pages translated. Knox only needed to walk a few hundred yards to Bar Italia, the twenty-four-hour Italian cafe on Frith Street, buy an espresso, and call in one of the many favours the cafe's waiters owed him. He knew he could rely on their tact – he'd owed them his fair share of favours over the years for secrets they'd kept and indiscretions they hadn't held against him – but he decided it probably wasn't worth the security risk in case the papers did end up containing something important. He'd have to send them on through official channels and wait for someone to be assigned to translating them.

The equations, however, he might be able to get help with sooner.

CHAPTER FIVE

Ledjo stood pressed against the front door, his nose rubbing the unvarnished wood and his mouth moving as he silently counted to himself. When he reached five he spun round and Valera, who had been creeping up on him from the kitchen, froze like a statue. He stared at her. Ledjo had inherited his mother's eyes, but also his father's, so they looked more like raindrops than almonds, with a slight upward curve at the edges that made him look permanently on the verge of breaking into a smile. He giggled and waited for her to make the slightest movement. She didn't budge.

He faced the door again, counting faster this time. When he turned back, Valera was already halfway across the living room. He started to spin round and round, giggling more with every turn until Valera reached him, scooped him up, and pulled him into a tight, bony hug.

'Be a good boy today at school,' she said into his neck.

'Yes, Mama.'

'I love you.'

'I love you too, Mama.'

She put him down and straightened his simple uniform of a white shirt and grey shorts.

'Goodbye, my little Pikku,' she said once she was done.

Then she took his hand in hers, opened the door, and stepped outside.

Ten minutes later she had delivered Ledjo to school and was heading back to her lab. As she passed the power plant, its own siren began to wail and men ran to deal with today's little crisis. Valera silenced the ever-present worry at the back of her mind that one morning the emergency at the plant would be really serious. Instead, she focused on the hope that she would get through the day without being summoned to see Zukolev. Unfortunately, when she reached her lab two of his goons were already there waiting for her.

Every ruble that came into Povenets B passed through Zukolev's office, and it showed – on both the man and room. Zukolev had grown fat on his excess. His GRU dress uniform, which he wore at all times, strained against his stomach, and his face was flushed red from too much rich meat and vodka.

His office was modelled on Stalin's own in the Kremlin, to which Zukolev had made a pilgrimage as a young GRU officer. The walls were covered in dark maroon wallpaper and hung with ugly paintings on revolutionary themes. A large wooden desk sat in the middle of the room. Marble busts of Lenin and Stalin stared at each other from either end.

Zukolev, of course, proclaimed his loyalty to Nikita Khrushchev, the current leader of the Soviet Union, but his heart belonged to Stalin. He had come of age at the height of Stalin's personality cult, and now that he had a little nation of his own to govern, he took his cues from the true father of the Soviet Union. However, where Stalin had been one of the shrewdest minds ever to rise to power in the long history of Russia and inspired devotion across the nation, Zukolev was heavily deluded about his own competence and how much the people of Povenets B loved him.

Valera sat on the single, small chair pushed against the wall opposite Zukolev's desk. She sat there for almost ten minutes while he silently pored over a stack of documents and fed himself from a large bowl of raspberries. It was a simple, childish power play, and one that Valera was extremely bored by after three years.

'Argon is a noble gas,' Zukolev finally said, his eyes still fixed on his papers.

'Yes,' Valera replied.

'That means it doesn't do anything.' He scooped up a handful of berries and tipped them into his mouth. He insisted on getting the best of the summer fruits that grew wild around Povenets B delivered to him every morning. No one else was allowed to forage for them, because no one apart

33

from Zukolev's lackeys were allowed to leave the *naukograd*.

Valera hesitated for a moment. 'Actually, it means that—' she started.

But before she could correct him, Zukolev slammed the report he was holding down on the desk and looked up at her.

'If it doesn't do anything,' he said. 'Why do you want five twenty-kilogram canisters of it?'

It was clear from his tone that he thought he'd caught Valera out. He hadn't. She tried to make her explanation for the supply request she'd put in a week ago as simple as possible.

'Argon is inert,' she said. 'It doesn't react to stimulation. However, it can cause a reaction in other things. It can, in certain circumstances, act like a catalyst.' She could already tell he wasn't following her. But he'd demanded she explain herself, so that's what she was going to do. 'It's an atmospheric gas. It makes up less than one per cent of the air we breathe, but we don't know exactly how much of it there is higher up. It doesn't affect radio waves near the surface of the planet, but in larger quantities it might.'

'You want to create different levels of the atmosphere?'

Valera, surprised that Zukolev appeared to have grasped the concept after all, nodded. 'I want to try.'

'Your job is to find a way to talk to space. Not go there, or bring it here.'

34

'I simply want to—'

'Is the ground not good enough for you?' He interrupted her again. 'Would you like us to put you on a rocket too? Spend untold millions of rubles so you can satisfy your curiosity?'

She couldn't resist the bait. 'I think it would make more sense to send scientists into space than someone who was chosen because he was short enough to fit in the cockpit.'

Zukolev slammed his hands down on the desk again. 'Major Gagarin is a hero of the Soviet Union!'

Yuri Gagarin was Zukolev's second idol after Stalin, though his affinity for Russia's most celebrated cosmonaut was primarily based on their shared first name. Valera knew this, and while she also knew better than to ever say anything critical about Stalin to Zukolev, Gagarin was a nerve she was happy to pinch to put him off balance.

Zukolev sighed deeply and squeezed the bridge of his nose with his fat thumb and forefinger, dramatically transforming in a moment from irate dictator to disappointed father. He pushed his chair back – it dragged loudly under his weight – and walked round his desk.

'We are a small part of a great family,' he said, raising his arms as if gesturing to the whole of the Soviet Union. The gold buttons on his jacket struggled to stay fastened. 'I want you to be happy, Irina. I want people to understand your genius. We must work together, to make life better for all of us, to protect each other from our enemies.'

He got closer and closer to her until Valera could see nothing but his large stomach and feel his sweet, heavy breath on her. His hand hovered over her shoulder, then drifted over to her face. She looked up at him before his palm could cup her chin and force her head upward. He met her stare, his eyes pleading. She could see the blood-red flesh of berries stuck between his teeth.

'But I can't protect you, or Ledjo,' he said, 'if you keep asking for things without giving anything back.'

It was a threat, and it didn't work. Valera had spent her whole life being threatened. Her family history was intimately connected with the darker side of the Soviet Union. Her father, a celebrated linguist who specialised in early Asian languages, had been killed in the Great Purge when Valera was eight years old, accused of being a spy for Chiang Kai-shek's nationalist China. Her mother, a gifted chemist, starved to death in the siege of Leningrad five years later. Valera herself only barely survived to see the city liberated. She was not a happy child of Mother Russia, and she was immune to intimidation.

'You cannot just keep experimenting,' Zukolev continued. 'Moscow is demanding results. And we must provide them.'

Valera had no desire to hear more of Zukolev's lecture and knew the quickest way to get out of his office would be to simply agree with everything he said and promise to do better.

'I believe I'm close to a breakthrough. I'm sure I can give Moscow everything they want . . .' She paused a moment for effect '. . . without any more resources.'

A broad smile spread across Zukolev's face. Victory was his.

'Very good,' he said.

He turned away and walked back towards his desk, a blunt signal that Valera was now free to go.

CHAPTER SIX

Malcolm White was stressed. One of Holland's ambitions had been to transform MI5 into a truly modern intelligence service that combined the best of both human and technological expertise. In Manning's new world order the pendulum was already swinging back towards something far more arcane, and MI5's head of research and development was not happy about it.

White, like Knox, had been one of the shining stars of MI5. In the three years that Holland had been director general, White had built up the Service's formidable research and development section from nothing to a point where it could rival America's and Russia's.

He was also the creator of Operation Pipistrelle. Pipistrelle, a top-secret bugging system, was MI5's most advanced piece of surveillance technology. It was the current jewel in the research and development department's crown, but Manning's first decision as acting director general had been to hand control of it over to his freshly appointed liaison to GCHQ, the UK's dedicated signals intelligence agency.

'If we aren't going to let our signals intelligence agency run our signals intelligence, then what's the point in having one?' Peterson, who had relayed Manning's orders, had said when White challenged him.

Intercepting communications and secreting listening devices in sensitive locations had been standard practice for every self-respecting security service since the war. But the technology was far from perfect. Devices were cumbersome, difficult to install, and easy to detect. A simple sweep for radio signals would reveal their presence, no matter how well they were hidden.

After the Americans had discovered 'The Thing', a passive listening device the KGB had buried in a wooden carving of the Great Seal of the United States given to the American ambassador in Moscow as a gesture of post-war friendship, intelligence agencies on either side of the Iron Curtain had been developing more advanced and less detectable bugs.

Operation Pipistrelle was the game-changer everyone was looking for. White had not only worked out a way to radically shrink MI5's listening devices so they could be installed in more places in less time and removed just as easily. He'd also introduced a failsafe into the bug's transmitters, which temporarily shut them down whenever a room was being swept.

When White had first unveiled Pipistrelle to Holland and Knox in its full miniature glory, they'd immediately seen its potential. Even the most secure rooms, buried deep in embassies and wrapped in layers of soundproofing, would become vulnerable to MI5 eavesdropping. Knox also couldn't believe how small and deceptively innocent it looked. Somehow White had managed to fit Pipistrelle's battery, aerial and transmitter in a simple square metal box half the size of Knox's thumb.

'How did you get it all in there?' Knox asked White as he nudged the tiny prototype across his palm with his fingertip.

'A lot of hard work,' White replied.

Pipistrelle was Britain's greatest intelligence weapon since Bletchley Park cracked the Enigma code, and was years beyond Venona, the joint project between the UK, America, and Australia that was still decrypting decades-old Soviet cables. For the last three years it had provided MI5 with invaluable intelligence and remained completely undetected. However, six months ago White had revealed the next step in Pipistrelle's evolution and it had driven a wedge between him and Knox.

'Our problem,' White had said when he presented his new proposal to Holland and Knox, 'is processing power. We need to be able to work on everything in one place, as soon as we get it.'

'You mean using a computer?' Knox asked.

'I've read the budget request,' Holland answered. 'He means more than that.'

'A supercomputer,' White replied. 'The University of Manchester's new Atlas machine is more powerful than anything IBM or CDC are working on in America, and far ahead of what we think the Russians are up to.'

The Atlas was built on a solid-state germanium transistor infrastructure, using 128 high speed index register and 680 kilobytes of memory, which was roughly the same amount of storage and processing power as every other computer in Britain put together.

Knox understood the value of technology – Pipistrelle had proven itself time and again – but he wasn't ready to hand everything over to it. He believed there were still some things machines just couldn't do.

'How many analysts could we hire for what this will cost?' he asked.

'Atlas can analyse much more information than a person, and in a fraction of the time,' White replied.

'But it can't make decisions, or draw conclusions.'

'Nor is it burdened by habit or narrow viewpoints,' White said, defensively. 'It uses every variable to make the most likely predictions.'

'Unfortunately,' Knox countered, 'our enemies don't tend to do the most likely things.'

Holland cut their argument short, approving White's request on the proviso that flesh-and-bone analysts would continue working on Pipistrelle intelligence and check everything that was run through Atlas.

It took almost a month for the research and development department deep in the bowels of Leconfield House to be turned into what was effectively one giant mainframe of blinking towers, cables, and stacks of index cards. By the time his team had finished enhancing and refining Atlas, White felt comfortable describing it as the most advanced computer on earth.

But now he was standing in front of its primary control panel, watching hundreds of thousands of pounds' worth of equipment do absolutely nothing. It had taken weeks to install Pipistrelle devices all over London ahead of the OECD conference, and thanks to Manning White had no idea what conversations any of them were listening in on.

The last person White wanted to see was Knox. He thought Knox wasn't just responsible for Holland's current condition, but his as well. And Knox was now very much *persona non grata* at MI5 headquarters, yet there he was, standing in the middle of what should have been one of its most secure departments.

White had wanted to give Knox a piece of his mind for several days. But instead of making a scene in front of his staff he simply smoothed back the thick shock of blond hair that had earned some distant ancestor of his their surname, straightened his jacket, and nodded towards his office door.

42

Before White could tell Knox exactly what he thought of him inside the small, gloomy room that had until recently been used for storage, Knox thrust the Italians' papers into his hands.

'These belonged to Bianchi and Moretti,' Knox said.

White's scientific curiosity immediately took over and he scanned the sheets for a moment before holding them out for Knox to take back.

'It looks like nonsense to me,' White replied.

'Don't be modest,' Knox said, trying to charm him. 'If anyone can make sense of this, you can.'

'I'm not, and I can't.'

'I know you don't exactly like me at the moment, Malcolm, but I need your help.'

'This has nothing to do with whether or not I like you,' White said, letting the sheets fall on his desk. 'I might think your obsession with Russian moles is a childish obsession. I might think you've betrayed the one man who deserves your complete loyalty. And I might think you're the reason I'm now stuck dealing with Manning and his cronies. But none of that has any bearing on the fact that these calculations don't make sense to me.'

'Then I'm sorry to have taken you away from your very important work,' Knox said, scooping up the papers and heading for the door.

It was already swinging closed behind him when White called out, 'Try Kaspar.'

'Who?' Knox asked, leaning back into the office.

'Dr Ludvig Kaspar. A German physicist up at Cambridge. One of the Dragons.'

'You think he'll know what they mean?'

'I honestly don't know if these symbols are some kind of code, or incredibly advanced maths, or total rubbish. But Kaspar had one of the most creative scientific minds in Europe once upon a time. If anyone can work out what this is, it'll be him.'

'Thanks,' Knox said. 'I owe you.'

'You owe Holland,' White replied.

Knox slipped back through the old fire exit that connected the subterranean car park to the rest of Leconfield House. He'd temporarily relieved one of the custodians of the master key for the building's emergency exits almost five years ago and made a copy. He'd been equal parts shocked and relieved to discover it still worked when he walked down the car park ramp ten minutes ago.

The car park smelled of old oil and stale air. He passed several grey and black Consuls, then the bays that housed the nicer cars of more senior officers. There were two empty spaces. One was his, which he'd never used – living in the centre of town, he saw no reason to own a car – the other belonged to Holland. At this time of day his dark green Bentley S2 should have been there, but it wasn't.

Knox walked unnoticed back up the car park's exit ramp and out into Mayfair.

When he made it back to Kemp House, there

was another Watcher waiting at his front door. This one handed Knox an envelope, sneered at him when he asked what was in it, and stepped into the closing lift before Knox had a chance to say anything else.

Knox didn't know if the silent treatment was just the traditional dislike Watchers had for their more menial tasks or a result of recent events. Given their low level in MI5's pecking order, the Watchers shouldn't know the details of Knox's review board and suspension. But if there was one place gossip spread faster than the halls of Parliament, it was the corridors of MI5's head-quarters. And if there was one person in the Service the Watchers weren't inclined to like, it was Knox. At the same time as Holland had been fighting to modernise MI5, Knox had made it his mission to retrain the Watchers, breaking them out of the stale techniques they used in their never-ending games of cat and mouse with foreign operatives. The Watchers considered themselves part of an ancient brotherhood and very much resented the interference from someone who wasn't one of their own.

The envelope contained a preliminary autopsy report on the Italians, and it threw up about as many questions as everything else about their deaths did.

Knox poured himself a drink and tried to make sense of it. The coroner now believed they had died closer to seventy-two hours before being discovered, which explained the slick liquid Knox had seen around their noses and mouths – it was lung fluid, expelled as rigor mortis started to wear off. The marks on the men's necks suggested they'd been choked to death, but on closer inspection their windpipes showed no signs of being crushed. Toxicology tests were being run but the results would take another day to come through.

So, Knox didn't know anything about the two dead men beyond the most basic information. He didn't know how they'd been killed, or why. It was hard for him not to feel like Manning was setting him up.

CHAPTER SEVEN

In her cramped, windowless lab, Valera thought about the lie she'd told Zukolev.

She didn't need the argon. He was right – it was inert. It didn't do anything. It wasn't a catalyst and it had nothing to do with her research. She'd just requested the gas because she wanted to know how much attention Zukolev was paying to her work.

She was telling the truth about something else, though. She really did feel close to a breakthrough. After years of struggle, toil, and setbacks, she was convinced she was on the edge of glory – because she had to be.

Valera's father had had two passions in life: early Asian languages, and British detective stories. Every evening when Valera was a child, he would read the Russian translations of novels by Arthur Conan Doyle to her. She was too young to understand the complicated plots, but one line from *The Sign of the Four* – the novel they had been reading the night her father was seized by the NKVD and never seen again – had been seared into her mind. The Russian translation was 'when you have removed every other possibility, the truth is all that's left'.

After three years of wrestling with the same problem every day, she'd eliminated so many possibilities that, by Conan Doyle's logic, she must be near the answer.

'What shall we try today?' she asked the portrait of Stalin hanging on the wall opposite her.

Zukolev insisted that a portrait of the great man hung in every office and workroom in Povenets B, so the city's workers could always feel him looking down on them. It was always the same portrait, and always shrouded in black velvet.

But to Valera the face hanging in her office didn't belong to Stalin. It was her lab assistant, her collaborator, her confessor. His identity changed day by day, depending on what Valera needed to keep herself sane – another little rebellion.

She had wasted her first year in Povenets B chasing theoretical dead ends. Eventually, she had realised she needed help and, with none on offer, she'd created her own. She started talking to the painting. It helped her externalise her thoughts, consider fresh perspectives, vent her frustrations. The painting never talked back. It didn't need to. It just needed to listen. Until one day, when Valera felt like she was lost and trapped at the same time. She had looked into Stalin's eyes and heard in her mind, in a voice that wasn't quite her father's but wasn't quite anyone else's either, the line from *The Sign of the Four*.

Protecting standard radio communications from interception was relatively straightforward. By encrypting signals across a broad spectrum of channels, constantly hopping between a preset range of bandwidths, messages could be sent between two locations without being jammed or listened in to. This was how all major militaries, intelligence agencies, and the more private of the world's global corporations kept their conversations secure and their secrets safe.

Unfortunately, this technique didn't work when it came to getting anything but the most basic messages from the Earth's surface to orbit and back again. This was because of the scattering effect of the planet's atmosphere. No matter how many bandwidths were jumped, messages never pierced the atmospheric barrier. Only the most simple signals that were barely a step up from Morse code could pass through.

Valera had convinced herself that the secret to breaking the barrier lay in unlocking some new, undiscovered realm of physics. It was an arrogant idea, and after months of questioning proofs, exploring half-cooked theories, and drafting calculations that didn't add up, she'd conceded defeat.

That was the day the portrait on her lab wall started talking to her, and she realised that if the answer wasn't to be found in creating something new, then it must be in doing something different with what she already had.

She broke down the problem into its simplest

49

form. There was a wall in her way, and she needed something to punch through it. She needed a bigger signal.

Zukolev may have been a skinflint when it came to supplies and equipment, but he had furnished Valera with an impressive library. He fed her a regular supply of papers by other Russian scientists, along with some of the latest research by physicists working in America, Britain, Germany, and Sweden, all clandestinely acquired by the GRU. He always handed them over with great ceremony, as if he himself had risked his life to bring them to her. The first few sets of papers had even been translated for Valera, but the efforts were so poor that she'd ended up just asking for the originals. She still struggled with German, but her Swedish was now passable and her English was almost fluent.

She reread every paper and report she had. Then she went to Zukolev and asked for two things. The first was a travelling wave tube amplifier, a technology developed by the British and Americans during World War Two to boost radio signals. The second was a set of plans for something called a rake receiver. Valera thought that combining a stronger signal with a more sensitive receiving system might be the key to opening up a hole in the atmospheric barrier and getting a message into space. She made her case to Zukolev and, after his usual complaining about time and expense, both pieces of equipment were delivered to her lab the next month.

Combining the travelling wave tube amplifier with the rake receiver did exactly what she'd hoped, but it wasn't a solution. For every broadcast that worked, another didn't. A fifty per cent success rate in lab conditions wasn't good enough. But she was convinced she was on the right track. So she repeated test after test, each time getting different results, and each time pretending that she wasn't getting closer and closer to the definition of madness.

After two more months, Valera had gone back to reading through her library for fresh inspiration. She was now halfway through.

She poured herself a weak cup of coffee from her samovar – another hard-fought-for gift from Zukolev – and carried the next stack of papers over to her desk.

Valera could read for hours, and she did, stopping only for occasional refills of coffee. She was happy losing herself in the theoretical world and forgetting the reality of Povenets B. But by late afternoon she'd found nothing to help her solve her problem. It was frustrating. She knew she couldn't rush the science, but she also knew after her meeting with Zukolev that she needed to deliver something resembling progress soon.

She emptied the last of the samovar and started on the next pile of papers. Halfway down was a slim report from 1957 by a military engineer called Leonid Kupriyanovich about his development of an experimental portable telephone. She

51

paced up and down the small amount of free floor space, clutching her coffee in one hand and Kupriyanovich's report in the other. By the third page she knew she was on to something.

Because of its diminutive size, Kupriyanovich's phone could only broadcast a very weak signal. He'd overcome this limitation not by trying to make his signals stronger, but by making them larger, wider. He used asynchronous code division to spread his transmissions across a much broader bandwidth than they needed, effectively increasing the odds of them reaching their destination. Instead of trying to turn the signal into a rocket, he turned it into the wind.

Before she had finished Kupriyanovich's report, Valera was already trying to work out if she could apply the same principle to her work. If one big signal couldn't break through the atmospheric barrier, could a hundred smaller ones? She asked Stalin what he thought. He didn't say yes, but he didn't say no either.

She recalibrated the amplifier and receiver to asynchronous code division and sent a basic test signal. It worked. She reset the equipment and encoded a more complex message. She transmitted the signal and, after a split second that felt like a year, the receiver captured it completely intact, with no degradation or corruption.

Valera almost didn't believe it. She might actually have found a way to talk to the stars. This could change everything. For Russia, for science, for her, and for Ledjo. She allowed herself the briefest moment of celebration before resetting her equipment to send another signal. She needed to prove it wasn't a fluke. She picked her message, encoded it, and sent it. But as soon as she did the room plunged into darkness.

The power to her lab had been cut. She looked around for a moment, confused. Then her eyes landed on the luminescent hands of the clock that hung above the lab's door. In her excitement she'd missed the double blare of the siren that had sounded a minute before. It was five o'clock, and the working day in Povenets B was over.

CHAPTER EIGHT

'They'll hate you for this,' Holland had said to Knox the day he'd asked him to become MI5's own grand inquisitor and mole hunter in his large, wood-panelled office on the fifth floor of Leconfield House.

'Most of them already do,' Knox had replied.

Knox knew he didn't have many friends in the Service. After a decade and a half, he was still an outsider. He didn't come from the right sort of family and hadn't gone to the right sort of schools. He was an orphan from the East End who had spent his childhood dodging Blitz bombs instead of learning the classics. He'd never doffed his cap to the great and good, or asked people to do something when he could just tell them, because with Holland's ever-present support, he'd never had to.

'I've already been told by various quarters that this is all baseless paranoia, sheer McCarthyism, a classic Russian misinformation tactic that we shouldn't fall for, and generally beneath the Service's attention,' Holland said.

'What do you think?' Knox asked.

'Frankly, I hope they're all correct,' Holland said. 'But the onus is on us to prove it one way or the other. We find ourselves in a rather precarious position, caught between two old allies. We can't afford any missteps.'

'Only one is still our ally,' Knox countered.

'True, but for every person in Whitehall who thinks we should be cosying up even closer to America there's someone else who wants us building bridges with the Russians,' Holland said. 'And if they end up firing nuclear warheads at each other they'll be flying over our heads.'

Britain's own nuclear defence development had stalled after the de Havilland Blue Streak missile programme had been cancelled a year earlier. And no rocket with the Union Jack on its side would be shooting for the moon any time soon. This was one of the reasons Pipistrelle was so important – the intelligence it collected gave MI5 a much-needed edge in a rapidly changing world.

'Or they'll get us to do it for them,' Knox said.

Desperate to make up for the UK's shortfall, Macmillan had authorised the RAF to carry US nuclear warheads. The arrangement was supposed to be built on clear distinctions: the missiles were American, and the planes were British. But it was never certain whose finger would really be on the launch button. The idea of the UK being dragged into a nuclear war because of a trigger-happy US general or president made a lot of people nervous, including in Leconfield House.

'Quite,' Holland replied.

'Which side do we pick?' Knox asked.

'Neither,' Holland said. 'We stay vigilant, and pay close attention to anyone inside or outside this building who might be trying to curry too much favour with either one. I don't like the idea of surviving the battering of two world wars just to end up as the fifty-first state or a tinpot Soviet republic.'

That conversation had happened three years ago, and ever since Knox had been hunting moles. He'd been exhaustive in his quest, but had found little evidence of anyone working against MI5 from the inside, until a throwaway revelation in Sandra Horne's testimony eventually led him to suspect that Manning, then an assistant director, was a Soviet agent.

While most of the information Sandra and Peter passed on to Moscow came personally from Montcalm, Peter would also travel into London once every two months to retrieve coded messages from a second-hand bookshop in Cecil Court. Knox had cross-referenced the times of these trips with Montcalm's movements and established that he hadn't been leaving the messages for Horne to collect. The question then was, who had?

Knox reviewed the records of the Service's most senior members, looking for signs that would point to one of them being the guilty party. After several late nights reading through old reports called in from record storage, Knox had begun to appreciate some of White's enthusiasm for the speed and efficiency offered by Atlas. But he still believed there was no substitute for studying the actual files, understanding their context and subtext, and reading the specific words that were used and – importantly – the ones that weren't.

When he reached Manning's service record he found it was littered with enough basic errors and operational missteps to convince Knox he should never have been allowed in the field, let alone made acting director general. But there was nothing in it to suggest malice was hiding beneath his incompetence. At least, not until Knox found one very odd and very deeply buried operation.

On 7 March 1947, Yevgeny Kuznetsov walked into a small, backstreet restaurant in Singapore. It was midday, and Paul Fenwick, a low-ranking member of Singapore's British Military Administration, was eating his lunch. Kuznetsov approached Fenwick's table, sat down opposite him.

'You are British,' the Russian said. 'I am MGB, and I want to defect.'

Singapore in 1947 was, to put it kindly, a mess. The British Military Administration was still restoring most of the colony's infrastructure after the Japanese occupation of the island during the war. Food was scarce, crime was rampant, and Chinese communist seditionists were stoking anti-colonial protests. In other words, the Military Administration was stretched thinly enough without worrying about a Russian walk-in. But Kuznetsov made Fenwick a tantalising offer.

'Get me back to civilisation, and I'll give you the names of all the Russian agents in your country.'

The Administration made a blanket request for assistance to Military Intelligence, MI6, and MI5. All three could have claimed jurisdiction over Singapore. But it was Manning, then working in MI5's counter-intelligence division, who quickly drafted a memo making the case that as Singapore was a colony, all intelligence operations there fell under MI5's purview. He also said that, given Kuznetsov's suggestion about Soviet infiltration, this matter was too serious to be handled by the MI5 security liaison officer assigned to Singapore and someone from counter-intelligence should fly out to interrogate him – and that he was happy to volunteer.

Neither MI6 nor Military Intelligence were inclined to put up a fight, and Manning was on a plane to Singapore the next morning.

It was clear from Manning's record that this was the moment he became tipped for bigger things. Everyone was impressed with how he handled the mission, and his conclusion after meeting Kuznetsov that every piece of information he'd offered up was entirely fictitious. The report's coda stated that two days after meeting Manning Kuznetsov's body was found on the edge of Singapore's north coast, washed up from the Johore Strait – the price, it seemed, of his failure to trick the British.

This conclusion made sense to Manning's superiors, but not to Knox.

Honeytraps were a favourite KGB tactic for keeping Russia's enemies on their toes. But Knox didn't know of any instance when an aborted trap had resulted in the death of the agent involved. They usually just faded away, disappearing overnight to pop up again somewhere else with a different identity and new deal to make. The only reason Knox could think the Soviets would have for killing Kuznetsov was if he really was a defector.

Manning's claim that all his information was false also didn't ring true to Knox. The best chicken feed always had at least some truth mixed in with it. Working in counter-intelligence, Manning of all people would know this.

To Knox, Manning's insistence that he should be the one to run the Kuznetsov case didn't look like healthy ambition and dedication to duty. It looked like someone acting very swiftly to remove a threat.

None of this amounted to hard proof that Manning was secretly working for the Russians, but Knox couldn't completely dismiss the possibility. He'd looked back through Manning's record again with different eyes. Suddenly all the little mistakes looked like part of a much larger pattern. He'd started to see connections between events separated by years, and Manning's whole career turned into a grand narrative of subtle manipulations.

Knox became convinced that Manning had played a very long, very calculated game. And now it felt like he was playing one with Knox. He knew Manning wouldn't have dangled the carrot of finally finding a solid link between him and Russia without being able to pull it away whenever he wanted. But Knox was determined to grab it before he did.

He needed to move fast, because he knew the longer Manning was acting director general the harder it would be to get him thrown out of Leconfield House, even with evidence that he was a traitor of the highest order. It was also very likely Manning had sent his own inquisitor hunting through Knox's records for a reason to get rid of him permanently. And if they looked closely enough they'd find one. Because in his files was the secret of why he hadn't shown up at Holland's house for dinner on Sunday. The old deep secret that bound Knox and Holland together. The secret that Knox knew could so easily be twisted to make it look like he was the traitor in MI5's midst.

CHAPTER NINE

Another morning in Povenets B, another relentless sequence of sirens. But this morning Valera wasn't running late. She was early. By the third siren, she'd already hurried Ledjo out of the house and halfway to school.

Today, Valera had dressed in a dull brown blouse and the same pair of old, worn trousers she wore almost every day, and Ledjo had a small, bright red neckerchief under his white collar. This short length of fabric was the symbol of the Young Pioneers, the Soviet Union's mass youth organisation. Technically, Ledjo was three years too young to join the Young Pioneers but Zukolev had made membership mandatory for every child in Povenets B. Young Pioneer neckerchiefs were also technically supposed to be a neatly folded triangle of plain red fabric, but Ledjo's had recently been part of the right sleeve of one of Valera's few brighter shirts, which she had sacrificed for her son's happiness. From a distance it looked plain, but up close it was an abstract pattern of intermingling triangles and squares.

Young Pioneer day was Ledjo's favourite day of

the week, and he would normally be pulling on his mother's arm to get to school as early as possible. But today he struggled to keep up with her. He kept tugging on her hand to get her to slow down, but it didn't work.

When they reached the school gates a full twenty minutes before the fourth siren, Ledjo decided it was time for his own small rebellion against Povenets B's draconian rules.

He let go of Valera's hand, stepped in front of her, and said, very loudly, 'Goodbye, Mama.'

His voice snapped Valera out of the swirling thoughts about radio waves and rake receivers that had consumed her all night. She looked down at him, really seeing him and the tears threatening the corners of his eyes properly for the first time that day.

'Oh, Pikku, I'm so sorry.' She opened her arms, and Ledjo rushed straight into them, his pout instantly dissolving. 'I've been very bad,' she said to the top of his head, 'but I'll make up for it. I think today is going to be a great day.' She kneeled down, holding Ledjo out in front of her. 'Be a good boy. I love you.'

'I love you too, Mama.'

Valera smiled, turned him round, and gave him a gentle shove to start him running through the gates.

As soon as he was inside the school, she turned away, letting herself get lost in her thoughts again. She ignored the other mothers with their plaited hair and children in perfect neckerchiefs passing her on their way to school, and the men in overalls rushing to deal with the latest problem at the power plant.

Valera would never say luck had played much of a part in her life. But she had been fortunate that her natural aptitude for physics had been spotted late.

When the siege of Leningrad ended, what remained of the city's population hoped their liberation would be cause for a national celebration. It wasn't. Stalin had never liked Leningrad or its people, and as the city began to rebuild, he worried about the influence its new generation of leaders was starting to wield. The Soviet Union could only have one seat of power – Moscow – and one unassailable leader – Josef Stalin.

Five years after the city was decimated by the siege, it was purged. The mayor was executed, two hundred city officials were sentenced to hard labour in the Siberian gulags, and two thousand public figures, including industry leaders, scientists, and university professors, were deemed to be anti-Soviet agitators and exiled from the city. By then Valera had become a junior member of the physics faculty at Andrei Zhdanov University. As a survivor of the siege and the daughter of an acknowledged anti-Soviet intellectual, she naturally fell under suspicion. But one thing saved her life. To make the purge as efficient as possible, an arbitrary combination of age and rank was used to decide who posed a threat. Valera was too young and too junior.

She suddenly had the run of Andrei Zhdanov's labs, with no old intellectuals blocking or belittling her. Then, with Stalin's death and Khrushchev's political thaw, her superiors began to return from the Siberian wilderness, and she was back to begging for respect. So, when the GRU agent approached her with the offer of moving to Povenets B, it wasn't just fleeing the penury of life in Leningrad that enticed her, but escaping the prejudice of academia as well. But Povenets B had just been another kind of cage. And not even a gilded one.

Valera dreamed of a different life, when she was awake and when she was asleep. Almost every night since Ledjo had been born she'd dreamed about the two of them in a small rowing boat, floating in the middle of a calm lake. The details of the dream changed over time – sometimes it was winter and they were bundled up, surrounded by distant, snowy peaks, other times it was summer and she could hear the far rustling of reeds and grassy fields – but the feeling was always the same: freedom.

With the promise of a new life in Povenets B, it felt like her dream might come true at last. She imagined lazy summer days on Lake Onega, fishing for their supper, or long nights curled up in front of a fire, reading stories together like she'd done

64

with her father. None of that had happened. Life in the *naukograd* was the same, day after grinding day. But last night her dream was the most intense it had ever been. The scenery constantly changed, mountains rising and falling as the sky moved through hues of blue, yellow, and pink, and the sound of Ledjo's laughter echoed across the water.

When she reached her lab, Valera checked that her equipment hadn't been tampered with overnight. It wasn't beyond Zukolev to go snooping when she wasn't there and try to uncover some piece of information she hadn't included in her latest official report. Unfortunately for him, he wouldn't find anything useful if he did. Valera wasn't stupid. She didn't keep notes. Everything she did, every experiment she tried, and every discovery she made was locked up in her head. And only a fraction of it made it into her official reports.

The travelling wave amplifier and rake receiver were both exactly as she'd left them. So she fired them up, encoded a test signal, and sent it. There was some slight degradation of individual signals, but the rake receiver easily reconstructed the full message. She encoded another signal, and threw in a couple of random problems of her own. This one came through perfectly. Then, just to be sure, she spent an hour taking the amplifier and the receiver apart and putting them back together again, and sent one more message. When this one was captured without any issues, she leaned back and burst out laughing. Then she stood in front of the portrait of Stalin, looked it square in the eyes, and shouted, 'The truth is all that's left!'

She'd really done it. She'd solved the impossible problem, and given herself and Ledjo a way to escape Povenets B.

She ran down the corridor to her research block's one communal telephone to call Zukolev's office and deliver the news that would finally free her of him. But before she reached the phone it flew past her, blasted off the wall by a massive shockwave. A split second later she was hurled off her feet, slammed into the floor, and knocked out as the ceiling collapsed on top of her.

CHAPTER TEN

Valera didn't know how long she was unconscious for, but she came to with her ears ringing and her chest pinned under a huge chunk of plaster. The wall where the phone had hung was in pieces, the wooden beams that had been holding it up exposed and buckled.

She knew only one thing in Povenets B could have caused this much damage. The power plant.

She pulled herself up, causing a loud creak to echo through the wrecked building, and crept backwards, away from the collapsed wall towards the staircase at the opposite end of the corridor. She didn't look into her lab as she passed it. She knew she'd only see her equipment destroyed and her library in ruins.

The staircase was made of thick wooden boards bolted to the bare concrete wall. Valera tested the first step. It held. So she ran down the rest, and burst out into the madness that was consuming the *naukograd*. She passed other scientists, stumbling out of their labs and offices into the street, and started to sprint towards the school. She outpaced the guards rushing from their posts and parents abandoning their jobs, all running in the same direction, all sharing the same terrifying thought.

The closer she got to the plant, the more damaged the buildings she sped past were. Some had holes blown out of their roofs, some had lost entire walls, exposing all the secret bits of life and work that had been locked up inside them.

She told herself over and over that if the explosion had happened on this side of the plant then the rest of the complex itself might have protected the school from the worst of the blast. That Ledjo and all the other children would be fine – shaken and scared but safe. That any second she'd hear their cries and sobs rise above the shouting of the grown-ups around her. But then she turned a corner and saw in the distance a sight that even her worst nightmares over the last three years had never dared to conjure up.

The cooling tower had collapsed and the plant had been ripped in two, a deep gouge cut through it. And beyond, where the school should have been, was only rubble.

She slowed to a walk, then stopped, frozen, in the middle of the road. She didn't register the people knocking into her as they ran past. She didn't notice the hot embers in the air stinging her eyes and burning her nostrils. She only felt a sudden and total emptiness.

Her head told her there was no use rushing towards the gaping void where the school should have been, no point screaming out Ledjo's name. No one could have survived such a violent explosion. But her heart refused to listen.

After a long, agonising moment she was running again. She clambered through the chasm that had opened up in the middle of the plant. She crushed wood and glass under her feet, climbed over lumps of twisted metal and chunks of brick. It was a gauntlet, and every few metres the carnage was punctured by the raggedy edge of an overall or the blank stare of dead eyes poking up through the rubble.

Then the fabric changed from the dark green of workers' uniforms to the grey, white and red of children's. Valera cried out Ledjo's name, just like all the other parents who were scouring the chaos searching for their babies.

She rushed from body to body, feeling sick and ashamed of herself for leaving them as soon as she realised they weren't her son. She couldn't stop until she'd found Ledjo. She couldn't even help the people who had heard faint, whispering voices and were racing to move the broken pieces of walls and desks on top of them. Any one of them could have been her son, but something inside her told her they weren't.

Valera reached a large slab of wall that had tipped over, jutting up into the air at a perilous angle. Half-torn posters of colourful Cyrillic letters were still pinned to it, fluttering in the gentle wind that had been stirred up by the city wrenching itself apart. She was in the ruins of a classroom. Jagged metal and glass blocked any other path than the way she'd come.

'Ledjo! Ledjo!' she finally screamed. 'Where are you, Pikku?'

She had to keep going, keep searching. The only route she could take was over the wall. She didn't know how she was going to scale it, but she knew she had to. She told herself it might even have saved Ledjo from the brunt of the blast, and he was trapped just on the other side of it, waiting for her to rescue him.

She looked for a foothold, something that would help her up onto the wall so she could test her weight. But another flash of red caught her eye almost directly beneath her. It was tiny, barely visible through a gap between two chunks of wall that hadn't survived the blast, and almost smothered in dust. But as she focused on it she saw the intricate, abstract pattern of triangles and squares that covered the fabric.

'No. No, no, no,' she whispered as she pulled away shards of glass and broken plaster. She dug, and dug, and dug. The wall began to creak and shudder as Valera shifted its new foundations, but she didn't stop until she uncovered the bruised, soot-covered face of her son.

CHAPTER ELEVEN

After a very short and very cold shower, Knox made himself a very strong coffee. He had no food in the flat for breakfast. This wasn't out of the ordinary. In fact, his cupboards were usually bare beyond a bag of coffee beans from the Algerian Coffee Stores, the shop on Old Compton Street that had been supplying caffeine addicts with their domestic fixes since 1887.

This morning Knox took his coffee short as he got dressed. He didn't like suits and only owned two that he'd had made on Savile Row several years ago for special occasions, like disciplinary review boards. Day to day, he preferred clothes that didn't obviously mark him out as a government servant.

He'd recently bought several summer jackets, shirts and trousers from Hardy Amies' new line of menswear, and picked out a suitable combination. He matched them with a pair of brown brogues from Crockett & Jones, his Omega watch, and a slim black leather wallet from Dunhill.

Dressing less conspicuously was another lesson he'd tried to teach the Watchers. Their dark suits and light mackintoshes, which had been intended

71

to make them blend in, were starting to date and become easy to spot as austere post-war fashions started to relax. Knox had encouraged them to broaden their sartorial horizons, but this had just resulted in more resentment. It had taken the Watchers a lot of hard work to earn enough to buy their uniform, and they wore it with pride.

He took an early train to Cambridge. It wasn't busy – most people were making their way into London, not the other way round – yet Knox still didn't have his first-class carriage to himself. Just before the train pulled out of King's Cross a man joined him in the small compartment. The day was already warming up and the man was sweating in his oversized three-piece suit. Even though it was summer he also carried a thick coat along with his bulging suitcase. He had the look of a travelling salesman.

Thankfully the man didn't seem interested in making conversation and sat silently across from Knox, reading his newspaper, until the train reached Hitchin. Knox watched him drag his suitcase down onto the platform and then, as the train pulled out of the station, reached over for the paper he'd left behind. Knox scanned the headlines as the countryside rolled by. Calder Hall, which had been front-page news a few days ago, was already relegated to a single column on page five, replaced by a large, close-up photo of Yuri Gagarin sipping champagne. Knox, happily, couldn't find any mention of Holland, Manning, or himself anywhere.

Once he reached Cambridge, Knox headed to the Cavendish Laboratory on Free School Lane, home to the university's physics department. The Cavendish was a warren of narrow passages, dead ends and staircases. He passed a steady stream of postgraduate students – some, he thought, more than once – who all shuffled quietly around him, their eyes glazed over from a summer buried in experiments and books.

Eventually, he stopped one and asked for directions. Two staircases and more corridors later he found the door with a little brass plaque next to it that read:

Dr Ludvig Kaspar, Emeritus.

Kaspar was German, and a polymath. He was a prodigious mind who had made a name for his young self across Europe by being able to take on almost any problem in any scientific field. Then the war came, and the Nazis put him to work on a task that in Kaspar's mind was entirely beneath him – improving the guidance systems of their V2 rockets.

At the end of the war, Kaspar, who had been brought to Berlin to avoid him falling into enemy hands, fell into enemy hands. He had been high on the GRU's list of prizes, and when Russian soldiers found him working in his temporary lab as if the Third Reich wasn't crumbling outside, he was transported to Moscow, where he was thoroughly and relentlessly debriefed.

Once the GRU had learned all they could from him to help them advance their own intercontinental ballistic missile programme, he was allowed to return to Berlin. Kaspar hoped to find his lab still intact. It wasn't. Deep inside the Soviet-controlled eastern sector of the city, the building had long since been repurposed and all traces of his lab gone. He wrote to several universities in the Bundesrepublik to the west seeking a position, but none of them wanted anything to do with someone now considered a Nazi and Soviet collaborator.

The CIA, however, did. He was approached, and then spirited out of East Berlin to Washington as part of Operation Dragon Return. When the US had extracted everything of value from him about both the Soviet Union's missile programme and life behind the Iron Curtain, the British were given their chance.

Kaspar had been a brilliant young scientist, but after almost ten years being traded between superpowers and endlessly debriefed, the light of his genius had become dim and jaded. There was little flesh on his intellectual bones for the British to pick on. But there was also nowhere else for Kaspar to go. He was almost sixty and had no family, and no desire to return to a Germany that didn't want him back.

In a fit of generosity, he was given rooms and a small office in Cambridge where he could live out his dotage quietly. In the last six years he'd given

74

two lectures, had published one short paper, and had generally been ignored by successive generations of students passing through the university. It was a stroke of luck that the postgraduate Knox stopped for directions knew about 'the old Nazi in the rafters'.

Knox tapped on Kaspar's door. There was no response. He knocked again, louder. Still no acknowledgement or movement inside. Thinking his luck might already have run out, Knox was about to give the door one last bang when it was suddenly pulled open by a short, flushed woman in a thin summer jumper and black capri pants.

'What do you want?' she demanded, in a strong Midwestern American accent. She looked very young, but that could have been her height, close-cropped dark hair, and flushed cheeks conspiring against her.

'I'm looking for Dr Kaspar,' Knox replied.

'He's not here.' She tried to block Knox's view of the office, but he could see straight over her head. The room was untidy. Open books had been left on every surface, and several trays containing the remnants of old meals were strewn across the floor. But the woman, who Knox assumed must be Kaspar's assistant, was right – he wasn't inside.

'Do you by any chance know where he might be?' Knox asked.

The woman checked her watch. 'It's twelve thirty. He'll be on Sheep's Green.'

'And how might I recognise him?'

'He'll be the one with the swans,' she replied. Then she slammed the door.

Knox decided there was no point trying to get any more information from her, so he traced his way back through the labyrinth of the Cavendish and made his way the short distance to Sheep's Green.

The warm morning was turning into a hot afternoon. The River Cam was clogged with punts, and day-trippers swarmed over the small plot of open land where the river split in two. It was one of the prettier patches in the city that wasn't locked behind a college's walls.

Knox could see several people trying to tempt the swans on the river with bits of food, but only one of them was having any success. An old man, leaning on a stick, was doling out crusts of bread to the birds. He also looked like he was deep in conversation with several of them. Knox wondered if this whole trip might have been a trick by White.

He kept a short distance between himself and Kaspar. Knox didn't want to get too close to the swans. He didn't like swans, and these ones looked like they didn't like anyone but Kaspar. Everyone else who approached them received either a hiss or a wide flapping of wings.

'Are you just going to stand there?' the old German said.

It took Knox a moment to realise Kaspar wasn't talking to one of the swans but to him. 'You think

76

after all this time I don't know when a spook is sneaking up on me?' he asked.

Knox took this as his cue. He sidled up next to Kaspar, facing the river and doing his best to ignore the angry noises coming from the nearest swan.

'I'm sorry for the intrusion,' Knox said. 'But I need your help.'

'I've already told your people everything I know. I've told everyone everything I know.' He broke another crust into pieces and threw them at the swans.

'This is something new. Something, well, something that we don't know what it is.' Knox pulled the bundle of equations half out of his jacket pocket so Kaspar could see them. 'We need an expert opinion.'

Kaspar threw the remains of the bread into the Cam, sending the swans scrabbling, and held out his hand. Knox passed him the papers.

He waited for Kaspar to review them, to tell him that they were indeed important, connected to Russia, and, ideally, had Manning's coded initials somewhere in them. But, after skimming over the first couple of sheets, Kaspar's face darkened.

'So,' he said to himself, 'I have become a joke.' Then he turned, forced the bundle back into Knox's hands, and started to walk away.

Knox, confused, followed him. 'What's that supposed to mean?'

Kaspar spun on his stick to face him, suddenly boiling with anger.

'Who put you up to this? Those bloody first-years? Who told you where I was?' He spat the questions at Knox.

'Your assistant told me you were here.'

'My assistant?'

'This isn't a joke,' Knox insisted. 'This is a matter of national security.'

But Kaspar wasn't listening. 'I won't be your stupid summer prank. I know what they say about me and I won't put up with this nonsense.'

'What nonsense?'

'These childish scribblings,' Kaspar said, reaching out and crumpling the papers Knox still held to his chest. 'Pathetic.'

'They don't mean anything?'

'You know damned well they don't. Now leave me alone.' Kaspar turned his back to Knox, spinning again on his stick. But he didn't walk away. His anger had tired him out.

After several long breaths he spoke again, his voice quieter, more defeated.

'I never was a Nazi. Work or die. For what? I had no choice.' He looked up at the sky, then down at the ground. 'But no one accepts the grey of life any more. It's all so black and white now. So much easier to decide who the heroes and villains are.'

After a few more breaths he started walking across the Green, back towards his little office up in the rafters. Knox let him go.

CHAPTER TWELVE

If Knox had been paying attention when he caught the next train back to London he might have noticed the woman with short dark hair lingering on the Cambridge station platform. But he didn't. He climbed straight up into the first-class carriage, chose an empty compartment, sat in the middle seat – a sign to anyone looking for a seat to keep moving – and settled into his thoughts about his encounter with Kaspar for the whole journey.

Knox also didn't notice the same woman following twenty feet behind him as he walked along the platform at King's Cross and down into the Underground. He was still lost in thought when he boarded a Piccadilly Line train and accidentally ended up in a smoking carriage. He rode the single stop north to Caledonian Road in a thick miasma of old, hot smoke.

The woman also took the tube one stop, and trailed Knox along Hillmarton Road. Then, as soon as she was sure where he was headed, she doubled back on herself, shaking her head as if she'd just realised she'd left something important at home, and went back down into the Underground.

The ornate turrets of HMP Holloway looked more like they belonged to a Cambridge college than the front of a prison in north London. The imposing architecture of Holloway prison, which was originally opened in 1852, was intended to inspire respect for the law. The castle-like facade was also apt as conditions inside for most of the prison's residents were positively medieval.

Once criminal charges had been brought against the four members of the Calder Hall Ring and the case became public, Sandra Horne had been transferred from the secure holding cell on the third floor of Leconfield House to Holloway. Knox didn't agree with the decision.

'We can't guarantee her safety if she isn't in our custody,' he argued. 'And Holloway is hardly the leniency we promised for cooperation.'

But he'd been overruled.

'It's not our decision to make any more,' Holland said. 'But I've been assured she'll be held in solitary confinement, away from any inmate who might wish to do her harm.'

It was a peculiar character trait of many prisoners that they developed a fierce patriotism for the country that had locked them up. To many of Holloway's long-term residents, Sandra Horne's role in passing on classified information to the KGB was as treasonous as trying to kill a member of the royal family.

Knox stepped through the stone arch entrance to the prison and into the guard's office. The man on duty recognised him from his previous visits to Horne and, luckily for Knox, waved him through without checking if his presence had been approved.

Five minutes later, he was sitting in a spartan meeting room, waiting for Horne to be brought to him. The room was cold. Its concrete and brick floor and walls were whitewashed, its heavy door was painted gunmetal grey. There were no windows. Knox sat on one of two chairs that faced each other across a small Formica table.

Knox knew Horne might not know anything about Bianchi and Moretti, but he still had questions about the mysterious contact in Cecil Court she'd alluded to when she'd first been persuaded to talk. Knox wanted to know if there was another Soviet agent operating in the city.

The bolt on the door shifted and Sandra Horne was brought into the room by a silent female guard. Horne looked like she'd aged ten years since Knox had last seen her. She was wearing the drab grey shirt and skirt all female inmates at Holloway wore. Her hair, which she'd managed to keep in high, gravity-defying curls throughout her stay at Leconfield House, now hung flat and limp in a straggly bob.

The guard pointed at the chair opposite Knox, waited for Horne to sit down, gave Knox a curt nod, and retreated from the room, locking the bolt across the door behind her.

It seemed to take a Horne a moment to recognise Knox, and when she did, she let out a long, irritated sigh.

'When are you people going to leave me in peace?' she asked, her voice thin and tired.

It didn't fool Knox. He knew how shrewd an operator the woman sitting across from him was. 'Drop the act, Sandra,' he replied.

Her face broke into a broad, bright smile. 'Oh, dearie, let me have my fun.' Her voice was suddenly alive and devious. 'I am popular, aren't I? You lot should move in. Save you making the trip over from Mayfair every day.'

Knox didn't like the idea of someone else handling Horne now. The Calder Hall case had been his operation, his victory, and he should have been able to see it through. But that wasn't an option right now. At least it looked like news of his suspension hadn't reached Horne yet.

'You know the deal,' he said. 'Unless you'd rather we put you on a plane and let you take your chances in Russia.'

Knox and Horne both knew what happened to most blown KGB assets when they went to Moscow looking for sanctuary. The lucky ones never made it out of Sheremetyevo airport.

'I'd have to talk to my husband about that,' Horne said, her grin turning cold. It was a thinly veiled barb. Sandra was the brains behind Calder Hall, and she blamed Peter for cracking and landing them both in prison. He'd been sent to

Pentonville when she had come to Holloway and, as far as Knox knew, she'd made no requests to have them reunited.

'So,' she continued, 'what do you want to know today? Where Montcalm drank all his money away? Or if Slaughter really is that stupid?'

It had become clear over the course of interrogating the ring's members that not only was Sandra in charge but that she'd also seemed to know where her collaborators were and what they were doing without ever leaving her house in Richmond. Montcalm had indeed spent most of the cash he received from the KGB via the Hornes drinking and gambling his way up and down the country, creating a vicious circle of debt and addiction that always led him back to London and Calder Hall. As for Slaughter, he'd maintained throughout his questioning that he had no idea he was working for the Russians. In fact, the security guard claimed he'd been slipping secrets to the Campaign for Nuclear Disarmament in exchange for money to supplement his meagre income.

But Knox hadn't come to Holloway to push Sandra for information about Slaughter or Montcalm.

'I want to know about Cecil Court,' he said.

'Oh.' The broad smile was back. 'That.'

'I want to know who was leaving the messages.'

'Well, I wish I could tell you, dearie. But I'm afraid my memory isn't what it was.'

'Sounds terrible.'

'I'm serious. It's the chloral they give us. Supposed to help us sleep, but half the poor loves in here can't remember what day it is, let alone why they're banged up. It's sinful.'

'I'm sure it is,' Knox replied. He had grilled Horne enough to know he'd have to play her game, but he wanted to shorthand it as much as possible. 'And what do you think would help jog your memory?'

Sandra leaned back in her seat, relishing the small piece of power she held over Knox.

'A stop to that chemical nonsense for a start. I just need some lavender on my pillows to help me sleep. Cotton pillows, stuffed with goose down, of course.'

'Of course.'

'Lord knows what the linens are made of in here, but they aren't very homely.'

'I don't think they're meant to be.'

Horne's smile turned cold again. 'Maybe for everyone else. But I'm different, aren't I? I'm special. And you want me to be comfortable.'

Knox nodded. 'Tell me about Cecil Court and I'll see what I can do.'

'Oh, dearie, you know that's not how this works. Get me a good night's sleep and then we can see if I remember anything about that ghost of yours.'

Knox knew if he pushed her there was every chance she'd shut down and not tell him anything. He might be in no position to give Horne anything officially, but she didn't know that, and there were

84

always ways to get things into a prison – even into high-security solitary confinement – unofficially.

'Right, then. I think it's time for my afternoon stroll round the grounds.' Horne pushed her chair back, stood up, and straightened her shirt. 'Oi,' she shouted at the door. A moment later it opened, revealing the same guard who had delivered her a few minutes earlier. 'I think we're finished now,' Horne told the guard, then turned back to Knox and said, 'I'll see you soon, dearie.'

The guard looked at Knox as Horne stepped past her. He nodded that they were indeed done, and the guard fell into step behind her prisoner, leaving Knox to find his own way out.

CHAPTER THIRTEEN

Abey Bennett loved London. The city was literally and figuratively thousands of miles from Lakin, the township in rural Kansas where she'd grown up. Lakin was a small, tight-knit community of weather-beaten buildings and grizzled prairie folk who were only a few generations removed from the great push west. London was the complete opposite. It was a real melting pot, where the tall towers and endless streets were full of people from all over the world.

Bennett felt free in London. Free to be who she wanted to be. Free to be as visible or invisible as she needed to be. And when it came to trailing members of MI5 across the city, she needed to be invisible.

Once she was sure Knox was going to see Sandra Horne, Bennett went back to the tube and rode the Piccadilly Line all the way to South Kensington. If she'd been following operational procedure properly, she'd have reported Knox's trips to Cambridge and Holloway to her superiors. But, as they'd already dismissed every attempt she'd made to convince them something was rotten at

86

the highest levels of British intelligence and she was currently acting alone and without authorisation, she didn't feel inclined to.

She knew who Knox was, and that he'd been suspended from MI5 just over twenty-four hours ago. What she didn't understand was why he'd then gone to see Dr Ludwig Kaspar, a man who still had suspected links to Russia, and then Horne, whose Soviet connections were certain.

At South Kensington, she changed onto the District Line and travelled another three stops. At West Brompton she got off the tube, turned right out of the station, walked a hundred yards along Old Brompton Road, and turned right again.

It was now late afternoon and Brompton Cemetery was quiet. Streams of light cut through knotty old trees, bouncing off row after row of ornate tombstones. Bennett's final destination stood just ahead of her, but she had another stop to make first. She turned off the wide central avenue and followed one of the smaller paths down towards the grand colonnades and catacombs that dominated the lower half of the cemetery. She weaved through the graves, following a route that almost entirely hid her from view behind tall headstones. She paused briefly at the top of one of the sloped catacomb entrances before walking down into the cool shadows.

Three bricks up from the ground to the left of the large, locked gate at the bottom of the slope, there was a wide gap in the mortar – wide enough for something to be wedged inside. Bennett eased a dull metal case out of its hiding place, adding to the scrapes that ran along its sides. The case was a dead drop. It was also an early warning system, and a trap. She opened the thin lid and checked that the small piece of paper she'd left inside weeks ago was still there. It was. If it hadn't been, she'd know that someone was watching her as closely as she was watching Knox. And whoever it was would have come into possession of something that looked like a long string of code but which, after hours spent trying to decrypt it, would reveal itself to be completely meaningless.

She put the case back, walked up into the warm sun, and headed through the cemetery to the sandstone cross that stood just inside the northern entrance. The headstone had weathered over the years, but the inscription on it was still legible. It read:

In loving memory of Emmeline Pankhurst, wife of RM Pankhurst LLD, in rest June 14th 1928.

People tend to latch on to the heroes they discover when they're young, but Bennett was probably the only child in the history of Kansas who had chosen to idolise a British suffragette. The other children of Lakin had their choice of brave pioneers and nation builders to look up to. Bennett, however, had been denied access to this pantheon, because she was half Native American. And, because she was also half white, she'd been just as shunned by the community that could have shared hundreds of years of stories about ancestors roaming the Great Plains with her. So, whenever she could she'd take the bus to the nearest big town to Lakin – the ironically named Garden City – and sit in the public library for hours on end, searching through book after book for her own heroes.

She found Emmeline Pankhurst in a biographical encyclopaedia of famous women in history. The book was short, ordered chronologically, and Pankhurst was the final entry. Bennett felt an immediate connection to this dead foreign woman, the cause she'd led, and her belief that acceptance was something to be claimed, not just asked for. This sentiment became Bennett's driving force, and it had pushed her all the way from Lakin to the CIA.

London was her first international posting, and she'd gone looking for Pankhurst's grave as soon as she'd arrived in the city. She visited it whenever she felt her own resolve wavering, whenever she felt beaten down by the constant struggle to be taken seriously by her colleagues or, like now, when she just needed to think about her next move.

Bennett's superiors were paying close attention to the fallout from Holland's mysterious coma and Manning's ascension to the top of MI5 days before the OECD conference. But they didn't think either of these strange events had anything to do with the lingering rumours about Russian infiltration. Bennett did.

Her suspicions had led her to Dr Kaspar, and she'd been extremely careful timing her visit to Cambridge so she'd be able to take a look at his office undisturbed. She hadn't expected to be interrupted halfway through her search of the old man's den by one of MI5's most senior officers, and she wanted to know why he'd been there. The obvious answer was that he was a mole hastily shutting down his network. Obvious and stupid. If Knox was a Soviet agent he'd have disappeared out of the country as soon as people had begun to ask questions about what had happened to Holland. The fact that he hadn't, Bennett thought, meant something else was going on. She wondered if Knox was still hunting the mole himself. And if he was, then she might be able to use him.

After a few more minutes standing quietly in front of Pankhurst's grave, staring at the details of the headstone that stood almost a full foot taller than her and that she knew so well, she left the cemetery.

CHAPTER FOURTEEN

Valera stood on a low rise looking out over the tundra. By her reckoning she was about thirty kilometres from the Finnish border. She had dug Ledjo's body out of the rubble and sat cradling it for over an hour in the ruins of Povenets B. Long enough for all the dust, soot, and whatever else the explosion had thrown up into the air to start falling back down to earth, blanketing the *naukograd* in a black, acrid snow.

Valera had cleared as much of it off Ledjo as she could. With his raindrop eyes closed, he'd looked almost peaceful, an angel somehow trapped in hell. With her body covered in ash and her hands cut and filthy from digging, Valera had looked like some kind of beast from the abyss. She wanted to bathe Ledjo in her tears, but they wouldn't come.

Povenets B had taken Valera's freedom, and now it had taken her child. She'd almost given in, lain down next to Ledjo and let the rubble consume her as well, but something deep in her mind had compelled her not to. It forced her up and onto her feet. She couldn't stop herself. She left her son in his horrible, open grave, and she walked home.

The further she got from the plant, the quieter the streets were. She passed building after building with cracked or smashed windows, and the odd person still running towards or away from the centre of the *naukograd*. By the time she reached her house she was completely alone. But even if Zukolev's entire battalion of guards had been standing at her door, she wouldn't have seen them in her shock-fuelled trance.

She stepped into the silent house and saw that the destruction had even reached inside here. Shards of glass from the windows that faced towards the power plant covered the floor, and a thick crack ran up the wall that she and Ledjo used to paint their fantastical worlds and stories on. She briefly looked at her faint half-reflection in one of the larger slices of glass. It was bad luck to look in a broken mirror – if she could have constructed the thought she would have asked the universe what more bad luck she could possibly endure.

She moved into the kitchen, and opened a cupboard next to the sink. She removed the thin wood panel she'd installed in it a year ago to create a fake back wall, and pulled two backpacks out of the hidden recess. She strapped the large one across her shoulders, and cradled the smaller one in her arms. Then, not rushing or racing, or looking at all like she was conscious of what she was doing, she walked away from her home and out through the unguarded entrance to Povenets B.

In her haze of trauma, she'd hiked west through the forest that surrounded the secret city until she hit a road. She'd continued on, one pack across her shoulders and the other in her arms, until the driver of a small truck picked her up just outside a village called Pindushi at the top of Lake Onega.

It was an unspoken agreement among the people who travelled Russia's vast landscape that they would help each other get where they needed to go, and not ask questions along the way. Valera didn't ask the driver why he was taking the long way to Leningrad, choosing the old country roads that meandered their way across Karelia instead of the modern highway that linked it directly to Petrozavodsk, the regional capital on the western side of Lake Onega. And he didn't ask why she was filthy, why she never let go of the small backpack she clung to her chest, or why she shrank down in her seat whenever they passed another vehicle.

They travelled for a few hours in silence on the old road that wound through forests and tundra, skirted small lakes, or crossed them on rickety bridges, and passed through the decayed remains of several abandoned villages.

Karelia's history was both long and bloody. Its vast network of interconnected lakes linked the Gulf of Finland and the White Sea, which meant whoever controlled Karelia controlled access to the Baltic and the Arctic. The region straddled the border between Finland and Russia, and twenty years ago, after centuries of tussling, the Soviet Union annexed most of it. The inhabitants of the area who wouldn't or couldn't flee west were moved out of their farms and villages, which were left to rot, and into internment camps. Povenets B had originally been one of those camps.

Valera barely registered the tundra, the lakes, or the empty villages as they drove on. Her mind was still trying to process what had happened. It was only when the sun started to stream through the truck's windscreen that she realised the road had turned south. She was running on instinct but she knew she couldn't risk going all the way to Leningrad. As soon as the GRU worked out she wasn't in Povenets B, they'd go hunting for her, and Leningrad would be the first place they'd look. So with a few quiet words she said goodbye to the truck driver, and continued her journey on foot.

She hiked through two more villages in quick succession. The first had been remarkably well preserved. Buildings were still standing and small flowers bloomed in overgrown gardens. It was like everyone had just gone on a long summer holiday. The second village she almost missed entirely. It must have been the site of a major battle in one of Karelia's many conflicts. A few broken walls were all that was left. There were no little flowers or any signs of life at all. And after that, there was just more tundra.

Another three hours of trudging across scrub and rock had brought her to this bluff, tantalisingly close to the Finnish border. It was late. She had no idea of the exact time, but the aching in her legs and pain in her stomach were finally starting to press against the fog of her shock and tell her she'd gone too long without food or a rest. She had two choices. Find somewhere to bed down, or keep walking.

This close to midsummer in Karelia the sun would briefly skim the horizon in a few hours' time, but it wouldn't get truly dark for another two months. Valera wouldn't have the protective cover of night if she kept going, but she would be putting more distance between her and anyone who might be following behind her.

She stepped down from the bluff, checked her bearings against the low sun, and forced her body to keep going.

CHAPTER FIFTEEN

I n an office deep in the NASA Langley Research Center in Hampton, Virginia, Patrick Dixon was on the phone.

'Is he happy with the latest set of images?' he asked, the slightest shadow of his Boston accent softening the middle *t* of *latest*.

'When is he ever happy?' the voice at the other end of the line replied. The voice belonged to Phinneus Murphy, Dixon's CIA liaison. And the *he* they were both referring to was the new president, John F. Kennedy.

Dixon was the chief scientist on the Corona programme, and knew better than anyone how much pressure the project was under from the White House.

Corona was the newest frontier in the global espionage war – a joint project between the CIA and NASA to create a network of satellites carrying ultra-high-resolution cameras that could be positioned above any location on the planet at a moment's notice. It was supposed to hand the US an eye on the whole world – and unassailable intelligence supremacy – but it was behind schedule.

'He's impatient,' Murphy said. 'He wants us on the moon already.'

'Who the hell signed off that speech?' Dixon asked rhetorically as he rubbed his free hand over the top of his stubbled buzz-cut head. 'I can't even get a decent radio signal into orbit, let alone two hundred and forty thousand miles into space.'

'It's three months since *Freedom 7* went up. He doesn't understand why we're still playing around with parachutes.'

Dixon sighed. 'Neither do I,' he said. He leaned onto his elbow, massaging his temple between his thumb and middle finger.

'You shouldn't be telling me things like that.'

'I know better than to try and keep secrets from the CIA. And I need all the help I can get.'

Despite years of work, Dixon and his team had failed to find a way to send data-heavy radio signals through the atmospheric barrier. This was why the Corona satellites relied on dropping capsules full of photographic film from the tips of their thick, cigar-shaped bodies, and why Alan Shepard had been blasted into near-orbit aboard *Freedom 7* with a communications system that was essentially a jumped-up walkie-talkie.

'We have the nation's best scientific minds on this, Patrick. There's not much more help I can get you.'

'The president's welcome to come down to Langley and lend a hand if he wants.'

'Let's not go down that road,' Murphy said.

Part of Murphy's job was keeping the president informed about strategic developments from the Corona programme; another part was stopping him from getting too personally involved.

Dixon looked down at the mess of papers on his desk. Each one was a pipe dream or dead end.

'Why do I feel like I've got a sword dangling over my head?' he asked.

'Because you do,' Murphy said. 'But if it's any consolation it's over both our heads. A few photos in a metal tube every couple of weeks isn't enough. He wants his parade down the Mall. And slightly more relevant to us, he wants to know what's going on in Russia.'

'Can't he send up the U-2s again?' Dixon asked.

'Not an option.'

A year ago, Gary Powers' U-2 spy plane had been shot down deep inside Russian territory by a rogue S75-Dvina missile. The incident hadn't just embarrassed America and handed Russia a major political victory. It had also effectively ended the CIA's aerial reconnaissance operations, and led directly to its interest in Corona.

The holy American trinity of government, military, and private industry had been experimenting with orbital reconnaissance since 1957. Under the codename Discoverer, Washington paid the RAND Corporation to build satellites, the Itek Corporation to design next-generation triple-lensed panoramic cameras, and Eastman Kodak to develop a new film stock that delivered three times the resolution of the best aerial photography film used in World War Two. The Air Force originally managed the Discoverer programme, but in May 1958 control was moved to the Advanced Research and Projects Agency, then when NASA was founded a few months later it was shifted again.

Progress was slow. Between January 1959 and May 1960, Discoverer attempted twelve satellite launches, and every single one was a failure. Two rockets never left the launchpad, five exploded before they reached orbit, and the five that did all malfunctioned. But as the shockwaves of the U-2 incident rippled around Washington throughout the summer of 1960, the CIA science and technology division was already taking over leadership of Discoverer and turning it into Corona.

Corona was named after the outer layer of the sun's atmosphere that only becomes visible during an eclipse, when everything else is black. Given how handicapped American intelligence gathering had become, it was an apt moniker. The research team, now led by Dixon, was given a new, dedicated lab at NASA's Langley Research Center in Hampton, Virginia. They were also told that, when it came to getting Corona working, money was no object and failure was not an option.

'Powers was a fluke,' Murphy continued. 'But intelligence says Russian missiles are more than capable of hitting the U-2's cruising altitude now.'

'I thought that was just Khrushchev banging his shoe.'

'For once it seems the old man isn't lying through his teeth. The Air Force is working on a new plane with a higher ceiling, but it's taking time.'

'Everything takes time.'

'Not for us. We're magicians, remember?'

'How could I forget?'

Dixon hung up the phone, leaned back in his chair, and wondered, for what felt like the thousandth time, why he'd ever left his tenured position at MIT and joined NASA. Of course, he knew the answer. He wanted to help America win the space race. But right now it felt like they were losing, and because of him.

He picked up a sheet of paper from his desk, hoping to find inspiration in its scribbles and half-finished calculations. It didn't come.

CHAPTER SIXTEEN

There was no Watcher at Knox's front door when he got back to Kemp House. But someone was waiting for him.

He found Peterson sitting at his dining table, leafing through the three bundles of papers from Bianchi and Moretti's flat that Knox hadn't taken with him to Cambridge and Holloway.

'What are you doing here?' Knox demanded. He didn't appreciate the invasion of his private space. He was also still irritated about his trip to Cambridge – guilty that he'd dragged up an old man's demons, and embarrassed that the whole thing had been a waste of time – and frustrated that Sandra Horne hadn't given him anything useful.

'Manning wants a progress report,' Peterson replied, eyes still skimming through the papers in front of him.

'He can wait.'

Knox could tell Peterson wanted to say something more, but he wasn't about to give him the satisfaction of asking what. So they just stared at each other across the table while Knox took off his jacket.

Peterson blinked first. 'Find anything interesting in Cambridge?'

'You had me followed?' Knox said, slamming his jacket down on the table for dramatic effect.

'Of course I had you followed,' Peterson said. 'In four days London will become the biggest intelligence target since the Paris Peace Conference. The last thing I need is a rogue element running around the place.' He picked up the address book and flicked through it.

'I'm not a rogue element,' Knox replied.

'You ignore orders. You're unreliable. And now you're my problem.'

'I'm doing what I have to to get answers.' He gestured at the papers, making it clear that they didn't hold any.

'From your perspective, perhaps. But let me give you another one. The director general is in a coma, two men have been found dead, and the man who connects them all ran off at the first opportunity.'

'You and Manning put me in the middle of this.'

'Where we could keep tabs on you.'

Knox's jaw hardened. He wondered exactly what 'keeping tabs' meant. Did Peterson's interest stretch to scrutinising his service record?

'I don't like what you're implying,' he said.

'Implying suggests I'm saying something open to interpretation. You're still as much a suspect as anyone else. More as far as I'm concerned. And fleeing the scene hardly does you any favours.'

'I was doing my job.'

'Your job is to find out who killed Bianchi and Moretti. Not to go showing classified evidence to old Nazis.'

The image of Kaspar, defeated, hobbling across Sheep's Green, rushed back into Knox's mind.

'He's not a Nazi,' he said.

'It's amazing how many of them weren't after they lost the war.'

'He told me he wasn't,' Knox countered. 'And I haven't seen anything that proves he was.'

'Did he, really? Did he also tell you he'd never been turned by the Russians? Or the Americans? Or both?' Sarcasm dripped off Peterson's questions. 'Don't be so naive, Richard. But maybe that's why you went straight to him. Maybe he's your KGB handler. The poor old genius everyone's forgotten about. It's a smart play. Hell, maybe you're the mysterious phantom of Cecil Court too. That's the only reason I can think of for you visiting Sandra Horne. Check in with Moscow, then make sure your operative hasn't sold you out yet.'

'I'm not a traitor,' Knox replied, spitting the words through clenched teeth.

In response, Peterson's face broke into a bright smile.

'Oh, probably not,' he said. His tone was suddenly light, almost conversational. 'All just idle speculation. Not very pleasant though, is it? Beauty is in the eye of the beholder, but remember, so is truth.'

'If you don't like my methods, take me off the case.'

'I don't like that you're acting as if you're still working for the director general who's been lying unresponsive in a hospital bed for four days instead of the one who's very much with us and gave you a very simple order. Your duty is to the Service, not Holland.'

'And yours?' Knox spat back.

'I do what I'm told.'

Knox was suddenly very tired of arguing with Peterson. 'If you want me to find out who killed Bianchi and Moretti I have to start with why,' he said.

'Exactly,' Peterson replied. 'Why two Italians died in the arse end of Deptford. Not how you can make this part of a grand conspiracy. Just because you want there to be a connection between them and Manning doesn't mean there is one.' He stood up and smoothed his suit jacket. 'You might not believe me, Richard, but I am trying to help you.'

He took one more look at the papers spread over the table, then started to make his way to the door.

'Manning's generosity isn't limitless,' he said. 'Find a lead worth pulling on. Quickly.'

CHAPTER SEVENTEEN

Valera's resolve lasted another hour. The sun never completely set in Karelia in July, but the nights still got cold. She passed another abandoned village without registering it. Its old church still stood, offering sanctuary, but she didn't seek it.

She ignored the pools and peat bogs she stepped in, and the gnats that had become a constant buzzing swarm around her. She stumbled over uneven ground, only changing direction for the largest of obstacles – a boulder deposited on the tundra by some ancient glacier or an inexplicable and long-felled tree trunk – until her body finally gave out.

Her legs crumpled under her and she collapsed onto a patch of moss and stunted bracken. As she hit the ground the small pack fell out of her arms. It was the first time she'd let go of it since she'd retrieved it from its hiding place. For almost a year she'd been collecting things, preparing emergency packs for her and Ledjo in case they ever got the chance to escape Povenets B. The chance had finally come, but only for Valera.

Her stomach suddenly demanded sustenance. She reached out and unfastened the flap of Ledjo's pack. A small parcel of nuts and dried biscuits sat on top of a thick jumper. The jumper was one of Ledjo's favourites from Leningrad. He'd almost grown out of it when they'd arrived in Povenets B, but years of feasting on scraps meant it still fitted him. Valera couldn't remember when she'd put the nuts and biscuits in the backpack – it had been weeks since there'd been any of either in the *naukograd*'s sole, undersupplied shop. She bit into a biscuit. It was dry, brittle, stale, and tasteless. But that didn't matter. It was food, the fuel she needed. Her body was slowly shifting from shock to survival mode. Next it demanded water and shelter.

She stood back up on her stiff, aching legs and took in her surroundings properly for the first time. In the midsummer twilight the tundra seemed to stretch away from her forever in all directions. So too did thousands of small pools. She hobbled over to the nearest one and used both hands to cup the first water to touch her lips in hours. It tasted of the Earth, and chemicals. She realised her hands were still caked in whatever substances the power plant had flung into the atmosphere and all over her. She plunged both hands into the pool and tried to scrub them clean. Then she took her own pack off her back and pulled out a large, rough wool jumper. She slipped it over her head, wiping her hands across the front of it.

The falling temperature had driven the cloud of gnats away and Valera started to feel the silence of the night around her. She realised just how alone she was. There were no distant cries or howls, no beasts calling out to their mates or taunting their prey. The only sound was Valera's own breath. It occurred to her that she hadn't encountered anything larger than the gnats on her long walk across the tundra. There had been no snarling wolves or skittish elk, no tracks to follow or avoid. Even the animals had abandoned Karelia.

She spotted the low remains of a building a hundred metres away – just two walls a few metres high on a slab of concrete. She couldn't tell if it was the final remnant of another lost village or some lone hut that had succumbed to the wilderness. But it didn't matter. It was shelter.

Valera picked up both her packs, carried them over to the walls and wedged them into the corner where they met. Then she curled up against them and finally let out all the pain and anger she'd carried across Karelia. She cried. She wept for everything she'd lost. She wept for her parents. She wept for her beautiful, innocent son. She wept because the cost of her freedom had been too high.

CHAPTER EIGHTEEN

I n the years following Stalin's death it became increasingly fashionable for high-ranking members of the Communist Party to move out of the centre of Moscow to the city's burgeoning suburbs. Apartments were swapped for houses, commutes by car replaced short metro rides. It was all part of the Soviet paradox.

General Grigor Medev had never made the move out to the pretty, manicured neighbourhoods of Zhukovka or Barvikha, like so many of his comrades. He still lived in the Narkomfin Building, El Lissitzky's grand communal housing project for Soviet workers in the centre of the city. He'd moved in in 1945 at the end of the Great Patriotic War, as the survivors of the Eastern Front returned home, and had lived there ever since.

His apartment, like all the others in the building, was small, and simple. Every home in the Narkomfin Building was open-plan and split-level. Medev's front door opened onto a short flight of stairs up to a living area. Another flight led to the second level with his single bed and bathroom. There was no kitchen. Medev knew some of the other residents had secretly installed makeshift pantries in their living rooms so they didn't have to eat every meal in the large ground-floor cafeteria. But he had kept the original layout of his – a small circular table surrounded by a built-in settee and chairs, and a desk bolted to the wall beneath the apartment's single, wide window. He'd added a few bookshelves and paintings but he'd more or less kept his home the same for sixteen years. He also ate every meal he could in the cafeteria.

Secrecy and solitude were fundamental parts of Medev's professional life, so he relished being surrounded by people whenever he had the chance. However, he hadn't just stayed in the Narkomfin Building out of a deep, personal commitment to the concept of collectivised living. He'd stayed because he enjoyed his hour-long morning walk to KGB headquarters at the Lubyanka far too much to ever think about giving it up for a few acres of land out in the sticks. He also didn't have anyone to move to the suburbs with.

Medev had given his life to the Party and the KGB. On his long but steady ascent to becoming chief of the KGB scientific directorate, he'd worked for many leaders and become privy to even more secrets. He was a near-mythical figure in the eyes of his staff, and had proven himself enough times to be left to run his directorate however he saw fit.

To the population of the Narkomfin Building he was something between an enigma and a contradiction. Everyone knew that he was a senior KGB officer. Some had even discovered his actual position and title. None of them understood why he lived with them, or why he was so friendly. Medev went out of his way to say hello to everyone he met in the building, asked after the parents and children of the people whose paths he crossed regularly (they were always, invariably, fine), and was on very good terms with the cafeteria staff. This was particularly important because Medev's responsibilities at the Lubyanka meant that he could easily miss the building's normal mealtimes.

For the last two days he hadn't left the Lubyanka before midnight.

'Good evening, comrade,' a disembodied voice said as Medev finally pushed open the cafeteria door at almost two in the morning. It belonged to Galina, one of the cafeteria staff, who had lived and worked in the Narkomfin Building almost as long as Medev had. She was a widow, and happy to take the graveyard shifts so the other workers could spend their evenings and nights with their families. Medev liked Galina. She had a good sense of humour, and was an excellent cook.

'Busy day?' Galina asked, appearing through the side door to the kitchen.

'Very,' Medev replied, taking a seat at one of the empty tables in the small section of the cafeteria that still had its lights on.

'And productive,' she said, her voice rising to mimic the Party messages that were broadcast on radios across the country every day about the value of hard work.

'Of course,' Medev said, smiling.

The last two days had, as far as Medev was concerned, been anything but productive. He'd spent them locked in an unmoving argument with Sergei Korolev. Many people only knew Korolev by his grandiose and somewhat made-up title of chief designer of rocket-space systems. Medev, unfortunately, was now far more intimately acquainted with the man and his overblown aspirations.

Kennedy wanted to take America to the moon, but Korolev wanted to take Russia to Mars. It had been his secret ambition for years, and he'd somehow persuaded Khrushchev that it should be a public one. He'd drawn up plans for orbital launching platforms and electric rocket engines, and was preparing to build an advanced life support system at the Institute of Biophysics in Krasnoyarsk in Siberia. The closed-loop system, codenamed BIOS-3, could theoretically sustain human life indefinitely with recycled air and water, food cultivators, and xenon lamps designed to mimic sunlight – all key concerns for getting people all the way to the red planet and back again. But, unlike NASA and its endless budgets, Korolev had to fight for funding and not even having Khrushchev's ear could get him everything he needed. It would take more money than he had to make BIOS-3 a reality, so he had travelled, cap grudgingly in hand, all the way from Siberia.

'BIOS-3 is crucial to establishing Soviet dominance of the cosmos,' Korolev had declared in their first meeting.

'That is very good,' Medev replied. 'But what will it give our comrades here on Earth?'

Korolev didn't like being questioned. Medev didn't care. He had to deal with people like Korolev on an almost weekly basis – people who, he suspected, were more interested in personal glory than advancing the Soviet cause.

'Hope,' Korolev said after a long pause.

'Communism doesn't need hope,' Medev replied. 'It needs protecting.'

It took another two long meetings for Korolev to grasp what Medev had dangled in front of him and start talking about BIOS-3 in more terrestrial terms. It could, he began to argue, be used to house brave comrades in hostile environments around the world, or high-value foreign assets from whom the KGB might want to extract information in complete secrecy.

Medev could see merit in both arguments. But just as Korolev didn't have infinite resources, neither did he. Considerable amounts of KGB money had already been funnelled into the Zenit satellite and Vostok rocket programmes as well as the constant surveillance of their American counterparts, the Corona programme and Project Mercury. He couldn't justify moving funds from any of these to research that would take years to produce even a proof of concept.

An hour ago Medev had finally sent Korolev on his way, empty-handed but with a promise to reconsider his request at some unspecified date in the future.

'I know you're desperate to tell me all about it,' Galina said, knowing full well that Medev couldn't. 'But I've got to get back to my stove. A bowl of *solyanka*, comrade?'

'That sounds perfect,' Medev said. A bowl of Galina's sweet and sour beef stew was exactly what he needed before heading up to his apartment and sleep.

CHAPTER NINETEEN

Knox slouched in his Eames lounger. He'd been sitting in it for hours, watching the sun drop over London as he slowly sank lower and lower himself. He was now near horizontal. There was a crystal tumbler on the floor next to him within easy reach. The events of the day had called for something stronger than gin, so he was drinking his best Ron Zacapa rum, neat.

He'd spent the whole evening staring out at the city, seething about his run-in with Peterson, and trying to work out exactly what he'd ended up in the middle of. He'd been given a puzzle to solve that didn't make any sense. There were too many parts, and he couldn't see how any of them fitted together.

He'd survived as an outsider within MI5 by always being one step ahead, always knowing more about an operation than anyone else, considering every outcome, and preparing for all of them. Knox was absolutely not in control of this situation, and he didn't like it. There had to be some angle that would make everything fall into place. But he had no idea what it was. And the longer he sat thinking about it, the less Kemp House felt like a castle in the sky and the more it felt like a giant plinth, giving a clear shot at him to anyone who wanted one.

The one thing he knew for definite this evening was that he was too drunk to visit Holland. This was a problem, because he'd only felt more lost than right now once before during his MI5 career. The first time he'd visited the Gresham Arms. The first and only time he'd been responsible for a fellow officer's death. And it had been Holland who had helped him find his way back then.

Holland had recruited Knox into the Service as his apprentice at the end of the war. Knox wasn't a typical candidate for MI5. But Holland had been impressed by his military record, and even more so when he discovered that he'd lied about his age to sign up to the army a week after D-Day.

Holland had become Knox's patron. Knox had become his pupil and, in turn, had recruited Jack Williams as his fellow disciple. Williams was Knox's complete opposite. He was from the right kind of family and had gone to the right school. He had the relaxed, carefree attitude of the extremely well off, and the bright eyes and skin of someone who grew up breathing country air on land their family owned. But he also saw through his privilege and knew it was hollow, built on nothing he or his parents had achieved themselves.

His mother and father were content to while away their lives on their large Hertfordshire estate, enjoying the silver spoon that Williams's father had had the luck to be born sucking on. Williams himself preferred to do something with his. When he was young, he used his money to travel, and his easy charm to make friends all over the world. Then, when it was time for more serious pursuits, he used his name to get into Sandhurst. His great-grandfather had been a brigadier in the early days of the Raj in India, and the army had a long memory.

Knox met Williams in Paris during the sombre yet heady days after its liberation from the Nazis. Williams was five years older than Knox, an officer in the 1st Royal Tank Regiment. He'd landed on Gold Beach during D-Day and had been in France ever since, pushing the Wehrmacht back village by village.

The proprietor of a small bistro on the Île Saint-Louis sat them together one night when they happened to arrive at the restaurant at the same time, both in uniform. Before Knox could point out that they didn't know each other, Williams had asked the owner, in perfect French, for a good bottle of Cahors wine for them to share.

'I'll show you mine and you can show me yours,' Williams said to Knox as their wine was delivered.

'Excuse me?' Knox asked, confused.

Williams unbuttoned his uniform jacket and pulled up his shirt to reveal a large patch of scar tissue that ran up the left side of his torso. 'Got caught a little too close to an incendiary on a trip to the seaside.'

Knox was momentarily transfixed by the swirls of flesh that stretched up towards his new dining companion's chest and down towards his hip.

'I like to think of it as my own, personal Van Gogh. Maybe I should get it painted,' Williams joked as he tucked his shirt back in.

Knox pulled back the thick lock of hair that he'd started to let fall over his forehead, revealing the wide scar that stuck out from his hairline. 'Goes all the way back,' he said.

'Normandy?' Williams asked.

Knox shook his head. 'Afterwards. I was on a patrol outside Rouen, looking for German stragglers. We got word there might be some holed up in the roof of an old manor house. It was late, and everyone was tired, so I volunteered to take a look. They were there, alright. Two young Germans who had been surviving on God knows what for weeks. One of them was too frail to do anything, the other decided to put me through a wall to protect his friend.'

'What did you do?'

'Lay half concussed in a pool of my own blood while the rest of my company came to the rescue.'

They shared more war stories over dinner and another two bottles of wine. And for the next week they spent every day together, dining, drinking, and touring the city.

Months later, demobbed and uninterested by the prospect of restoring his family's pile to its pre-war state (it had, like many country homes,

117

been taken over by the military for the duration of the war), Williams looked up Knox in London.

Knox introduced him to Holland over a long dinner and drinks at the Garrick Club, where Holland was a member. Williams fitted the rarefied surroundings more than Knox ever had, but his irreverence for them still shone through. Holland liked him, and by dessert they were discussing his prospects. Within a week Williams was cleared to join MI5. From that point Knox and Williams trained together, worked together, and spent most of their free time together. Then, after fourteen years of friendship closer than Knox ever thought he'd experience in his life, he got Williams killed.

In 1959, President de Gaulle decided to pay a visit to Prime Minister Macmillan. Freshly elevated to the highest office in France, de Gaulle felt he deserved all the pomp his new title would afford him. It was to be a state visit.

He sailed across the Channel aboard the *Surcouf*, one of the French navy's new T 47-class destroyers, passing within ogling distance of the naval ship-yards in Plymouth so everyone there could get an eyeful of the latest symbol of France's post-war resurgence, before arriving in Southampton.

Of course, some people wanted a closer look at the destroyer, and a plan was hatched between MI5, MI6, and Naval Intelligence to do just that. There was a rumour that the *Surcouf* had a new underwater guidance and torpedo detection system installed on the underside of its forward hull, and the navy wanted to know if it really existed before they made overtures about an official exchange of information.

Knox was put in charge of the mission, and Williams, who had spent six months training with military divers for exactly this kind of operation, led the dive team.

The night that de Gaulle was in London being wined and dined at Buckingham Palace, the clouds over Southampton were thick and the harbour water dead calm – perfect conditions for a clandestine dive.

Confidence was high as Williams and his team slipped into the sea outside the harbour and made their way towards the destroyer. But when all the divers but Williams surfaced on time, Knox became concerned. When he hadn't appeared after twenty minutes, concern turned into worry. Williams had enough air in his tank to last an hour, but that window came and went with no sign of him. This was the one outcome Knox hadn't prepared for. He ordered people to comb both sides of the Southampton estuary all the way up to the Solent. They found nothing. He wanted to send every diver back into the water, requisition boats to start dredging the harbour. But by then it was morning, and doing either would make it obvious to anyone within fifty miles that Britain had been flagrantly spying on an ally in the middle of a state visit. So, nothing was done.

The next day Williams was quietly listed as missing in action, and the operation, which had only proved that the guidance and detection system was just a rumour after all, was officially forgotten.

Without his closest friend, and racked with guilt over his death, Knox started to unravel. While his colleagues may have only seen his usual professional mask harden, Holland could see cracks starting to show in it. He arranged for a short leave of absence after the painful debriefing at which Knox was absolved of any responsibility for Williams's unfortunate but accidental death. And when the leave ran out and Knox didn't return to Leconfield House, Holland went looking for him.

He found him in the Gresham Arms, unshaven, unkempt, and cradling his fifth pint of the day. Holland sat down opposite Knox, lifted the pint glass from his hands, and told him that this wallowing wasn't doing anything to respect Williams's memory and that he needed to pull himself together and get on with his job.

The next day Knox was back at headquarters, and the following week Sarah Holland arranged a small, private memorial for Williams.

'He'll be with you for the rest of your life,' she'd told Knox when he'd said he wasn't ready to say goodbye to his best friend. 'You need to carry more than his death.'

Knox went back to work, but without Williams it felt like there was an invisible wall around him,

120

an impenetrable distance between him and everyone else that only Holland, sometimes, could cross.

Since then Knox had stepped away from running all but the most important active operations – like Calder Hall – and dedicated more and more time to sifting through MI5's past. It had given him a focus, a purpose, but it had also widened the gulf between him and everyone except the few people he was closest to.

Now, Knox felt almost as adrift as he had after Williams's death. But this time Holland wasn't here to help him through it.

He had no idea what he should do next. The problem was a lack of concrete, tangible evidence to guide him. He hadn't found anything to suggest Bianchi and Moretti were more than the couple of chancers he'd originally dismissed them as. There was nothing that connected them to the Russians. And nothing to link them back to Manning, either. So, why was Manning so interested in them? Or Knox, for that matter? Why go to the trouble of kicking him out only to bring him back in? Why not leave him out in the cold where he couldn't cause him any more trouble?

Was it just as Manning had said himself, to use Knox to prove his innocence, all the while enjoying watching him squirm and chase false leads? With Manning now sitting in Holland's seat, the only higher powers Knox could turn to for support were political ones, and they wouldn't dare touch the acting head of MI5 without a cast-iron case against him.

Knox had nothing, and he needed something. He needed to do something. He decided he needed, in the words of Holland, to pull himself together and get on with his job. So, he climbed out of the Eames lounger, and took himself out of his flat and down the two streets that led from Kemp House to Bar Italia.

CHAPTER TWENTY

Even at his most maudlin, the streets of Soho at night had the power to make Knox feel better.

After his parents' deaths, Knox had gone to live with his grandmother, who had tried to keep him safe by limiting his world to the few streets of the East End where she'd spent her whole life. It hadn't worked. As soon as he was old enough to understand there was a vast city out there beyond Bethnal Green waiting to be discovered, Knox became a person of two distinct halves – the well-behaved grandson by day, and the night owl who would pound the capital's pavements and alleys for hours.

The city's lights and spirit dimmed during the war, but Soho had still shone, once you knew where to look. The old men in ragged suits still pushed their carts of meagre wares along the gutters. Open doorways leading to staircases lit with tealights reminded passers-by that London's oldest and hardest workers were still open for business. And basement bars and clubs still catered for the brave souls who didn't want to spend their nights cowed in their beds, waiting for German bombs to fall.

Knox was too young to do much more than watch all this go on. But watch he did, a nocturnal *flâneur* soaking it all in. He'd choose a street corner or bench and let the city's nightlife pass him by, or he'd pick someone out from the throng and follow them to whichever theatre, club, or inconspicuous doorway they were heading for. He didn't know it at the time, but it was all good training for his future career.

It was Soho that Knox missed when he was fighting in France. So, when it was all over and he returned to London, it was in Soho that he settled. He'd lost count of the places he'd lived before Kemp House. He'd had a room above a restaurant on the corner of Haymarket and Panton Street, lived in what could kindly be described as a garret in Golden Square, and even spent a year in the basement of a grand old townhouse in Bloomsbury Street, next to the British Museum.

A lot had changed since the war. The glow of the city had returned. The first generation that had grown up untouched by the war was coming of age, testing their boundaries and pushing the world to see how far they could make it move. Collars were getting longer, skirts shorter. But some of the old Soho was still there. The men hauling carts now wore demob suits, newcomers and veterans alike were beckoned into dark doorways, and, at any time of day or night, there was coffee to be had.

124

Bar Italia was never quiet, but Knox hit a lull between the pub-goers needing a shot of caffeine to carry them home and the late crowd after a fix to get them through the night.

He ordered a double espresso at the counter and watched the young waiters with their rolled-up white shirt-sleeves and greased hair cleaning up small cups and plates. The older staff spent their time actually making the coffee, checking their immaculate beards in the counter's mirrored panels, and harassing the junior staff in rapid Italian. Above them the high *wa-wa-was* and clavioline notes of Del Shannon's 'Runaway' played from an invisible radio.

Knox finished his espresso, pushed his empty cup across the bar, and, realising that there wasn't anyone waiting to steal his spot from him, ordered another with a brief raising of his finger and the slightest nod – the unspoken language of the regular.

Knox and Williams had spent endless late Friday nights propping up Bar Italia's counter and it had taken Knox considerable effort to keep the cafe as a home for only good memories.

The two men used to play a game over their late-night espressos – guessing which of the cafe's customers was most likely to be an agent of some foreign power, and inventing ever more sinister backstories for them.

'Eldest daughter of a Cypriot shipping magnate, became a gunrunner for the Turks when Daddy

125

wrote her out of the will,' Knox would say about a woman in a jet-black trench coat and sunglasses at ten o'clock at night.

'Soviet sleeper who gave it all up for love and is now on the run,' Williams would say about a pensive man lingering over his third milky coffee.

Now Knox played the game by himself over his second espresso. This evening he had his pick of a man in a dishevelled suit who looked like he was in a worse state than Knox, two couples talking very quickly over each other, someone Knox could only half-see past the couples sitting in the window, wearing a light jacket with a trilby perched on the back of their head, and another suited man lingering in the door, alternating between sipping his coffee and sucking on a cigarette.

He settled on the man in the doorway, who kept eyeing people as they walked past the cafe. He decided he was the frontman for a Balkan smuggling operation, waiting to make contact with someone who wanted something only he could supply. Not his best creative work, but it would do.

Knox finished his espresso and, considerably more alert, gave up his space at the counter and headed back out into Soho. It was one of those hot London nights that brought people out onto the streets. Lovers strolled arm in arm from bar to bar. Groups of teenagers flirted with each other across traffic junctions. Theatregoers lingered outside tube stations, putting off the end of their evenings as long as possible.

At the corner of Old Compton Street and Greek Street, Knox realised he'd been wrong to finger the man in Bar Italia. As he crossed the road he noticed a figure twenty yards behind him turn quickly away – a figure in a light jacket and hat. Someone had taken an interest in him.

Peterson hadn't been exaggerating when he'd said he'd be keeping a close eye on Knox. Unfortunately for this Watcher, no matter how well they might know London there was no way they could compete with Knox's years of night-time wandering. He turned into Moor Street, heading towards Cambridge Circus, then quickly doubled back down Romilly Street, along the side of the Palace Theatre. He crossed over Shaftesbury Avenue and Gerrard Place before approaching Cambridge Circus again, this time from the south. He could see the trilby trying to push through the crowd that was still outside the Palace, discussing the performance they'd just seen of the new musical, *The Sound of Music*.

Knox decided to have a little fun at Peterson's expense. He made his way round the circus slowly enough for the Watcher to spot him again before turning into the warren of streets that made up Seven Dials. Here he could really play with his tail, appearing at random down the narrow, cobbled lanes that, by a quirk of the city's ancient beginnings, radiated from a single junction like the spokes of a wheel. The Watcher followed him into his trap and chased his shadows and echoing

127

steps in circles for fifteen minutes before giving up in the hub of the Dials, refusing to be tempted down another alley.

Knox quit while he was ahead. He slipped away and headed south to Long Acre and through Covent Garden, before dropping down onto the Strand. Halfway along, he slipped through the side entrance to the Savoy Hotel, then back out through its gilded foyer to the line of taxis idling in front of its grand entrance. It was an old trick Williams had taught him for getting a cabbie to take you south of the river late at night. They never wanted the fare, but they knew if they refused it the hotel doormen would make sure they didn't get any more.

Half an hour later, Knox was back in Deptford.

CHAPTER TWENTY-ONE

Abey Bennett loved London. But sometimes she also hated it. Like when the mark she'd been trailing realised he was being followed and gave her the slip.

If her surveillance of Knox had been approved she'd have had a whole team working with her, blanketing Soho so he couldn't have gone anywhere without her knowing. But, as with so many times in her life, Bennett was working alone.

It was a skill she'd learned young. Too young.

Bennett's mother was a member of the Kiowa tribe, who had once roamed all over Kansas and the surrounding states before their land was taken from them, and her father was a white man with a drinking problem who'd walked out on his family.

Bennett and her two brothers had been born in quick succession in the late thirties, as Kansas was being ravaged by the Great Depression and the Dust Bowl. Three years later her father disappeared without a trace. The only things he'd ever given her were her surname and her large, piercing blue eyes. Her mother had given her children their thick hair, golden skin, and three traditional tribal first names. She'd wanted to give each of them something to live up to, and honour their mixed heritage, but she'd just ended up alienating them even further from both the white and Kiowa communities. Bennett's brothers were named Enapy and Hori, which meant brave and strong. But they were dull, absent-minded children. Abey was an old Sioux word for 'leaf'. It was supposed to encourage Bennett to be nurturing, and it did, but it also inspired her eventually to blow away from Lakin.

When Bennett was six, her mother developed acute emphysema. All the dust storms had finally caught up with her. She couldn't work, and she didn't have enough money for medicine. Bennett's brothers were too lost in their empty heads to even notice. She was already growing up fast, and after her mother's diagnosis she had to do it even faster.

The white doctors had no interest in treating 'a sick squaw and her half-caste kids,' and the Kiowa elders still considered Bennett's mother's union with a white man too much of a betrayal to offer any help. Bennett had forced them both to change their minds.

It was this same strength of will that Bennett had used to get herself through school and then, after years of trying, into the CIA. She was the first Native American to work for the agency since the Navajo code talkers in the war. Her posting to London should have felt like a triumph. And sometimes it did, but a lot of the time it also felt like the latest fight in an unending series of battles to prove her worth.

Bennett had thought Knox might be the key to getting her bosses to take her seriously after shadowing him from Cambridge straight to Holloway prison. Now she was sure.

She'd almost taken the direct approach, sliding up next to him in Bar Italia. But she'd held back, waited to see where he was headed – because anyone who drank two double espressos that late was definitely heading somewhere. It had been a mistake. She'd tried to be inconspicuous, even wearing the trilby a man had left on the seat next to her on the tube a few weeks ago so Knox wouldn't recognise her. But it had just made her more obvious.

She'd let herself get cocky and thought she could play the game as well as one of MI5's best on his home turf. She'd underestimated Knox and been left looking like an idiot. Bennett hadn't just lost him in Seven Dials, she'd let him toy with her, and prove just how far out of her depth she was.

She wished she had someone to turn to, even just to be put through the wringer for her failure and told what she needed to do to make up for it. But there was no one to debrief her, no one she could vent to or run scenarios with. All she could do was wait for her anger to fade, shove the trilby in a nearby bin, and go home.

CHAPTER TWENTY-TWO

Knox approached the old tenement building off Deptford High Street. He wanted to take a more thorough look at Bianchi and Moretti's flat and see what Manning's investigators might have missed. Unfortunately for him, the policeman standing watch outside didn't want him to.

Knox tried to step past him, flashing the kind of half-smile that communicated something along the lines of 'You've seen me before and I probably live here,' but it didn't work.

'Where do you think you're going?' the officer asked, moving to block Knox's way.

He was a large, stocky man. His heavy brow, lit from behind by the light from the tenement's entrance, made it almost impossible to see his eyes.

'I'm investigating the murder,' Knox said.

That didn't work either.

'Ain't nothing like that here.' The officer shifted his weight, squaring up to Knox. 'Jog on.'

Knox decided it would be easier to play the fool than call up the chief of the Met, who he happened to know personally, and get him to put the fear of God into this jobsworth on his behalf. So he turned on his heel, tripped over his feet for added effect, and headed back to the high street. Then he darted round to the building's back door, waited for the headlights of a passing car to fade, then gave it a hard, sharp shove, catching it mid-swing before it hit the wall.

There was no guard standing watch outside the flat itself, which, if Knox had really thought about it, made it even stranger that a policeman was guarding the entrance to the building more than forty-eight hours after Bianchi and Moretti's bodies had been removed. But that tiny piece of the puzzle was too small for him to notice.

After making sure the curtains were pulled closed, Knox turned on all the lights and started to make his way through the flat, room by room. It looked like it had never been lived in. Everything apart from the most basic furniture had been removed. Knox wondered what had happened to the men's possessions. They must have had more clothes than the ones they'd been found in, more bits and pieces of everyday life that would have helped him build a picture of who they were, what they were doing, and why they died. He'd hoped for a treasure trove of clues, but he found nothing.

He left the small office until last. It was as bare as the rest of the flat. The desk was clear, the boxes gone, the bookcase still empty. He was about to give up, until he realised that one side of the large set of shelves wasn't quite flush with the wall. It was only off by less than half an inch, a small enough gap for most people to miss, but it caught his attention.

He squinted behind it, but couldn't see anything in the narrow, dark void. So he grabbed both sides and started to walk it away from the wall. He heard a low thud as something fell to the floor, finally free from its hiding place. Knox reached behind the case and pulled out what he'd dislodged. It was another bundle of pages covered in equations. But these ones weren't made up of nonsense symbols. They were letters and numbers, maths he could recognise. And, in the middle of the bundle, were two brand new Swiss passports.

CHAPTER TWENTY-THREE

The sun was on its way back up into the sky when Valera woke up. For the briefest second her mind allowed her some peace before it reminded her where she was and what had happened. Her stomach cried out again for food, but she had no more to give it. All she could do was get up, stretch out her tired body, and wait for different kinds of pain to smother her hunger.

She shouldered her pack, picked up Ledjo's in her arms, and started walking again. She didn't know how long she'd been asleep, but even though the sun was already getting higher the air was still cool. She might only have been unconscious for a few hours. She stopped at pools and small creeks for water, but with nothing to eat she quickly became light-headed.

After two hours of walking she reached a single, vast step in the ground. She stared at it for a moment, her mind unable to process its strangeness until she realised it was a road, raised up to protect it from the freeze-thaw swelling of the tundra, and she had hit it side on. Valera could either cross over it and keep going the way she was, or follow it and find out where it went. Her body decided it was too tired even to guide her by instinct, so she stepped up, turned right, and let the road lead her. Twenty minutes later she stopped dead in her tracks. There was a sign in front of her and it wasn't in Cyrillic. Its letters were from the Latin alphabet. She wasn't in Russia any more. She was in Finland.

The nearest place worth being on a road sign, somewhere called Ilomantsi, was only a few kilometres away. It turned out to be a small village, just a few paved streets and a few more muddy tracks rutted by cartwheels. But in the middle of its little square stood a large memorial to a battle that had been fought somewhere nearby. There was also, more importantly for Valera, a bus idling next to the monument.

The engine was running and a short queue of people was waiting to get on. Valera didn't know where the bus was headed, but even her foggy, malnourished brain reasoned it wouldn't be back across the border. So she joined the end of the line and pulled a purse out of the top of her rucksack, hoping the small amount of rubles she'd been able to secrete away over the last three years would be enough to buy her a ticket somewhere.

It turned out that Finnish bus drivers were as uninterested in asking questions about their passengers as Karelian truck drivers. It also turned out that Valera was not the first person to try to pay her fare with Russian coins. The driver took a few coins from the handful she offered him, and nodded at her to take a seat.

CHAPTER TWENTY-FOUR

Medev knew that one day someone, somewhere would decide he knew too much about something he shouldn't and he'd suddenly become a threat to the people he'd spent his whole life serving. He'd been part of the Soviet intelligence apparatus long enough to have worked for the NKVD, the MGB and now the KGB. He'd survived Stalin's purges of his own spies, and the jostling for control that had followed his death. Medev was now as near to the heart of the Party as he could be without being chairman of the KGB himself. His position as chief of the scientific directorate came with many powerful allies and untold, invisible enemies. But, for the moment, his standing was still good and his authority unquestioned.

He'd slept well, Korolev was already making his way back to the far side of the Urals, and he could enjoy his morning walk to the Lubyanka in peace. He strolled down Bolshaya Nikitskaya ul., and across Alexandrovsky Garden and Red Square, watching the city come to life around him in peace. Babushkas hurried their grandchildren to school,

137

and the street sweepers went through their daily ritual of cleaning the pavements outside old pastel-stuccoed villas as the bright summer sun rose over the spires of the Ministry of Foreign Affairs.

Like every other day, Medev reached his cavernous office at ten minutes to nine, and brewed himself a sour cherry and honey tea. Six five-metre-high windows flooded the room with light during the day, and a row of large, orb-shaped pendants hanging from the ceiling did the same at night. The room was far too large for one man in Medev's opinion, but he knew its size was intended to reflect the power and importance of his position rather than Medev himself.

He sat at his desk, surrounded on all four sides by three metres of meticulously maintained parquet flooring, savouring his favourite drink and toying with the set of figurines he kept next to his blotting pad. The small figures were abstract human shapes, fashioned in clay by Kazimir Malevich, the great Modernist artist who had been lauded by Lenin and then derided by Stalin.

Medev loved the figures for their myriad contradictions. They were anonymous, homogenous, each without a face and all of them made up of the same basic shapes. But they bore such unique markings and indentations from Malevich's tools that they were all completely individual. The same but different, different but the same.

No one knew if Khrushchev admired Modernism, and few officers would have risked displaying something so provocative as Malevich's figures in case they were not to his taste. But Medev reasoned that the leader of the Soviet Union probably had more important things to worry about than this. If Medev was going to find himself bundled onto the back seat of a car and driven out to Khimki Forest, it wouldn't be for a minor artistic indulgence.

At exactly nine o'clock there was a knock at Medev's door. Medev's assistant, Lieutenant Vadim Rykov, had arrived for his morning briefing. Rykov was barely into his twenties but he'd worked for Medev for almost two years and was well trained in his boss's preferred working methods. So, as ever, he got the incidentals out of the way before the day's big stories.

This morning's less important news included the acquisition of a new wrist-mounted Tessina subminiature camera by a KGB agent from the manufacturer's factory in Grenchen, Switzerland, and the progress of MIR and BESM research groups working on the development of the Soviet Union's first solid-state computer. Then Rykov moved on to the three pieces of information that might require Medev's review.

'Our informant at Cooke airbase has confirmed the next Corona retrieval is still scheduled for tomorrow morning, Pacific time.' He gave Medev a moment to file this away in his head. 'And results for the latest SP-117 tests will be delayed again as more volunteers are recruited.'

SP-117 was the codename for the KGB's range of psychoactive drugs. They were as close as the KGB had come to creating a real truth serum and were a cornerstone of its interrogation processes. But the latest generation, which should have gone into general circulation two months ago, was having teething problems. It either didn't work, caused test subjects to become delirious, or killed them.

The lieutenant expected Medev to be angry about this latest setback, but if he was, he didn't show it. He remained silent, turning one of Malevich's squat figures over in his hands.

Rykov cleared his throat and moved on to the final item on the agenda. 'A major explosion has caused significant damage to the Povenets B *naukograd* in Karelia.'

This got Medev's attention. He held the clay figure still as Rykov read through the truncated initial report that had been sent overnight to Moscow.

'The explosion occurred at the city's power plant while the GRU administrator was inspecting it,' Rykov continued. 'Part of the plant was destroyed, causing an overnight blackout . . .' He paused again at the line that had shocked him when he'd first read it half an hour ago '. . . and levelling the school building next to it. The administrator and surviving plant workers have been transported to the hospital in Petrozavodsk. Initial indications suggest all children and teachers in the school were

killed. The GRU is confident the site is now secure.'
He waited for Medev to respond.

Medev placed the small statue back on his desk.

'What research was being done at Povenets B?'
he asked.

Rykov consulted his notes. 'A variety of advanced
radio and electronics projects. Primarily remote
guidance systems, and long-range, experimental
communications.'

Medev sat for another long moment, then looked
up at his young assistant and said, 'Get me a plane.'

CHAPTER TWENTY-FIVE

Knox marched through the front door of Leconfield House, full of righteous indignation. After security reluctantly waved him through, he made his way across the ground floor's large typing pool to the bank of lifts that would take him up to confront Manning. By now the MI5 rumour mill had done its work and row after row of people averted their eyes as he passed. Colleagues he'd worked with for over a decade pretended they couldn't see him, but he didn't care. He was about to give them something new to talk about.

Knox hadn't needed another trip down to see White or up to Cambridge to confirm that the new papers he'd found in Bianchi and Moretti's flat were legitimate and dangerous. He'd looked through the papers when he'd got back to Kemp House, and a couple of the equations felt familiar, though he couldn't remember where from. In the morning he took them to the library in Senate House, the towering grey obelisk that loomed over Bloomsbury, and ten minutes in the physics section jogged his memory: they were a set of radio wave frequency calculations.

Knox had gleaned enough from briefings with White to know that frequency identification was a fundamental part of the science behind Operation Pipistrelle. Now the Italians were no longer just a mystery for Knox to solve; they were a potential threat to national security, and the timing of their deaths was suddenly extremely significant.

The OECD was the direct descendant of the Organisation for European Economic Co-operation, which had been formed to administer the thirteen billion dollars America and Canada pumped into Europe after the war via the Marshall Plan.

After the continent's economies were shored up, the OEEC's members decided to expand both the organisation and its remit. America and Canada were allowed to join, a belated thank you for their money, and the members magnanimously decided that the new OECD's mission would be to help the world's less-developed economies grow and prosper. Whether these economies wanted this help was a detail that would be ironed out later.

Now, the organisation's inaugural conference in London was just three days away. The main event would, of course, be mostly a show. A chance for heads of state to posture and have their pictures taken. But Holland had made it clear to every department head in MI5 that the conference needed to be a success. Politically, it gave Britain a much-needed platform in the nascent new world order – a way to align itself with America but with the buffer of a grand international project firmly

143

rooted in Europe, which would hopefully also stop the continent from falling into another war no one could afford. And from an information-gathering perspective, while the politicians were enjoying their receptions and photo opportunities, their London embassies would become the world's most tantalising intelligence targets. This was because the OECD delegates included the most senior members of NATO, the North Atlantic Treaty Organization, set up to coordinate and consolidate the West's opposition to the threat of Soviet Russia.

Everyone wanted to know whose egos needed stroking, whose noses had most recently been put out of joint, and what intrigues and stratagems were being hatched against friends and foes. MI5 had toiled for years to gain its home field advantage, creating and refining the Pipistrelle devices, then installing them in embassies, hotel rooms, and conference facilities all over the capital.

If Bianchi and Moretti had found a way to replicate them, and someone else was able to listen to what was being discussed behind closed doors, all of MI5's hard work would be undone. It also, in Knox's mind, shortened the list of the Italians' potential killers to three possibilities: someone they were working with who didn't want them working with anyone else, someone who knew about their discovery and killed them when they wouldn't hand it over, or someone who was scared of being exposed by it.

As for the passports, Knox had seen a lot of

forgeries in his time, and these ones were good. Very good. So good, in fact, they could only have come from either an expert and expensive forger, or from a source that regularly produced high-quality fakes, like a security service. He had no proof that they'd come from MI5. They could just as easily have been made by MI6, the CIA, KGB, SDECE, or any of the other acronymed agencies with a presence in London who used identity documents like currency. But he also couldn't say for certain that someone in the Service hadn't produced them.

By the time Knox reached the fifth floor, Manning's secretary was waiting for him. Rachel Taunton had worked for Manning even longer than Peterson, and, just like everyone else close to him, was enjoying her recent rise to the Service's highest echelon.

She let Knox step out of the lift, but blocked him from getting any further.

'I'm here to see Manning.'

'The director general's busy.'

'Acting director general,' he corrected her.

'Not any more,' she replied, her face breaking into a crocodile smile.

'What?'

'Didn't you hear? He was called to Whitehall this morning.' She made a show of checking her watch. 'It's been official for almost an hour now.'

Knox couldn't believe it. Holland had been out of action for less than a week, and he was carrying evidence that raised serious questions about MI5's operational security and Manning's personal agenda. This wasn't the time to hand the Service permanently over to someone else. Knox had to get to Whitehall, confront Manning, or make his case directly to the Home Secretary that he shouldn't be given absolute power over the Service.

Another lift arrived and he stepped inside as the doors started to close.

Taunton, still smiling, called after him: 'They'll be celebrating by now.'

She'd meant it as a twist of the knife she'd just buried in his chest, but she'd actually just told Knox there was no point going to Whitehall after all. If Manning was celebrating, there was only one place he'd be.

CHAPTER TWENTY-SIX

The Fountain restaurant opened in Fortnum and Mason's in 1955, and ever since had attracted the kind of person who liked their consumption extremely conspicuous. The restaurant's plush, velvet booths gave the illusion of privacy, while their low backs made sure that everyone could see and be seen. Likewise, its windows were set low and fringed with curtains but still managed to provide a perfect view of the restaurant's diners from the street.

Knox wasn't at all surprised to find Manning in one of the Fountain's larger booths, flanked by Peterson and two younger men he didn't recognise. They looked like they'd been shipped up from Oxford that morning – they were bright, eager, and were both wearing the same Prince of Wales check suit as Peterson.

The four men were all tucking into the restaurant's signature welsh rarebit. To Knox's non-gourmand eyes it looked like pretentious cheese on toast, but people who had actually sampled the dish described it in near-transcendental terms.

'Enjoying your meal?' Knox asked the group.

The four heads turned as one, no doubt expecting to see the maître d' dutifully checking in on them.

'Ah, Richard, care to join us?' Manning said, gesturing to the edge of the booth.

Knox didn't move.

'Phillips here was just telling us a charming story about Fortnum's sending hampers to some suffragettes who had been sent to prison for smashing their windows.' One of the Oxford men smiled, enjoying his moment in Manning's spotlight. 'Rather gentlemanly, don't you think?' He cut a large slice of the rarebit, then gestured again at the banquette. 'Please, sit.'

'No, thank you,' Knox replied. 'I hear congratulations are in order.'

'Yes, well, the PM thought it was for the best.'

'Of course he did.'

Peterson coughed loudly into his napkin, a less than subtle warning that Knox should check his tone. Knox ignored him.

'Would you like my report, sir?' he asked.

'Report?'

'Into Bianchi and Moretti.'

'Oh, yes.' Manning turned to his two young acolytes. 'Phillips, Harris, if you could excuse us for a moment.'

'No need,' Peterson said, placing his napkin on the table and shuffling out of the booth. 'You can give it to me, outside.'

'I really think the director general should hear it,' Knox replied.

'He will. Through me.'

Peterson guided Knox quickly out of the restaurant. Then, on the corner of Jermyn Street, asked him what exactly he thought he was playing at.

'First buggering off to Cambridge and Holloway without approval, and now trying to make a scene in public. What the hell's got into you?'

'You sound stressed, Nicholas,' Knox replied, his voice full of mock concern.

'We're in a period of transition,' he replied. A political, neutral answer. 'Everyone is feeling the strain.'

'They look pretty relaxed to me.' Knox pointed through the window at the three men still enjoying their lunch, Phillips and Harris hanging on to whatever anecdote Manning was telling them.

'They haven't spent all morning keeping the Spanish and Portuguese delegations from each other's throats,' Peterson said, somewhat less neutrally. 'That thankless task fell to me.'

'And I'm sure you put up a fight.'

Peterson let out a long sigh. 'I don't have time for this, Richard. What's going on?'

'I know why they were killed.'

'So?'

It wasn't the response Knox had expected.

'You think that justifies talking to Manning like that?' Peterson asked.

'They weren't just troublemakers. They'd worked out a way to replicate Pipistrelle.'

Concern suddenly flickered across Peterson's face. He stepped closer to Knox.

'You have proof?' he asked, lowering his voice.

'I have their equations. Their real equations.'

'What the hell does that mean?'

'Another set of papers. Hidden in their apartment, and not very well.'

Peterson glanced through the restaurant's wide windows at Manning. Knox enjoyed imagining the cogs turning in his mind.

'Your conclusion?' he asked, when he turned back to face Knox.

'Either they were hiding it from the person who killed them. Or they were hidden after they died, by someone who didn't want me to see them.'

'That sounds a little like putting the cart in front of the horse.'

'Not if this whole thing is a set-up. They were behind a bookcase in the study, where Manning was waiting for us.'

Peterson sighed again, and took half a step back. 'And that sounds more than a touch paranoid.'

'Everyone's a suspect,' Knox replied, throwing Peterson's line from the previous night back at him.

'You seriously want me to believe the director general hid evidence in the middle of a crime scene and a whole team of investigators missed it?'

Peterson's tone was dismissive but he still peered through the Fountain's windows again, checking that Manning was still distracted by his lunch guests.

Knox shrugged.

'It's unlikely,' he said. 'But it's not impossible, is it?'

Peterson paused before he answered. Knox wondered if Manning's faithful servant was finally starting to have doubts about his master.

'If Manning was behind all this, why would he have sent for you in the first place?' Peterson asked. 'He could have taken whatever he wanted from that flat and no one would have questioned him.'

'I don't know,' Knox conceded. 'But it's a bit too much of a coincidence when the city's about to become the world's biggest intelligence powder keg.'

'And we're doing everything we can to make sure it doesn't go off. Which includes not jumping to conclusions. For all we know half of these new calculations are gibberish, and they just stumbled onto something that looks like Pipistrelle by dumb luck.'

'Or,' Knox countered, 'this is just a fragment of what they had, and the fuse has already been lit by someone.'

Peterson thought for another long moment. 'Even if you're right,' he said, finally, 'and the security of the conference is in question, and your conspiracy is real, you still have to follow proper procedures. Give what you've got to White for review and we'll reassess the threat.'

'Then what?'

'Then you go home.'

CHAPTER TWENTY-SEVEN

Medev's Tupolev Tu-104 jet came into land over Lake Onega a few minutes before one o'clock in the afternoon. He'd been lucky that none of the planes kept on standby for the KGB at Chkalovsky airbase north of Moscow had been requisitioned for other emergencies that morning. He'd left the Lubyanka at half past nine, and was in the air an hour later.

He was the only passenger on the plane, and for the last two hours he'd let his mind reach back into his own memories of Karelia.

He'd been to this corner of the Soviet Union once before. In the winter of 1937 he'd been stationed on the Solovetsky Islands, five hundred kilometres north of Petrozavodsk in the middle of the White Sea. The islands were home to the Solovki special prison camp, where the people who had been deemed the greatest threat to Stalin's authority were sent during the Great Purge. The islands had originally been a single, vast Orthodox Christian monastery before they were taken over by the Party and turned into what would become the model for all the other gulags that would spring up across the country's more remote areas.

The islands were not hospitable. Living conditions for the NKVD interrogators, their staff, and the prison guards were harsh. For the prisoners, they were wretched. Many of the academics and intellectuals imprisoned at Solovki lost limbs either to frostbite or to forced labour. Others simply died overnight as temperatures, already below zero during the short days, plunged even further in the long nights.

Medev was a promising, young NKVD lieutenant when he was sent to Solovki. It was a formative experience. For five months, he saw first-hand the casual ruthlessness of absolute power, and learned how much ambition could advance your standing in Stalin's world, and how much could see you ending up in a mass grave. He also saw that doing what was right and doing what was right in the eyes of the Party were not always the same thing, even if they looked like they were.

The Solovetsky Monastery had originally been taken over to house forced labourers during the construction of the White Sea Canal, which would eventually link the Arctic coast to the Baltic Sea. By 1937 the first section of the canal had been completed and work had moved west.

The White Sea froze over in winter, and the thick ice could damage the entrance of the canal if it was left to build up. So, every day during winter fifty prisoners were taken out across the frozen sea to break the ice at the mouth of the canal. Because of the obvious opportunities for escape, extra men were drafted in for guard duty, often including Medev.

Prisoners, wearing whatever heavy rags they could find, would be marched from the camp before the sun rose, watched over while they worked for six hours without rest or food, and then marched back after the sun had fallen again. Some perished before they even reached the canal, and more as their bodies finally gave up after hours and hours of brutal work. The ones who managed to survive the day tended to make it back to the islands, the prospect of a metre or two of dry floor to rest on suddenly enough to keep them going.

None of the guards paid particularly close attention to how many prisoners died on any day, but one night, as the men were being lined up to head back across the ice, Medev sensed that there weren't enough of them still standing. He quietly left his position at the back of the loose column and walked towards the forest that ran near the edge of the canal. He immediately saw a messy path cutting through the trees. It looked like two sets of footprints, lopsided as if each was dragging the other.

Medev followed them into the forest, lifting his feet up to his knees with every step he took through the deep snow. The weak light of the day was almost completely gone, but after ten minutes of following the path Medev saw two hunched-over figures a hundred metres ahead of him. They turned, saw him, and began to desperately scramble away. Medev called out to the men to stop, but they wouldn't. He was forced to chase them. By now the snow was up to his thighs and pushing through it was exhausting. He had no idea how the prisoners were managing it, or how long it had taken them to get this far.

'Stop!' he shouted again.

But they kept struggling through the snow, grabbing onto each other and the bare trunks of trees to push themselves on until they finally tripped over something hidden in the snow and crashed into a drift.

It took a full minute for Medev to reach them. When he did, he saw that one had a makeshift splint on his right leg, and they were both so gaunt and grey he could barely believe they were still alive at all. He knew there was no way they could survive the journey back to Solovki, or whatever punishment the other guards might inflict on them for their attempted escape. He also knew they'd never survive a night in the snow without shelter. From the looks in both men's eyes, they knew all this too.

They gave up trying to struggle to their feet and just half kneeled, half slumped in the snow.

'Please,' one of them whispered.

It was so dark by then that Medev couldn't tell which one of them had said it, but he understood what they both wanted. He pulled his pistol from

155

the leather holster on his hip and shot them each in the head. The deep scarlet blood was slow to seep out of their frail, withered bodies. Ten minutes later two more guards arrived, alerted by the sound of gunfire. The next day Medev was promoted.

He was brought out of his memory as the Tu-104 touched the runway at Petrozavodsk airport. The plane taxied to a halt next to a large, black GAZ M21, freshly polished by the local KGB office in preparation for his arrival.

As he sat in the back seat he was handed a slim manila folder – the latest casualty and assessment report from Povenets B. It was considerably more detailed than the one that had been dispatched to Moscow. It also showed just how much that report had played down the scale of the disaster.

He read through the initial findings about the cause of the explosion, the city-wide loss of power that still hadn't been restored, and the multiple fires that had broken out overnight. Then he scanned the list of the deceased: twenty-seven power plant workers, sixteen children, and two teachers. Finally he reviewed the missing: three more workers and five more children, all presumed dead, and one scientist, unaccounted for. He recognised the scientist's surname from the reports he received from the GRU. But he was sure he'd seen it somewhere more recently too, much more recently. He checked the names of the dead, and found it halfway down the list of children.

CHAPTER TWENTY-EIGHT

It hadn't taken long for Zukolev to be moved to a private room in Petrozavodsk hospital. He believed this was because the hospital staff had realised just how important he was. But in reality the doctors had needed their intensive care beds for the more seriously wounded, and Zukolev's injuries had been relatively minor – just a broken arm and a deep gash across his chin, once all the dust had been cleaned off him.

Now he was propped up in his bed, his injured arm strapped to his side, and his stomach held down by tight sheets. He had a bandage across his jaw, but he was still feeding himself raspberries with his free hand. When he'd demanded them as soon as he'd been transferred to his private room, the nurses looking after him had thought it was some kind of delirious joke brought on by shock, until a man in dusty overalls arrived at the ward station, punnet in hand.

He was savouring a particularly large berry when the door to his room opened and Medev stepped inside.

'Who are you?' he asked, berry juice slipping across his lower lip.

Unlike Zukolev, Medev preferred the more anonymous attire of a dark suit to the general's uniform he could have worn. So Zukolev had no idea that he was talking to someone unfathomably more powerful than him.

Medev quietly closed the door behind him before responding, 'I'm the person who has to clean up the mess you've made.'

Then he crossed the short distance to Zukolev's bedside, picked up the bowl of berries, and moved them out of reach.

'How dare you come in here like this.' Zukolev couldn't believe this stranger's impudence. 'Don't you know who I am?'

'You're Major Yuri Zukolev,' Medev replied, now at the foot of his bed. 'GRU administrator of Povenets B. Charged with the safe keeping of three hundred souls.' His voice was measured, emotionless. 'And responsible for the deaths of fifty-four of them.'

Zukolev's face paled. Suddenly, for the first time in a very long time, he was scared.

'You're KGB,' Zukolev said, his voice faint.

Medev didn't need to confirm Zukolev's suspicion. His presence was enough.

'Do you have anything to say in your defence?' Medev's voice was still calm.

'You can't blame me for the incompetence of my workers,' Zukolev spluttered.

'Yes I can.'

Medev moved up the bed towards Zukolev. Zukolev frantically tried to claw his way out from under the sheets holding him down.

'The GRU will protect me from these baseless accusations,' Zukolev said. His voice was now high and desperate.

Medev put a hand on Zukolev's shoulder, as if trying to soothe him. Zukolev stopped moving, frozen in terror.

'They won't,' Medev replied.

The GRU and KGB might trade occasional jurisdictional blows, but everyone knew who held ultimate power. Medev tightened his grip on Zukolev's shoulder, then pulled a syringe from his jacket pocket and plunged it into Zukolev's neck. Zukolev tried to call out, but no sound came from his mouth. He was dead by the time Medev slipped quietly back out of the room.

As Medev made his way back down the corridor to the nurses' station, his mind finally made a connection it had been groping at since his morning briefing from Rykov.

He asked the nurse on duty if he could borrow her phone, then dialled the long list of numbers that could connect him securely to the Lubyanka. When Rykov answered, he told him that under no circumstances could the Americans be allowed to retrieve the next Corona payload. With twenty-two million square kilometres of

Soviet Union for them to spy on it would be terrible luck if the Americans had managed to photograph one small, smouldering *naukograd*. But it wasn't a risk Medev wanted to take.

CHAPTER TWENTY-NINE

Bennett made her way across the north side of Grosvenor Square towards the US embassy. It was an imposing presence. Its hard-edged, Modernist facade took up the whole western side of the square, and a large sculpture of a bald eagle with outstretched wings looked down from its roof on everyone who approached it.

The embassy had opened just over a year ago, and its interior had been designed to be as much of a statement about America's sense of importance as its brash exterior. The six above-ground levels contained vast conference rooms, banks of communications stations, and row after row of offices – each one's size correlating precisely with the rank of its occupier. The CIA took up the entire fourth floor, as well as a considerable amount of the building's subterranean levels, which had been given over to the agency's local archives.

This was where Bennett headed after flashing her security credentials at an uninterested guard and slipping through one of the small staff entrances on the side of the building.

161

The embassy was a piece of the United States on British soil, so American social mores ruled. In the rest of the city the golden hue of Bennett's skin and ice blue of her eyes might make her look like a northern European who had spent a long summer in warmer climes. In the embassy, they singled her out as what she really was – someone whose very existence made her fellow countrymen uncomfortable.

Many of the women who worked at the embassy lived together in houses in the area of the city bound to the north by Hyde Park and the south by the Thames. They were attracted by famous names and landmarks like the King's Road, Harrods, and the Royal Albert Hall. Rooms were often shared, and beds passed on to newcomers as people returned to America or found a Brit to marry and moved out. The embassy encouraged the system as it created a kind of sisterhood and support network that helped its female staff feel safe and settled.

But when Bennett arrived in London, she was told there was nowhere for her in any of the women's houses. A month later, after she'd found her own room in a boarding house off Gloucester Road, another woman had arrived, a blonde, white woman from New England. The embassy houses practically fought each other for her. There had been plenty of space all along, Bennett just wasn't wanted.

People did their best to ignore Bennett in

162

Grosvenor Square. Most of the time it irritated her, but today she was more than happy to let it work in her favour, especially in the archive, where the file clerks on duty chose not to see her moving through the aisles of record stacks.

First she went to the set of thick files the CIA held on Bianchi and Moretti. The agency had kept the two Italians under surveillance since they'd arrived in London to see if they posed a threat to local operations or if they were worth recruiting. Bennett wanted to see if anything had been added to their records since they'd been found dead. There was just a note saying MI5 were investigating their suspected murder. The front file had also been tagged with a green strip – code that all records relating to Bianchi and Moretti should be moved into deep storage during the next reconciliation cycle.

Her superiors may have stopped caring about the Italians, but she was still very interested in them. And so, apparently, was MI5. Bennett didn't know where Knox had gone after he'd given her the slip in Soho the night before, but she was willing to bet he'd gone to Deptford and Bianchi and Moretti's flat. Now she wanted to know what connected Kaspar, Horne, and the Italians. Unfortunately, the CIA didn't have any records on Horne or the Calder Hall Ring, and Bennett had already exhausted the information held on Kaspar in London. She could have put in a request to the central records store in Virginia for whatever

163

they held on him, but that would take too much time and probably earn her a reprimand.

Before she gave up completely on the archive, she stopped by the large pile of new files waiting to be carried off into the stacks and quickly scanned through them. The fourth folder just held a single photo. It was of a woman, her hair caught mid-turn as she walked into a building. The image was slightly blurry, taken with a long lens. The woman's narrow eyes looked more like sunken slits, and wisps of loose hair hung over her cheeks. But the expression on her face was clear enough. She looked long past the point of exhaustion. But more than that, Bennett thought she looked haunted, like something unspeakably awful had happened to her. She turned the photo over, reading the location and timestamp: Swedish embassy, Helsinki, 16:47, 16 July. Yesterday afternoon. It must have been sent to London almost as soon as it had been taken.

The woman's name was written underneath in different-coloured ink, added by someone once a source inside the Swedish embassy had confirmed her identity: Irina Valera. Bennett recognised the name, but she had no idea how she'd ended up in Helsinki. She turned the photograph over and looked at it again, trying to work out what had happened to her.

Bennett had a choice: put the photo back in its folder or do something else, something that could end up with her facing much more than a reprimand. She stood still for a moment, deciding if she was ready to cross a very big line. Then she took the photograph to the unattended Xerox machine next to the chief clerk's desk and made a copy of it before slipping the original back onto the pile of filing.

CHAPTER THIRTY

An hour after the bus left Ilomantsi, it had deposited Valera in the city of Joensuu. Joensuu was the biggest place she had been since she'd left Leningrad, and it was well away from the border with Russia. It felt like a metropolis compared to Povenets B. Well-fed people walked along its streets and riverbanks, cars drove on its roads, and a never-ending stream of boats sailed beneath its bridges.

Valera could have stayed in Joensuu, found somewhere out of the way to rest and build up her strength for a day or two, or stowed away on a ship heading out onto Lake Pyhäselkä and disappeared into the network of waterways that criss-crossed Finland. But she couldn't shake the feeling that at any moment she might be snatched up and taken back to Russia. The ties that bound Finland and its neighbour ran almost as deep as the divisions that separated them. Russia had exerted influence over Finland for centuries, and even after independence and multiple, bloody wars there were still plenty of people whose loyalties lay to the east. For every good Samaritan

166

Valera might encounter, she might also meet someone looking to curry favour with Moscow.

She'd decided that she had to keep moving.

Her ride from Ilomantsi had dropped her off in the middle of Joensuu's old town and, not wanting to expose herself as an outsider by asking for directions, she had spent almost an hour finding the main city bus station.

She'd tried to buy a ticket to Helsinki, but this time the clerk had refused her rubles. He'd said something to her, but Valera had no idea what. She'd tried, quietly, speaking to him in Swedish and then English, but he didn't understand either.

Valera had felt the eyes of the queue behind her boring into her back, and then she'd felt a hand gently rest on her shoulder. She'd looked at the fat fingers curling round her clavicle and for one terrifying moment thought they belonged to Zukolev. But they didn't. They were attached to an old man who had taken pity on her and translated the clerk's instructions to go get her money changed into Finnish markka two desks down.

After she'd bought her ticket she went to the station's small cafe, where she ate her first proper meal in days – a thick, meaty stew that she had to coax slowly down her throat. Then, an hour later, she'd got on another bus. Seven hours after that, she'd arrived in Helsinki. And just before five o'clock in the evening she'd walked through the doors of the Swedish embassy on the waterfront of the Finnish capital and requested political asylum.

Valera had no way of knowing that the CIA had a car permanently stationed in the ferry terminal car park across from the embassy and that the young agent sitting behind its steering wheel had taken her photo as she crossed the road and went inside. America had received its fair share of Soviet defectors in its European embassies over the years, and since Rudolf Nureyev, Russia's greatest ballet star, had requested asylum in Paris a month ago the CIA had been watching at a long list of potential crossover points all over the continent.

Most of the Swedish embassy's senior staff had already left for the day when Valera walked in, and had to be urgently called back. All except the ambassador himself who, it was decided, would be better off not knowing about Valera until the Swedish security service, RPS/Säk, had worked out what to do with her.

The embassy was used to Russia dangling fake defectors at its front desk, promising the earth or begging for help. But they'd never seen anyone like Valera – someone who truly looked beaten down by despair but who refused to be defeated by it, and who spoke almost perfect Swedish.

However, it still took three hours of conversations and phone calls, including to the physics departments at Stockholm and Uppsala Universities, to establish that Valera was who she said she was, and another one to decide that instead of making her

168

the ambassador's problem, a seat should be found for her on the 10 p.m. SAS flight from Helsinki to Stockholm.

She'd been given twenty minutes to freshen herself up and change into a clean set of clothes kindly donated by one of the embassy secretaries. Then she was driven out to the airport.

CHAPTER THIRTY-ONE

Knox knew trying to confront Manning had been a mistake. An amateurish, egotistical mistake. It was the kind of rash behaviour he'd drag a junior agent over the coals for. Manning wasn't going to confess to being a double agent just because Knox wanted him to. And if Knox's concerns about the security of the OECD conference and Operation Pipistrelle were as serious as he claimed, then Peterson was right and he should have taken the Italians' papers straight to White. But he hadn't. And he wasn't going to.

Knox walked south, away from Fortnum's, cutting through Green Park and then St James's and down to the river. The hot night had turned into a muggy day, heavy with clouds. It was the kind of weather that reminded Londoners of pea-soupers and the Great Smog of 1952.

Knox needed to clear his head and stop letting his emotions and distrust of Manning get the better of him. He needed a more rational perspective.

He made his way east along Victoria Embankment. Opposite him the South Bank was still suffering its decade-long hangover from the Festival of Britain. Skylon, the slender spire that had been suspended over the riverbank as a vision of the nation's bright tomorrow, was long gone. As was the grandiosely named Dome of Discovery that had been built next to it. The festival was supposed to be a beacon of hope and change, a celebration of a nation emerging from post-war austerity. And it had been, for the few months it was open.

Knox and Williams had visited the festival, along with everyone else in the city, it seemed, over the summer of 1951. It was a welcome distraction from their office hours spent monitoring the swelling ranks of American and Russian agents treating London as their playground, all the while wondering if the stalemate along the 38th parallel would break and turn Korea into another world war.

Only the Royal Festival Hall was left standing now. The rest of the festival grounds had been cleared for redevelopment. So far only the new twenty-seven-storey headquarters of Royal Dutch Shell had started to rise in Skylon's place.

He crossed over Blackfriars Bridge, stopping briefly to feel the wind blow past him. Even on the most stifling days, the air still moved on the Thames. He watched a heavy barge float downstream and under the bridge to the docks that lined the south side of the river from Blackfriars to beyond Tower Bridge.

He didn't know what he was going to say to

Holland, but he wanted to see him. Maybe sitting with him would help him accept how easily he'd let himself be manipulated, or maybe it would push him to do something about it.

Knox had visited Holland in Guy's hospital every evening since he'd been rushed there from Highgate. Every evening except yesterday. The nurses who worked nights had no idea how Knox managed to appear at Holland's bedside out of thin air at the start of their shifts. They'd just check Holland's private room during their rounds, and suddenly he'd be there. Then, ten minutes or an hour later, they'd look in again and he'd be gone.

The hospital was busier than Knox was used to this afternoon. Visiting hours were in full swing and wives, husbands, parents, and children swarmed through the building. The grown-ups looked worried, resigned, or dog-tired. The children either stared excitedly at their unusual surroundings or ignored them.

Every bed Knox passed on his way to Holland's room had someone next to it, talking, fussing, or just sitting quietly. And so did Holland's.

Sarah Holland hadn't slept properly in days. She'd found her husband lying face down on a thick-pile rug in their living room when she'd come home on Sunday evening after an afternoon visiting friends, his body limp, eyes closed, and breathing shallow and slow. She phoned for an ambulance, then she phoned Leconfield House. And for the last week her whole life had consisted of sitting at her husband's bedside for two hours every morning and afternoon, and the rest of the time sitting at home, waiting to come back to the hospital, or for someone at Leconfield House to call and tell her something.

'Sorry, I didn't realise you were here,' Knox said, as the door clicked shut behind him. 'I'll leave you alone.'

Sarah looked up at him from Holland's side. She didn't seem surprised. She looked like she'd been expecting him. She was immaculately dressed in a muted, floral dress. Her hair was neat, her make-up perfect, but Knox could see how tired she was.

'No you won't,' Sarah replied. Her voice was cool, measured. 'Stay.'

'How is he?' Knox asked, looking at Holland. He still wasn't used to seeing him in his hospital bed, asleep, unable to wake up. Holland was a man with a powerful presence and it didn't seem right for him to be so reduced, tucked under sheets in a pair of flannel pyjamas instead of behind his desk in one of his dark, pinstriped suits.

'You'd know as well as me,' Sarah said. 'The nurses tell me you visit James every day.'

'It's the least I can do.' Knox had known Sarah for years, but he found himself falling back on the formalities people used when talking to the grieving.

'Is it?' Sarah asked, her voice suddenly changing from cool to cold.

'I'll come back later,' Knox said, sensing the change in her tone.

'The hell you will.'

'I don't want to upset you.'

'You think you're upsetting me? My husband lying in a coma no one can do anything about upsets me. The one person who could help him refusing to do anything bloody infuriates me.'

Sarah had been privy to most of the details of MI5's investigation, including Knox's lack of cooperation.

Knox knew he owed her the truth. Holland had been more than a patron and mentor to him. Though neither of them would ever say it, the older man had become a kind of father to him, a replacement for the one he'd never had the chance to know. And in many ways Sarah had been his surrogate mother, offering her own support, ear, or advice whenever needed.

Knox wanted to tell her where he'd been the night Holland had fallen into the coma. He wanted to tell her she was right to blame him, that it was his fault. He wanted to share with her the secret he and Holland had kept for fifteen years. But he couldn't, because Holland himself had sworn him to secrecy, and because the more people who knew about it, the more people could be hurt by it.

Sarah, however, didn't care about that. She just wanted to know what had happened to her husband.

'Please, just tell me where you were,' she said, her exhaustion creeping into her voice.

Knox couldn't bring himself to betray Holland's trust in him after so long, even to the one person closer to him than Knox was. 'I can't,' he said.

'After everything we've done for you? I'm his wife, for God's sake.'

Sarah knew her husband's life was built on secrets, but they'd never kept any from each other. Apart from the one he shared only with Knox.

'I can't,' he said.

'That's not your decision to make.'

'No, it was James's.' As soon as the words left Knox's mouth he knew he'd made a mistake.

Sarah's face set hard, her tiredness and worry finally turning to rage. But she didn't explode at Knox. Instead, she got up, kissed Holland on the forehead, and straightened his gold-rimmed glasses that sat next to his wedding ring – a thin band of bronze shaped like a belt buckle – on his bedside table.

She smoothed down her dress, picked up her handbag, and walked past Knox.

'Say goodbye,' she said in a quiet voice. 'And don't come back.'

Then she left.

Knox didn't say goodbye to Holland. He didn't say anything. He just sat with him, going over and over his encounters with Manning and Sarah in his mind. His reason for not breaking his pact with Holland and telling Sarah where he had been was that it could ruin both his career and her husband's. But, if Manning was now permanent director general and Knox's professional life already lay in tatters, how much did it really matter?

After several, silent hours he decided to go up to Highgate and tell Sarah everything. It might not bring her husband back to her, but perhaps it would make her feel better to know that even if he had kept something from her, it had been to protect her.

CHAPTER THIRTY-TWO

Knox's London had almost been destroyed twice. Once by the Luftwaffe, and once by his parents' deaths. Now, with Manning in control of MI5, his world was on the brink of collapse again. What no one knew was how his parents' deaths were connected to his mentor's coma. No one apart from Knox, Holland, and, soon, his wife.

Knox left Guy's, walking back along Southwark Street towards Blackfriars Bridge. Rush hour was over, but there were still plenty of people about. The man who Knox had noticed following him since he'd turned out of St Thomas Street may just have been making his way to the tube and home after a long day in the office. But that didn't explain why he was wearing the international uniform of street muscle – a large, black leather bomber jacket and a flat cap tilted low over his eyes in the middle of summer.

Knox reached the entrance to Blackfriars station at the northern end of the bridge. He passed two paper sellers trying to get rid of their last copies of the *Evening Standard* and the *Evening News*.

Both were leading with stories about the rapid build-up of American military in West Berlin. Knox slowed down to read the headlines, and see if the man following him would carry on past him or linger on the bridge. He headed straight into the station and, after a moment, so did Knox.

He made his way down to the tube and stopped in the middle of the platform, already anticipating his change at Charing Cross to the Northern Line, which would take him up to Highgate.

The man in the bomber was further down the platform, keeping enough distance between him and Knox to put them in different carriages when the tube arrived. If he was following Knox, he was being smart about it. And if this was another round in Knox's game with Peterson, he'd sent a much better player. Out of the corner of his eye, Knox watched him lean against the wall next to one of the station roundels. With the sudden context he realised the man was a giant. Six foot five, at least, and built like the side of a house.

A bright red Circle Line train pulled into the station, screeching loudly as its worn brakes grabbed at the tracks. The doors opened with a judder and a few commuters got off. Knox hung back on the platform. So did the giant. At the last moment, Knox hopped through the closing doors. So did the giant.

The train lumbered its way to the next stop, speeding up only to slow down again over and over, as if it wasn't sure what lay ahead in the dark tunnel. Knox resisted the urge to look at the other passengers. He wanted to be as inconspicuous as possible, and the easiest way to stand out and draw attention in London was to make eye contact with people on the tube.

Temple station was empty. No one got off, and no one got on. Knox snatched a glance through the open doors before they slid shut again, but couldn't see any movement in the next carriage.

Charing Cross was next. This time, as soon as the doors opened, Knox burst off the train and sprinted down the stairs his carriage had lined up perfectly with. He didn't look back, so he didn't see the giant pushing his way down the platform and into the tunnel, trying to catch up with him.

Knox reached the northbound platform of the Northern Line as a train was about to depart. It was one of the new silver deep-level trains. He stretched his arms out, jamming the nearest set of doors open. Several of the carriage's other occupants tutted loudly as he climbed inside, angry that they'd delayed their journey home by a few seconds. But Knox ignored them. He kept his eyes on the platform, watching the giant reach the platform too late to stop the train pulling away.

Knox had lost him. But he couldn't risk the chance that the man had guessed his destination and would follow him all the way to Highgate.

He got off at the next station, Strand. From there he could have run the short distance to Trafalgar Square station and the Bakerloo Line, or doubled back on himself and taken the Northern Line under the river to Waterloo. But he needed to make sure he'd slipped his tail, and that would be a lot easier above ground where he wouldn't be trapped in trains and tunnels.

Both of the station's recently installed escalators were cordoned off, so Knox took the spiral stair-case that climbed a shaft next to the station's old, original lifts up to the ticket hall. It was quiet. Knox knew that once he made it up to street level he'd be exposed as he crossed Trafalgar Square, but only for a minute.

He made it three steps up the exit that led to the south-east corner of the square before a boot slammed into his chest and sent him flying back down. He skidded several feet across the floor, sliding to a halt as the body the boot belonged to reached the bottom of the stairs. It was another man wearing an unseasonably heavy coat. This one was a few inches shorter than the giant who had followed Knox to Embankment. But he was almost as wide as he was tall and, from Knox's viewpoint on the ground, it looked like it was all muscle.

Knox scrambled up to his feet. He heard the sound of footsteps approaching behind him. It was giant number one. Somehow they'd known where he was going and how he'd react if he real-ised he was being shadowed. He tried to back away as the two giants circled him, but there was nowhere for him to go. In the end, he held up his hands and managed to say 'Gentlemen—' before they lunged at him.

Giant number one struck first, followed by his shorter friend. They alternated their assault, keeping Knox off balance as they hit and grabbed at him. The attack was brutal but calculated. They wanted to do damage, but Knox could tell between blows that they were holding back. Instead of just one of them holding him down while the other laid into him, they kept switching roles and going after different parts of his body. Knox realised they wanted something more than just to hurt him. They were searching him. Not for his watch or wallet, but for the papers and passports he was carrying in the inside pocket of his jacket.

Knox twisted and squirmed, taking every hit while not letting them hold him still. Eventually the giants ran out of patience and the smaller one grabbed both of his arms and kicked his legs out from under him, pinning him down on the tiles as the larger giant started working his way through his pockets. He reached inside Knox's jacket. His fingers brushed the papers, but before he could pull them out a voice shouted out behind them.

One of the station guards had finally noticed what was happening. He was ancient, small, and bent over under the weight of his uniform. The old man couldn't have done much to help Knox, but just interrupting the beating he was taking was enough to spook the giants. The taller one let go of the papers as the smaller one let go of Knox.

Then, after both giving him one last kick in the side, they ran past the guard and disappeared.

Knox used the tiled wall to help push himself back up onto his feet as the guard approached him.

'Not fair that, two on one,' the guard said.

'A case of mistaken identity,' Knox replied. 'They thought I was a friend of theirs.'

He thanked the old man for his help, but declined his offer of calling the police. Instead, he straightened his jacket, patted himself down, and made his way up the staircase he'd been kicked down a minute before.

At the top he looked out across the square, just in case the giants were waiting for round two. They weren't. He checked the papers and passports were still in his jacket pocket, held a hand to his side where it felt like the final kick had cracked a couple of his ribs, took a breath, and ran.

He sprinted across Trafalgar and Leicester Squares, then through Piccadilly Circus, weaving his way through the people bustling under the giant glowing adverts for Wrigley, BP, and Coca-Cola, and avoiding the policemen in their jet-black uniforms and bleached white gloves trying to control the traffic and early-evening crowds. His side throbbed as he ran, and the scar across his head that itched whenever he pushed himself too hard felt like it was on fire.

He struggled to keep his breath even and shallow enough not to add more pain to his side. He finally slowed down as he cut through the grim, narrow Ham Yard to Archer Street, and was walking at a normal pace by the time he turned north into Rupert Street. Instead of continuing on the short distance to Kemp House, he turned right into Tisbury Court and stopped outside a small, anonymous door halfway down the alley. He didn't want to risk going home yet, just in case the men from Trafalgar Square knew where he lived and had got there ahead of him. He needed somewhere to hide and recover, somewhere people wouldn't think to look because they had no idea it existed.

He knocked on the door three times and after a long, pregnant moment, it opened.

The basement bar was dark, lit only by a few scattered candles. There was no way of telling how far back the room stretched, how many tables there were, or who was sitting at them. The only clues were the murmur of intimate conversations that mingled with the quiet, mournful jazz that played from somewhere, and the occasional candlelit glint of a cocktail glass or flare of a burning cigarette.

The bar was private, members-only in all but dues. It served a clientele who didn't want to be seen, who craved respite from the city above and wanted to be alone, or sometimes together, away from prying eyes.

It would normally take a few minutes to adjust to the dimness, but Knox had been to this particular clandestine refuge from the world enough times to know his way through it with his eyes closed. He walked in a diagonal across the room, avoiding the tables and legs of the other patrons, to a long counter lined with stools and a row of low lamps.

A man sat at one end of the counter. His body was lost in the dark but his tanned face and perfectly quiffed hair were haloed by the lamp hanging just above them. Knox chose a spot at the other end, suddenly conscious of how much of a mess he must look after his sprint across Soho. He slouched on his stool, craning his body to avoid the pool of light on the counter in front of him, and nodded to the bartender, a woman in a three-piece suit whose pompadour hair matched the man's.

'You look like you've had a time of it,' she said. 'What'll it be? Vodka? Whisky?'

'Both,' Knox answered.

'Sure thing.' She poured two generous measures of the spirits over ice and passed the two glasses across the bar to Knox.

He swallowed the vodka in one go, then started to swirl the whisky, encouraging the ice to melt a little and take the edge off the deep-brown liquid. Eventually the vodka did its job. His side stopped aching, his scar stopped feeling like it was burning into his skull, and he started to calm down.

CHAPTER THIRTY-THREE

The crew of the Hercules stationed at Cooke Air Force Base understood why the timings of their recovery flights had to be kept secret until the last minute. But they didn't enjoy the endless days spent on standby, waiting for the go signal. It also irked them that no matter when they flew, day or night, the *Shining Emerald* was always waiting for them in the target zone over the Pacific. It seemed like the KGB knew their mission parameters before they did.

Evening was always the worst time to fly. Heading west out over the coast, it took every pair of eyes on board to spot the parachutes attached to the Corona payload capsules against the fierce rays of the setting sun. At least this evening the *Shining Emerald* would have just as much of a problem as the Hercules. A thick blanket of low cloud stretched over the ocean, cutting visibility to just a few thousand feet from sea level.

Fortunately, luck was also on the Hercules' side, and just as the plane entered the target zone, several shouts went up. The parachute had been spotted twenty degrees off their current path,

185

roughly five miles away. The pilot altered course and altitude to give them plenty of time to reach it before it was lost in the clouds.

When the Hercules was about a mile from the capsule, a strange shadow started to appear on the surface of the clouds in front of the plane. It looked like it was projected a few feet ahead of the cockpit, but it couldn't have been because the Hercules was still flying into the sun. The pilot made a small course change, and the shadow matched it. He came back onto his original trajectory, and so did the shadow.

Then the shadow pulled away. It rose out of the clouds and solidified. First a long, silver tube. Then two vast, swept-back wings. A Soviet Tupolev Tu-95 long-range strategic bomber.

The huge Russian plane gleamed in the sunlight as it climbed in front of the Hercules. It continued to pull away from the American plane, its huge engines roaring as it accelerated towards the falling capsule. There was no time for the Hercules to overtake it. All the American crew could do was watch as the Tupolev got further and further away from them and closer and closer to the parachute.

The Tupolev had no hook hanging behind it, but it did have a long, thin refuelling probe projecting out from its nose. The Russian pilot lined the probe up with the gap between the parachute and the Corona capsule, and squeezed one more push from the throttle. His aim was true and the probe

186

shot through the parachute lines like they were the eye of a needle.

Everyone in the Hercules sat in stunned silence as they watched the Tupolev descend back into the clouds and vanish with the Corona payload pinned against the underside of its cockpit.

CHAPTER THIRTY-FOUR

The Hercules returned to Cooke Air Force Base at 9 p.m. Pacific time. It was 11 p.m. by the time the crew was debriefed, which meant it was 2 a.m. Eastern time when the phone in Patrick Dixon's hallway started to ring.

He'd told Langley that the post-flight report could wait until the morning. He'd stayed late at the office too many nights recently and needed some decent sleep. If he was being called now, something must have gone very wrong.

NASA had offered Dixon one of the apartments in the research centre grounds when he'd moved down from New England, but he'd preferred to keep a little distinction between his work and home life. He'd found an old colonial-era villa in Armstrong Gardens on the far side of Hampton, south of Langley, that looked out over Chesapeake Bay. Its fretwork veranda and bright painted walls stuck out among the more recent red-brick houses that dominated the neighbourhood. They had been built to survive whatever the Atlantic threw at them, but the villa already had. Dixon loved it.

He dragged himself out of bed and along the

dark landing. He almost tripped over Loki, his jet-black cat, who had taken to sitting at the top of the stairs at night, but remembered he was there just in time to clumsily hop over him and land heavily on the first step. He reached the bottom of the staircase intact and picked up the phone. He didn't even have a chance to say hello before the voice on the other end of the line started telling him exactly how badly things had gone with the evening flight. Thirty seconds later he'd hung up and was making his way back up the dark stairs to get dressed.

The security breach Dixon had feared for months had finally happened. And in dramatic fashion. Questions would now be asked, arguments had, pounds of flesh claimed. Worst of all, people would want to know what progress he'd made on coming up with a more secure way to control and retrieve the intelligence Corona gathered, and the answer to that was still vanishingly little.

The only saving grace of the Russians picking this capsule to intercept was that its payload was relatively low-value. All they'd find when they cracked it open would be an experimental pressurisation system containing a few strips of unexposed film. If they'd wanted to score a major intelligence coup, they'd picked the wrong day for it.

Langley was quiet when Dixon arrived at the research centre twenty minutes later. The night-watchman waved him through the security gates and he drove across the empty car park to his reserved spot outside the building that had been given over to the Corona programme.

The only light in the building came from his office. Someone was waiting for him.

Phinneus Murphy had worked for the CIA for a long time. He looked like it, and he smoked like it. Dixon had never seen him without a cigarette between his fingers and another lined up to take its place. He was slouched in the easy chair that sat in front of Dixon's desk, lighting up, as Dixon stepped into his office. They'd worked together long enough to dispense with pleasantries, so as soon as Murphy was finished taking his first, long pull on his cigarette, he got down to business.

'What are we going to tell the president?' he asked.

Dixon had anticipated Murphy's question. 'They didn't get anything important,' he answered. 'Maybe we even let them take it. Something worthless to keep them occupied.'

'Is that true?'

'It could be. We got lucky.' Dixon took a cigarette from Murphy's case and sat down at his desk. He only smoked when he was stressed.

'We got lazy,' Murphy replied, between drags.

The Marlboro Man had sold America on the image of smokers as rugged and masculine. Cigarettes were to be savoured, smoked slowly by powerful people thinking serious thoughts. Murphy

190

didn't smoke like the Marlboro Man. He smoked like nicotine was his air and oxygen was poison.

'We've known they've been on to Corona for months. We should have been expecting this,' he said.

'Not my area of expertise, I'm afraid,' Dixon replied.

'It doesn't take an expert to guess that the more times you let someone get on a podium and tell the world how great we are, the more everyone's going to want our stuff.'

'We could always just share Corona,' Dixon said. 'You know, for the collective good of humanity.'

'You going commie on me?' Murphy asked.

Dixon let out a short laugh. Murphy lit his next cigarette.

'Speaking of which,' Murphy continued, 'next on the president's list is sticking a bunch of satellites over Vietnam. Got it into his head Corona is the key to nipping this Cong problem in the bud.'

'He knows it can't see through things, right? Unless we start clearing jungle it won't be much help.'

'He's been told. But the practicalities aren't his problem, they're ours.'

'My hands are full,' Dixon said.

His recent late nights had involved a succession of increasingly bizarre experiments to try to crack the atmospheric barrier problem. Dixon and his team had come at the problem from every angle they could think of. They'd explored the idea of vast ground-based aerials, or high-altitude radio balloons. They'd considered developing reusable space planes that could take off and land from regular airstrips. They'd even thought about somehow shrinking down the IBM 7090 mainframe computer that was currently being used by the Mercury programme so it could actually be launched into space. Each experiment was approached with fresh optimism, but each one failed. It was tiring.

'You know, it's cute how you think you have a choice,' Murphy said.

Dixon finally finished his cigarette. 'I thought we were winning, anyway.'

'Of course we are,' Murphy answered. 'America doesn't lose. But we could be winning faster. Ideally before the next election.'

'There it is,' Dixon said.

'Don't act so surprised. Everything's always about votes.'

A dark thought suddenly struck Dixon. 'He'd use Corona on our own people, wouldn't he?'

Murphy pulled himself up out of the easy chair. 'I wouldn't recommend it, at least not letting the electorate know it was happening. But I can see the logic.'

'That's not something I want to help happen,' Dixon said.

'It's been happening for years,' Murphy replied. 'Did you know in the thirties the Nazis worked out which US states had the highest numbers of

German migrants in them so they could run adverts about the joys of National Socialism in the local papers and swing US public opinion against intervening in Europe? I saw the map they made.'

'We're using Nazis as our reference point, now?'

Murphy smiled. 'I'm just saying this is nothing new. Finding people, working out what they want, and giving it to them. It's basic advertising.'

'That's not what either of the As in NASA stand for,' Dixon said.

'You sure?' The grin on Murphy's face faded as soon as he finished his joke. 'This is a mess, Patrick.'

'That it is, Phinn.'

'Want another one?' Murphy asked, offering Dixon his cigarette case.

'Thanks, but one's enough for me.'

'Suit yourself.' Murphy prepared another cigarette for himself as he made his way to the door. 'See you tomorrow, if we both still work here by then.'

CHAPTER THIRTY-FIVE

Knox's hangover was vicious. His head was pounding, his mouth was dry, and he could barely focus. He couldn't remember how long he'd stayed at the bar under Tisbury Court. The taste of whisky was still on his tongue, but it was mixed with enough other flavours for it to feel like a drop in a large ocean of alcohol. He wasn't sure what else he'd drunk, or eaten, but given how queasy he felt he was fairly sure he'd skipped dinner.

He also had no idea how or when he'd got home. Or who with. Someone was lying next to him in his bed, completely covered in sheets that rose and fell in time with their unconscious breathing. Knox had no memory of meeting anyone last night. But he clearly had. At some point he'd work out what had happened. But first, he wanted to know who was in his kitchen, loudly grinding coffee beans.

He slid out of his bed and slipped on a robe. He left the stranger under the covers and walked out into the kitchen, half-expecting to see Peterson waiting to question him about his ungentlemanly nocturnal habits. Instead, he found a young woman pouring two cups of fresh coffee.

This was the second time in three days someone had surprised him in his own home – the third if he counted the person still asleep in his bed. Through the haze of his hangover it took him a moment to recognise her pixie-cut hair and realise that he'd met her before.

'So, you're not Kaspar's assistant, then?' he said. His voice was croaky. He picked up the coffee she'd made for him and took a tentative sip, letting a small amount of the hot liquid mix with whatever was still sloshing around in his stomach.

'Afraid not,' she replied, her Midwestern accent coming through even in this short phrase.

'Are you working for Peterson?' he asked, realising she was also the right size and build to be the person in the hat who had followed him two nights ago.

She shook her head. 'I'm a friend.'

He resisted the dismissive grunt he felt in his throat. 'What were you doing in Cambridge?' he asked instead.

'The same thing as you, I reckon,' she replied. 'Not finding the answers I was looking for.'

Knox made a mental note to have some better locks fitted to his front door as she slid a photograph over the kitchen counter to him. It was a slightly blurred, blown-up image of a woman on a street. Knox reached out to pick it up, wincing as his side reminded him of the kicking it had taken last night. He didn't recognise her, or any details in the background of the picture that would tell him where it had been taken. All he could see was that whoever she was, she looked like she'd been through hell.

'Who is she?' he asked. 'And who are you?'

'I'm Abey Bennett, CIA. And that is Irina Valera. She is, or was, one of the Soviet Union's most promising physicists. She disappeared in Leningrad three years ago, and no one has seen or heard of her since. Until she walked into the Swedish embassy in Helsinki yesterday afternoon.'

Knox looked at the photo again. 'Very interesting, but I don't see what that has to do with me.' He took another, larger gulp of the coffee and briefly wondered about finding some food before his gut confirmed it wasn't ready for that just yet.

'Before she disappeared, Miss Valera was working on manipulating radio waves. The same kind of manipulation your dead Italians were working on' – she took her own sip of coffee for dramatic effect – 'and that Mr White is so fond of.'

Knox slowly lowered his cup. He'd been happy to entertain Bennett, whoever she was, while he woke up and got his head straight. The photo of the woman meant nothing to him, and she could easily have learned Bianchi and Moretti's names from Kaspar just by waiting for him to return to his office after his encounter with Knox. But her knowing who White was and about Operation

Pipistrelle told Knox two things. First, she was a bona fide member of the intelligence community. And second, one of MI5's most closely guarded secrets was out. He needed to tread very carefully for the next few minutes and find out exactly what she knew.

'Bianchi and Moretti were just a couple of opportunists,' he said, giving her MI5's de facto official line.

'Maybe they were. But they were killed because of their work.'

'That's supposition.'

'This is all supposition,' she replied, a smirk on her lips. 'That's what spies do. We suppose.'

Knox had to give her that. 'The investigation into Bianchi and Moretti is no longer active.'

'Your behaviour suggests otherwise,' she said.

Knox wondered how much she really knew, and how much she was fishing. He'd stored the crate from the Italians' flat in his bedroom wardrobe after he'd found Peterson rifling through its contents. And she definitely couldn't know about the new papers he'd found in Deptford, unless everything she'd told him was a lie and she was working for the people who had come after him under Trafalgar Square. But he doubted it. However, he also doubted that she wasn't above having given the rest of his flat a quick once-over while he was still asleep.

'MI5's interest in them has ended,' he said.

'Which makes sense, if someone's trying to cover

their ass,' Bennett replied. 'You're not the only one who thinks there's a wolf in your henhouse.'

'There's no proof MI5 has been compromised.' Knox was aware he sounded like Peterson when he'd voiced the exact same idea to him outside the Fountain.

'Well, you sure are acting like there is, and here's the evidence,' Bennett said, pointing at the photo of Valera.

'That's a big leap,' he said, covering his relief with another swig of coffee.

'This is a big problem.' She wasn't smirking any more. 'We were watching Bianchi and Moretti too. They were murdered, and now there's a Russian genius in the same field suddenly in play. There's no way they aren't connected.'

Bennett had made the link herself the night before. It was what made her finally decide it was time to talk to Knox.

'And, for argument's sake,' Knox replied, 'so what if they are?'

'We're peering through the keyhole of a door that's about to be thrown open. Whoever is at the front of this technology will have the power to spy on anyone, anywhere, any time.'

'Big Brother isn't real,' Knox said.

'Not yet he isn't,' Bennett replied. 'But one day he will be. If we're lucky it'll be a friendly face watching over us. But what if it isn't? Living under constant surveillance. No more privacy. Never knowing who we could trust.'

If Knox had any other job, he'd think she was crazy. But he was a spy, and as alarmist as he thought Bennett was being, he knew what she was suggesting wasn't beyond the realms of possibility.

'You can't stop progress,' he said after a moment, now repeating the phrase White had used on him countless times over the last six months whenever he'd expressed doubts about Atlas.

'No,' she replied between sips of coffee, 'but you can guide it in the right direction. Make sure the right people are in control.' She picked up the photo of Valera. 'This will be circulated to the heads of MI5 and Six this morning as part of our regular information exchange. By now, the Russians will have realised one of their prized scientists is missing, and they'll want her back. If they've turned someone here, they'll send them after her. But if we get Valera first, we can secure a vital asset for both our countries, and set a trap for the mole.'

That felt less like fiction to Knox. If this woman was as important as Bennett believed, the KGB would do everything they could to stop her spilling her secrets. And if those secrets were as potentially world-changing as Bennett thought, every Soviet agent west of the Iron Curtain and north of the Alps could be put on her tail.

'If there is one,' he said.

'If,' she repeated, the smirk back on her face.

'But why come to me?' he asked. 'Why not keep this in Grosvenor Square?'

Bennett decided to tip the last card in her hand. 'Because you have a vested interest,' she replied. 'And so do I.' She took one last swig of coffee. 'You need something to get you back in. I'm surrounded by colleagues who think I should be doing their filing. We both need a win.'

She picked up both of their empty cups and put them in the sink. 'And, besides, what else have you got going on today?'

Knox quickly considered his options. The easiest, of course, was to send Bennett on her way. But he had no more leads beyond the Italians' equations and passports, and there was every chance the men who had come after him last night were still roaming the streets looking for him – for all he knew, under Manning's orders. Now he was permanent director general, Knox would need something big to bring Manning down. Something very big. Something like catching him red-handed working for the Russians. Knox might not be able to save Holland from being dethroned, but maybe he could still avenge him. He decided he may as well take a look down Bennett's rabbit hole and see where it led.

'Nothing,' he answered, now smirking himself.

With perfect timing, his front door swung shut. Knox's overnight companion had finally decided to take their leave.

'Great,' Bennett replied. 'Now go get cleaned up. Our plane leaves in two hours.'

CHAPTER THIRTY-SIX

Stockholm looked like a chocolate-box fantasy to Valera. Its ancient buildings and winding streets were immaculate. No cobbles had been pulled up for makeshift weapons, no old doors taken off their hinges for firewood. The bridges between the islands that made up the city were lit up, even late into the night.

Valera had been taken to the Hotel Reisen, on the edge of Gamla Stan, the ancient heart of Stockholm, as soon as she'd arrived in the city. The hotel building dated back to the 1700s, but its rooms were spacious and modern. Valera's was almost as large as her entire home and lab in Povenets B combined.

After devouring a small plate of meat and cheese and a glass of *akvavit* that had been sent up to her compliments of the night manager, she was left alone. She'd carefully placed both backpacks in the room's large closet, which had been filled with more clothes for her, then stood at the window, staring out at the water below her until the adrenaline she'd been running on finally ran out and she crawled into the large, soft bed.

In the morning, she was woken by a knock at the door and a week's worth of breakfast. She ate all of it. Then she chose an outfit from the closet – a simple, plain tunic and pair of wide-legged trousers – and got dressed. Half an hour later there was a second knock. This time it was a tall, blond, young man.

'I am Alve,' he said. No surname. 'I am from the security service.'

'What do you want?' Valera asked.

'I am here to help you navigate the coming days.'

Alve embodied that unique Scandinavian quality of compassionate pragmatism. When Valera asked him what was going to happen to her, he said, 'There are many serious conversations that must be had, but we will have them when you are ready.'

She was happy to speak to Alve's superiors about life in the Soviet Union and, more specifically, about what it was like to live in a closed city. She was also happy to meet with the head of the physics department at Stockholm University in his bright, light-filled office and talk in broad and tantalising terms about the mysteries of spread-spectrum broadcasting and signal code division. But she drew the line when she was introduced to a lady with a large bun of grey hair perched on top of her head who asked her if she'd like to talk about how she was feeling.

Valera didn't know how to put into words the exhaustion and elation she felt about escaping Russia, or the total and utter despair that consumed her over Ledjo's death. She didn't know how to articulate her rage and failure and loss. Or explain how it felt to suddenly have to live without the person you were living for. Or the fear of her memories of him becoming old and faded without any photographs or mementos to keep them alive. Or that last night her recurring dream had returned, monochrome, the lake so flat it felt solid, the boat shrinking smaller and smaller, and Ledjo, no matter how much she grabbed for him, always facing away from her and out of her reach. And if she had known how to talk about any of this, there was no way she was going to discuss it with a psychologist employed by an intelligence agency.

Eventually, Alve returned Valera to the Reisen and informed her that her evening was hers to do what she wanted with. He could arrange for food to be brought to her room, or recommend a restaurant for her, or simply leave her in peace so she could rest or explore the city. Valera was surprised. She'd expected to be kept politely under lock and key while she wasn't being politely inter-rogated. But Alve assured her that wasn't the way things were done in Sweden, and that the security service wanted her to feel as comfortable as possi-ble before another day of meetings tomorrow.

'How many more will there be?' she asked him.

'That I cannot say,' he replied. 'As many as it takes for everyone to be . . .' He paused, searching for the right word, '. . . satisfied.'

He placed a small stack of Swedish krona and

a slip of paper with a phone number on a side table.

'The hotel staff are at your disposal. If there is anything you want to know you can ask them, or call this number and ask for me.'

'Am I safe?' she asked. It was a blunt question.

'Please do not worry,' Alve answered. 'We do not harass the members of the international community who have chosen to make Stockholm their home, and they do not harass us or our guests.'

With a reassuring nod, he withdrew, leaving Valera to decide what to do. She wasn't used to having options, and for a moment she stood in the middle of the room, paralysed by the possibilities. Then she went to the window and looked out at the city. To her right she could see a grey tangle of roads and walkways that linked Gamla Stan to its southern neighbour, Södermalm, and above them a row of tall buildings clinging to the side of a hill. In front of her was another small island and, beyond it, another much larger one covered only in trees. She decided that was where she wanted to go.

Valera picked up the money and the slip of paper, and a minute later she was on the street, looking out over the water at Djurgården, the tree-covered island she'd seen from her hotel room window. She turned north and walked past the imposing stone and stucco facade of the Royal Palace towards the bridge that would take her to the island. Valera couldn't make herself completely believe what Alve had said. She'd lived too long under constant, watchful eyes to suddenly imagine them not there. But she told herself she hadn't come this far to hide, and that if anyone was paying attention to her, then the Swedish security service would be doing the same to them.

CHAPTER THIRTY-SEVEN

Knox should have spent the two-hour flight
from London to Stockholm deciding if he
believed Bennett really was who she said
she was. He knew the CIA had a handful of female
agents in the field, but for one to show up in
London without any word making its way to
Leconfield House via the inter-agency grapevine
was very odd.

However, two more immediate issues stopped
him from focusing his attention on the woman
sitting next to him. The first was that he was not
a very good flyer, especially when hungover. For
too many of Knox's formative years planes had
been omens of death, their presence a sign to run,
hide, and hope for the best. And once he'd signed
up to the army, he never felt more vulnerable than
when he was airborne. While other soldiers would
relish the momentary reprieve from action, Knox
spent every minute in the air on edge, knowing
all it would take was one well-aimed rocket or
engine malfunction to kill him instantly or send
him falling thousands of feet to his death.

He'd only crossed the Atlantic twice after the

war. Both trips had been to make nice with counterparts in American intelligence, and neither had gone particularly well.

The most recent trip had been for a joint conference with MI6 and the CIA and FBI eighteen months ago. Washington was in the grip of a long, hard winter, and after almost ten hours in the air Knox's BOAC Comet was forced to spend another one circling Washington airport in a blizzard before air traffic control let the plane land. Knox had spent ten hours flying backwards in one of the rear-facing seats in the plane's first-class compartment and avoiding making polite conversation with his fellow passengers, and the whole time circling Washington staring unblinkingly at the bright silver engine embedded in the wing barely five feet from him.

The conference was equally unpleasant. In fact, Knox was convinced the two American agencies were running a double act designed to discourage further visits from their British cousins. His meetings with the CIA were short and curt, and his roundtables and seminars with the FBI were interminably long and dull. His evenings were swallowed up with dinners and receptions full of people telling him how great a town Washington was.

Two days later, he was back at the airport for his overnight flight to London. The blizzard had lasted the whole time he'd been in Washington. He'd been on the last flight in, and he was getting the first flight out. As he sat in the departure lounge, watching the crew board the plane that would take him back to London – another Comet, painted white and silver, with a black slash reaching back from the cockpit along its sides, as if pointing the way home – his only hope was that the in-flight meal would be served early so he could get some sleep and start to forget the whole trip as quickly as possible.

The second thing that kept running through his head was where Bennett's fear of discoveries like Bianchi and Moretti's – and inventions like Pipistrelle – could lead.

The world of science fiction was full of societies where malignant forces watched over downtrodden populations, eternally hunting for traitors and the not quite loyal enough. But not the real world.

Spying, like war, had strict rules of engagement, and they were followed by most sides, most of the time. People were regularly trailed or tapped by intelligence agents, but only when necessary, not simply out of interest. Neither America, who probably had the money to attempt some kind of mass surveillance programme, nor Russia, who probably had the manpower, had ever tried something so ambitious. Even the deep, penetrating reach of the Stasi, Europe's most invasive intelligence operation, was achieved more through myth and rumour than actual, active surveillance.

Would real science change those rules?

Knox instinctively wanted to dismiss Bennett's

worries. But he knew that he couldn't. He knew deep down that in the wrong hands something like Pipistrelle could give someone the power to create the world that scared Bennett so much. A world where every act, thought, or statement was recorded and scrutinised. He'd almost said as much to White and Holland himself, back when they first discussed using Atlas, and it was only Holland's reassurances that had calmed his concerns. But Holland was no longer in charge of MI5 or its technology.

Knox had spent the last fifteen years peeking through proverbial keyholes and curtains in the name of national security. But when he wasn't, he had no interest in the private lives of others. Everyone carried secrets with them, hiding their true selves or things too personal or difficult to explain to others. Knox's own life was full of secrets. He'd been expertly trained to hide them. But what if he couldn't?

As the plane started to descend over what seemed like a thousand tiny islands towards Stockholm, he wondered who would want to find out every little detail about him if they had the chance.

CHAPTER THIRTY-EIGHT

Knox and Bennett's flight landed at Bromma airport shortly after two o'clock, and by three they were in Stockholm. They took a car from the airport, and Knox spent the whole journey into the city craning his neck to check the driver's rear-view mirrors. It was highly unlikely they'd been followed from London, but he wanted to be sure.

Stockholm looked to Knox like what would have happened if one of Britain's ancient capitals like York or Winchester had managed to hold on to their title a few hundred years longer. The narrow streets, looming spires, and stone arches felt familiar, but he was keenly aware that he was in foreign territory, and that he was being guided through it by someone he knew almost nothing about.

In his younger years, Knox had hated the Swedish. Or, more precisely, he'd hated anyone who had remained neutral during the war. As far as he was concerned, being neutral was the same as collaborating. If people like the Swedes weren't on the Allies' side, then they were on the

210

Nazis'. One of the first lessons Holland taught him was to let go of such hard and fast views of the world. He'd reminded Knox that Britain had avoided its fair share of fights it probably shouldn't have – self-preservation may not always seem noble, but it's a feature of life. Holland also told him that Sweden had secretly provided vast amounts of intelligence to the Allies throughout the war, which, given the country was surrounded on all sides by Nazi-controlled territories, was an incredibly brave thing to do.

Knox and Bennett made their way straight to the Hotel Reisen, where they spent the last hour nursing cups of dark, strong coffee in its salon. Knox also spent the time gently testing Bennett. He had to admit he was impressed by her.

When they arrived, he let the waiter guide them to a small, private booth in the corner of the salon, which Bennett turned down in favour of a table next to the bar that gave them a clear view of both the salon's side door and the hotel foyer. After half an hour, he'd suggested taking turns to stretch their legs. She told him he could take a walk if he wanted, but she was going to stay where she was. And, when he asked her why she was so sure this was where they'd find Valera, she'd explained that the Swedish security service was closer to the KGB than to MI5 or the CIA. It was a super-agency that covered every aspect of the nation's security, from espionage and counter-espionage to basic policing and dignitary protection. Like any other major organisation, a combination of inertia and efficiency had caused it to fall into certain habits. And one of those habits was accommodating international guests at the Hotel Reisen.

Knox finished his third cup of coffee and was about to ask Bennett if she wanted another when a flicker in her eyes stopped him. He glanced down the length of the salon into the hotel foyer and saw what had caught Bennett's attention. Irina Valera was being escorted across the lobby by a tall, blond man.

Bennett handed Knox a couple of krona notes. 'Settle up, and stay put. I'll wait outside in case they're just stopping by.'

'And if they're not?'

'Then we'll need to work out a way to get rid of Blondie.'

There was no need to worry about Valera's companion. Five minutes after Bennett stepped outside the man left the hotel. And two minutes after that, so did Valera.

Knox waited a moment to let her clear the entrance, then left as well. He didn't pause at the door, or look down the street to see which way she'd gone, but crossed straight over the road to where Bennett was waiting for him. Without a word she nodded to the right and they both set off north, trailing twenty yards behind Valera.

CHAPTER THIRTY-NINE

It turned out Djurgården wasn't just an island of trees. As Valera crossed the low, ornate bridge to it and passed through a high, wrought-iron gate, she saw wooded paths busy with people branching off all over the island. Old men sat on benches talking, couples strolled arm in arm, and parents struggled to control children who wanted to run everywhere but on the path.

Valera had gone looking for solitude and she hadn't found it. But she wasn't ready to go back to the hotel yet. Despite having cleaned herself up in Helsinki and at the Reisen, she could still feel grains of dust under her fingernails and smell the carnage of Povenets B in her hair. They were a constant, taunting reminder of what she'd lost. She wasn't sure she'd ever get rid of them, but she knew that if she went back to the Reisen she'd just fixate on them.

She wanted to taste at least some of the freedom she'd gone through so much for, so she picked a path and started down it, falling into step with the other people who had chosen it for their

213

late-afternoon stroll and letting them guide her deeper into the island.

The woods became very dense, very quickly. The background hum of the city faded. Valera was reminded a little of Leningrad. It was also a city of islands, and some of them had been left wild. But few of their trees had survived the siege. Their wood was needed for shoring up defences or burning for heat, and their bark, in the most desperate moments, for food. A couple of the islands had been replanted with fresh stock, but they were saplings compared to the huge, old trees of Djurgården.

If it hadn't been for the other people on the path her mind might also have taken her back to the forest surrounding Povenets B. But before it could the path opened up to reveal a wide, neat lawn. On the far side stood a low, curved building, painted yellow and white. It was flanked with Swedish flags, and the word *Skansen* was written above it in more iron.

Valera joined a queue of people making their way through an archway in the side of the building and discovered, as she handed over one of the notes Alve had given her, that Skansen was some kind of amusement park and open-air museum.

She walked past small farmhouses with country gardens that butted up against clapboard cottages with thatched roofs, and bright, red-painted halls. People in old-fashioned clothes passed her by on horse-drawn carts, or cleaned the steps of townhouses, or mingled with visitors, chatting with parents and explaining things to children.

Coming from somewhere that devoted so much time and energy to erasing its past, Valera was shocked to see such a celebration of history.

She moved from human exhibits to natural ones, passing several large animal enclosures. In one, three wolves lay together on a wide, flat rock, sleeping. In another a brown bear sat in the branches of a tree, staring back at her as she stared up at it. These were the animals she should have encountered in her hike out of Russia, but here they were instead. The bear looked comfortable, content soaking up the last of the day's sun, but it was still in a cage. She wondered if it recognised a kindred spirit in her, and if it would have stayed happily sitting in its tree looking down at her if there wasn't a high wall separating them.

She kept walking and came to a deserted Viking village. As she passed its large meeting hall and longhouses, it occurred to her how much Ledjo would have loved this place. He'd have been as excited as all the other children straining at their parents' arms, running in and out of buildings, hopping through history and rushing to share everything he discovered with her. She wondered how different their lives would have been on this side of the Iron Curtain. They could have spent their weeks working and studying, and their weekends visiting the animals at Skansen or sailing around the Stockholm archipelago – everything she'd promised and never given him.

She stopped at a bench in front of one of the longhouses. She could feel her emotions starting to get the better of her and wanted to sit down before she fell down. But her sadness instantly turned to fear as she watched a man in a dark suit appear from behind the longhouse and sit next to her.

CHAPTER FORTY

'H ello, Irina.'
Her blood froze at the sound of her
name, pronounced in perfect Russian
with the drawn-out emphasis on the middle
syllable. In an instant she knew they'd found her,
and they'd come to take her back.

'Who are you?' she stuttered, staring straight ahead.

'My name is General Grigor Medev. I am the
head of the KGB scientific directorate. And I have
come to apologise to you.'

'Apologise?' she asked, turning to face him.

'For everything you've been through,' he replied.
'For the last three years.' He turned, finally making
eye contact. 'I want you to know that Povenets B
has been decommissioned, and Zukolev has been
dealt with.'

Valera had waited a long time for Zukolev to
face some kind of reckoning, and she hoped he
had, but she had no reason to believe Medev.

'He was a vain, arrogant man,' Medev said, trying
to calm the doubts he'd anticipated. 'He did not
deserve the responsibilities given to him.'

★   ★   ★

'Who the hell is that?' Bennett whispered to Knox.

They were standing in a narrow gap between a large, thatched hall and a smaller building, which, from the smell, Knox reckoned was some kind of barn. They'd followed Valera all the way from the Reisen, splitting up as she'd wandered around Skansen to make sure she didn't somehow give them the slip and reuniting out of view of Valera and the man who had appeared from nowhere.

'I have no idea,' Knox whispered back. 'But they're speaking Russian.'

'We have to get her out of there. We can't lose her.' Bennett tried to edge past Knox, pushing him into the thatch and making it rustle until he gently put his hand on her shoulder to stop her.

'Wait,' he said. 'Look at her. She's not going anywhere.'

Medev took in the view from the bench. The quaint, perfectly preserved longhouses, the well-maintained paths, the dappled sunlight. He watched two swallows dance in the sky above them, feasting on invisible insects.

'I understand why you left,' he said. 'I think I would have too under the circumstances. But I have to ask you to come home.'

Valera let out a short, hard laugh. 'I don't have a home. Anything I ever had was taken from me.'

'I know,' he replied. 'We've failed you terribly, and there's nothing we can do to make up for the debt we owe you. I can give you an apartment, a dacha, a laboratory. But I cannot give you your life back. Your parents, or Ledjo.'

Valera knew how short-lived promises were in her homeland. Medev might offer her something today, but would she get it tomorrow? Every ruined village she'd walked through as she fled Povenets B had once been teeming with life, hope, and happiness, and they'd all been destroyed.

'Problems are caused by mistakes,' Medev continued. 'Wars if we let them. The way you've been treated was an unforgivable mistake. I don't want it to turn into something even worse.'

Valera thought of Ledjo. Was Medev calling him a little problem, a mistake? Something that could never be fixed? She was about to tell him she would never go back, but before she could he turned to face the big, thatched hall across from the bench and said, 'Would you care to join us?' loudly, and in English.

Knox, whose hand was still resting on Bennett's shoulder, gestured at her to stay put, but she shrugged him off and stepped out into the open. After swearing under his breath to himself, Knox followed.

'It only seems fair that everyone gets to make their offer to Miss Valera,' Medev said, smiling at Bennett and Knox. 'Now, neither of you look like members of the Swedish security service, so may I ask who you represent? My name is General Medev and I, as you have probably guessed, am Russian.'

It was an obvious ploy, and Knox refused to fall

for it. But Bennett was too caught up in what was happening to realise she was being tricked.

'You need to leave the lady alone,' she said.

'Ah, American,' Medev replied. 'I must have our records updated. We didn't think the CIA had any female agents in Europe.'

'Maybe Soviet intelligence isn't as smart as it thinks it is,' Bennett said.

'Maybe.' Medev smiled at her. 'The world is full of surprises.' He turned to Knox. 'And you? Do you work for the CIA also?'

Knox couldn't avoid a direct question. But he also didn't want to give Medev any more ammunition. So he just said, 'No.'

'British? Then, my friend, I think you do,' Medev said with a chuckle. 'But who we are really is not so important. This is about Miss Valera, and what she wants.'

He stood up, gesturing for Bennett to take his place on the bench. But before she could sit down next to Valera and recite the speech she'd prepared about everything America had to offer her, about how important her research was, and how she and the CIA could work together to create a safer, better world, a crimson plume erupted from Medev's forehead.

Blood splattered Valera as his lifeless body slumped back down onto the bench. She screamed, but it was drowned out by the sound of more shots being fired at them and Knox shouting for all of them to get down.

Three men wearing balaclavas and dressed completely in black ran towards them. Two of them had their guns raised at Knox and Bennett, covering the third, who lunged for Valera, still sitting on the bench, motionless from the shock of seeing Medev die in front of her. But as soon as his gloved hand touched her arm she burst back into life, much to her attacker's surprise, shaking off his grip and launching herself off the bench.

Knox and Bennett seized the momentary distraction and both rushed their attackers, grabbing the guns pointed at them and trying to wrestle them away. Bennett was much smaller than her assailant, but she was faster. She weaved around him, twisting and pulling on his wrist so he couldn't grab hold of her or get off another shot.

Knox's opponent was a tougher customer. Every move he made against him was instantly countered. Knox took multiple hits to his head, and his side, which was still tender from the kicking he'd taken in Strand station.

Valera made it almost twenty feet from the bench before a gloved hand grabbed her again and slammed her down into the ground, stunning her for a moment before she started kicking and screaming at the man standing over her.

Bennett bent the wrist of her attacker so far back that he let out a growl of pain. But he still didn't drop his gun. She tried to pull it back even further, but she was concentrating so hard on the man's wrist that she'd stopped ducking and diving, or

221

paying attention to his other hand. He finally caught her and held her against him as he drove her into the wall of the longhouse, winding her and pinning her against it.

The man fighting Knox did drop his gun, but not because Knox made him. He took a step back, let it fall to the ground, and goaded Knox to come at him with both hands. Knox couldn't see the man's face under the balaclava but he was sure he was sneering at him. Knox wanted to throw himself at him and wipe the invisible smile off his face, but he knew that was just what the other man wanted. So he tried his own trick on him, backing away and forcing the man in black to keep moving forward until his patience ran out and he sprang at Knox. Knox ducked down. He'd planned to drive his shoulder up into the man's abdomen, but instead the man tripped over Knox's curled-up body, lost his balance, and crashed full speed and head first into the edge of the bench Medev's body was still slumped limply on.

The sound of the man's skull cracking against the metal corner of the bench stopped everyone else. For a moment no one moved. Then the two other masked men gave each other a look. The one holding Bennett against the wall drove her into it one more time, winding her again, then let her drop to the ground. He ran over to the man who had managed to pin Valera down and sedate her somehow. Then he turned the gun on Knox, who was separated from them by the bench and the two dead bodies. The other man slung Valera's body over his shoulder, and they both started to back away.

As soon as the men disappeared behind the longhouse, Knox ran over to Bennett, who was already pulling herself up off the ground.

'What just happened?' she asked, rhetorically.

The whole encounter, from Medev first sitting down on the bench to the masked men carrying Valera off, had lasted less than five minutes.

Bennett walked over to the dead attacker. She nudged him with her foot to make sure he wasn't just dazed, then reached down and pulled the balaclava off his head. It was already sticky with blood from the deep gash across the top of his skull.

'Anyone you know?' she said to Knox.

It was another rhetorical question, but as Knox looked down at the man, he recognised his heavy, almost Neanderthal brow, and the sneer that was still on his face, even in death. It was the policeman who had been guarding Bianchi and Moretti's building.

CHAPTER FORTY-ONE

The SAS flight to Amsterdam left Stockholm just before six o'clock. It was a popular route, and the two-hour flight time meant that the early-evening flight was always busy with business travellers keen to leave Sweden after their afternoon meetings and reach Holland in time for more business, or pleasure, or both. This evening's plane was almost full, but the SAS desk agent managed to find two seats together for the English gentleman and American lady who had arrived at Bromma shortly after 5 p.m.

Knox sat in silence for almost the whole flight. The only time he opened his mouth was to order two double whiskies in quick succession. The rest of the time he spent brooding. For once, he didn't like being right. He also didn't like how he'd been proved right. He'd been blindsided by events unfolding around him yet again. And he'd wilfully walked into a situation almost identical to the one at the centre of his suspicions of Manning. There was even the death of a Russian agent to complete the parallel. But there was also a significant difference between them – Manning's mission to Singapore had been sanctioned, and Knox's trip to Stockholm had not. If it hadn't been for the dead man from Deptford, Knox's anxiety at breaking one of MI5's most basic operational rules would have outweighed his anger at finding and then losing Valera. As it was there wasn't much between them.

At Schiphol, Knox and Bennett were lucky again. There was a KLM flight to London leaving at nine thirty, and it had plenty of seats available. They had an hour to kill before boarding, and tacitly agreed not to spend it together.

Knox found a bar in the terminal and ordered another whisky to tide him over as he tried to get his head round everything that had happened. He imagined Williams and Holland sitting opposite him, Williams joking about the man who had killed himself by tripping over Knox, and Holland calling him a bloody fool for letting himself get in such a mess in the first place.

The attack on Valera had proved Bennett right. And the dead man was the evidence Knox needed to prove there was a direct line that ran from Bianchi and Moretti to Valera and led straight back to MI5 and Manning. Seeing Valera snatched by a fully armed strike team dispelled any notion that she might have been some sort of elaborate honeytrap, and also showed Knox just how much he'd underestimated Manning. He wondered what else the man might be capable of. The KGB had mastered the art of incapacitating targets without any signs of foul play. For all Knox knew, they'd helped get Holland out of the way to clear a path for Manning.

One question still lingered. Medev. Was Manning so valuable the Russians were ready to sacrifice one of their own to protect him? It was possible, but it gnawed away at Knox's mind, not quite making sense, alongside what Medev had said about the CIA not having any female agents in Europe. Knox had no reason to believe Medev, but it still made him second-guess the rapid faith he'd developed in Bennett.

Knox hadn't paid attention to where she'd gone after they'd landed. She might have disappeared into the Dutch night, but Knox had a feeling she was somewhere very close, keeping her own tabs on him. He'd tested her in Stockholm; now he decided he needed to push her, and see if a little more pressure on top of everything they'd been through would make her break and reveal some hidden motive or allegiance. He reminded himself that just because they shared enemies that didn't necessarily mean they were friends.

They reunited in the gate line. The flight hadn't filled up and they boarded quickly. This plane was smaller than the ones they'd taken to and from Stockholm. The aisle was off-centre, with single seats running down the left side of the cabin, and sets of two down the right. Their seats were halfway down the plane, near the wing. Bennett took the window, leaving Knox with the aisle. He glimpsed one of the plane's two propellers starting to turn through a window and immediately fastened his seatbelt.

Bennett was the one who spoke first, but only after take-off, when the stewardess arrived with the drinks trolley.

'Nothing for either of us, thank you,' she said to the stewardess, leaning across Knox. Then, patting his arm, she added, 'You've had enough, darling.'

Before Knox had the chance to protest the stewardess moved on, and by the time he turned round to beckon her back after snatching his arm from under Bennett's surprisingly firm grip she was already several rows away. He wanted another drink, but he didn't want to be the man who chased a trolley down a plane to get it.

'Just keeping up the act,' she said.

But instead of winking back, Knox took the opportunity to put her on the spot.

'Who sent you?' he asked, point blank.

'What?' she replied.

'You heard me.'

'No one sent me,' she said, her voice turning as hard as his.

'Really? You just turned up at the right moment saying all the right things to get me to come on this jaunt with you?'

'And you just couldn't resist the little lady stroking your ego?' she shot back. 'I didn't force you to come. I needed help, so I asked for it. It's not my fault everything went south.'

'Things went south as soon as I started to trust you. Are you even CIA?'

'You're going to believe a KGB agent trying to destabilise a situation? If you're that easy to manipulate I should've just told you I found out Stalin was alive and well and living on a fishing boat on the Stockholm docks.'

She sounded genuinely hurt, but Knox knew she was evading him. 'Do you work for the CIA?' he asked again.

'Give me some credit.'

Bennett turned away from him, staring out at the North Sea, now thousands of feet beneath them. Suddenly she looked very young to Knox, like a child who had been sent on a long journey alone.

They sat in silence for ten minutes. When Knox spoke again, his voice was softer.

'I need to know,' he said.

'Yes,' she replied, refusing to take her eyes off the dark, churning waves. 'I work for the CIA.'

'Doing what?'

'File clerk.'

'Christ.' Knox barely mouthed the word, but she still heard it.

'Oh, I'm sorry,' she spat, finally turning back from the window to face him. 'Is this embarrassing for you? Have I taken you away from all that important work you were doing drunk off your ass on suspension? Let me get you a drink or three to make up for it.'

Knox tried to defend himself, but she cut him off before he could get a word out.

'Nothing I told you was a lie. Nothing. I work for the CIA. I see everything that comes through London, including all the intelligence my bosses choose to ignore. We'd been watching Bianchi and Moretti. We knew about their deaths before the ink was dry on the autopsy report. But no one cared, it was none of our business. I didn't buy that, but when I went to my boss he laughed at me. Told me not to worry my pretty head and go back to doing the filing.'

'So you ignored his orders?'

'Didn't you?'

'That's different.'

'Of course it is. You're a man. You can break all the rules and just get a slap on the wrist. You live in a world where you're right even when you're wrong.'

'You don't know anything about me,' Knox replied. 'I've fought for everything I've ever got.'

'And you got it too, didn't you? Because you really, really wanted it. Do you want to know about the world I live in? A world where my father decided he didn't like the family he'd been stuck with and left us with nothing. Where I put myself through school, aced every test, got a job working for the goddamn CIA, beat out a hundred other people for an international posting, and still get told every single day that what I think is wrong and what I do isn't important.'

229

'I haven't exactly had it easy,' Knox said, breaking the short but deep silence that had fallen between them. 'Both my parents died when I was a child.'

'And I'm sorry for you,' she said. 'But don't try to make this a competition. Because I've got plenty more I can tell you about how tough life can be, and you're the one who lives in a penthouse.'

Knox's confidence in his ability to read people had taken a battering over the last couple of days, but he couldn't deny the intensity of Bennett's emotions. If she was just a bit player in a larger game, drafted in to run interference on him, he was sure she'd have taken her leave by now. There was no reason for her to still be sitting next to him unless she really did believe in the conspiracy she'd sold him and thought he was the only person who could help her prove it was real.

'We knew about the suspicions you and Holland had about Manning,' she said quietly, her eyes looking down at her lap. 'It was obvious you were being hung out to dry. I thought you could help me, that we could help each other. My mistake.'

'Well, you were right about one thing,' Knox replied after a moment. 'This is definitely bigger than a couple of Italians. The dead man who attacked us. I did know him.'

Bennett looked up at Knox. The scarlet had left her cheeks and there was even the hint of a smirk on her lips again. Knox explained that he'd seen the attacker before, standing guard outside Bianchi and Moretti's flat.

'So someone in MI5 is behind all this,' she said, when Knox had finished. 'And now they have Valera.'

'It looks like it.'

'Do you think she's already on her way back to Russia?'

'I doubt it. They'll take her somewhere quiet first. Maybe see what they can get out of her themselves before they hand her over.'

'Then we still have a chance to find her.'

'If they've taken her back to the UK.'

'Which, with any luck, they will have.'

'I'm not sure that would be so lucky,' Knox said. 'With everyone in London focused on the OECD conference it'd be the perfect place to hide Valera. Or put her to work.'

A stewardess interrupted their conversation, telling them the plane was about to begin its descent.

'By the way,' Knox said after the stewardess had moved on and he'd checked that his seatbelt was still tight across his lap, 'how long has the CIA known about Pipistrelle?'

'What?' Bennett replied.

'White's bugs.'

'Oh.' Bennett smiled. 'That was just a guess. Lucky for you my bosses wouldn't believe me if I told them about it.'

As the plane came in to land at London Airport they agreed on a plan for the next day. Bennett would see if there was anything else she could find at the American embassy, and Knox would talk to the one other person in MI5 he might be able to trust.

CHAPTER FORTY-TWO

It was midnight by the time Knox reached Soho. The hot, heavy air that had sat over London for days had finally broken into a storm and he had to move between shop doorways and awnings, dodging the last of the downpour as he made his way from Oxford Circus to Kemp House.

Soho was quiet, its usual nocturnal wanderers driven indoors by the rain. Knox walked down Argyll Street, turning left onto Great Marlborough Street opposite Liberty, the department store's black and white Tudor panelling shining in the wet. He thought about his conversation with Bennett on the flight from Amsterdam. He understood better now why she was so scared of her dark vision of the world after everything she'd already gone through. He was starting to become as scared himself. Someone in London was so desperate to get their hands on the next generation of surveillance technology that they'd killed for it. Now, barely twenty-four hours before the opening of the OECD conference, they had kidnapped Irina Valera as well, leaving a trail of more death behind them. And Knox was convinced that this someone was his boss.

At the top of Poland Street two fire engines passed him. He wondered where they were headed at this time of night and in this weather. Then, as he turned into Berwick Street, he realised they weren't on their way to deal with a fire, they were leaving one they'd just put out.

Small groups of people were gathered on the street, some in raincoats and holding umbrellas, others looking like they'd come straight from their beds, wrapped in whatever they could find on their way out of their homes. They were all looking up at Kemp House, where black scorch marks circled the top of the building and wisps of smoke were still reaching out from the blown-out windows of Knox's flat.

Knox stood paralysed, staring at the destruction. He reached for his chest and felt the bundle of papers that were still in the inside pocket of his jacket. He knew this wasn't an accident. He didn't know if the fire had been meant to burn him and the papers along with his flat, or if it was some kind of swift retribution for the death of the man in Stockholm. But either way someone was sending him a very direct message.

He wanted to push past the gawpers and see just how much damage had been done, but he knew that if he did, or even if he just stayed on Berwick Street much longer, anyone waiting to make sure he got the message would spot him.

And he didn't have enough energy to cope with whatever else they might want to throw at him.

He turned away from Kemp House and slipped into D'Arblay Street. He hugged doorways as he moved quickly across Wardour Street and through the narrow cut-through of St Anne's Court, before doubling back north up Dean Street and into Soho Square.

He paused at the edge of the old public garden, watching the corner he'd just turned around. After a moment a figure appeared, lingering on the kerb. It was a man, wearing a heavy mackintosh. His face was obscured by the umbrella he was still holding up even though the last of the rain had stopped falling. He may have just been a drunk businessman trying to decide which way to take home, but after he'd spent almost a full minute looking up and down Dean Street and towards Soho Square, Knox decided he was trying to do something else.

Knox was tired of being watched, followed, and attacked. But he was also physically exhausted. He decided that right now his best course of action was to retreat. He waited for the man to turn away from the square, then he burst into a run, leaving his hiding place in the shadow of a large old plane tree and making a break for Tottenham Court Road.

The tube station was shut, the last train gone. But there were two double-decker night buses idling on the north side of the station's New

Oxford Street entrance. The first bus started its engine as Knox reached it, and pulled away just as he jumped on its backboard.

His respite lasted twenty seconds until the second bus also started to move down New Oxford Street, apparently taking an identical route. There was a chance the man looking for Knox had missed his quick, echoing footsteps around Soho Square and had been too slow off the mark to catch the bus behind him. But after what Knox had gone through over the last twenty-four hours he wasn't inclined to hope.

Knox's bus quickly filled up with people who had stayed too late at work or given up the idea of walking home after an evening in a pub. The windows on the lower level began to steam up thanks to all the warm, breathing bodies and Knox was forced to abandon his rear-facing seat next to a man who had definitely spent the evening hunched over a bar rather than a desk. He stood on the backboard, keeping his eyes fixed on the second bus, which was still following, always just one stop behind.

He let his double-decker take him down High Holborn and deeper into the city's history, past Chancery Lane towards St Paul's, then along London Wall, which traced the path of the ancient Londinium's battlements.

Knox could have stayed standing on the back-board as the bus took him further and further away from the West End, but constantly watching the second night bus follow him was making him impatient. He suddenly wanted to flush out and face the man from Soho Square, so as the bus slowed through a deserted junction he took a chance, jumped off the backboard, and started to run.

Cripplegate was a black hole all hours of the day, but especially at night. Once one of the most heavily populated parts of the City of London, it had been almost completely flattened by the Luftwaffe, and immediately after the war its residents numbered in the tens. It took Knox just a few seconds to disappear into the darkness that seemed to stretch away into eternity from the streetlights of London Wall, and only a couple more before the ground under him became uneven and he felt himself kicking rubble as he ran. He was sure he was making enough noise to be easily tracked, but he slowed down to make sure of it – and to stop himself slamming too hard into some unseen chunk of building or something else where it shouldn't be.

After a hundred yards Knox's instincts told him to stop, and he held his hands out into nothing. He caught his breath as his eyes adjusted to another level of darkness and he discovered he was teetering right on the edge of a chasm-like bomb crater.

He crouched down and inched his way round the rim of the crater, feeling with his hands and feet until he found a slab of wall that would hide

236

him but also give him a clear view of his pursuer hopefully tumbling full-tilt into the abyss. He waited, and waited. He was tense. The fear and anger of Stockholm and the decimation of his home burned inside of him, and he wanted to take it all out on someone. But the longer he waited, squatting in the dark, the more he started to wonder if he'd actually been followed at all.

Knox shifted his weight, leaning against the wall. The old bricks crumbled under him and sent him skidding down into the hole in the earth. He grabbed at the wet dirt but couldn't stop from crashing into the waterlogged, pitted floor of the crater. He pulled himself up, wiping his hands on his trousers and feeling filthy liquid pooling in his shoes and soaking his feet. For a brief, hysterical moment he stood in the centre of the void, daring his imaginary tail, or anyone else, to show themselves and take a shot at him, but there was only silence and darkness. After a few seconds he came to his senses and hauled himself back up out of the crater.

He thought about walking back to Soho, but decided to head in the opposite direction instead, to the one part of London he knew even better.

The night gave him one final stroke of luck when he was back on London Wall – a taxi to flag down. The driver had just dropped someone off at Liverpool Street station and was heading back into town to pick up some more late-night custom. He had no desire to go east again, but Knox persuaded him by offering double his fare.

Twenty minutes later the cab dropped Knox off on Roman Road, which, as its name suggested, was the old straight-arrow Roman route out of the city. He walked north towards Victoria Park. The park, as its name also suggested, was a gift from Queen Victoria to the people of the East End, a space where they could escape the drudgery of life for a few hours. It was a kind gesture, but it assumed that the people it had been created for could afford to take time off from working all hours every day to make ends meet to promenade through the park and smell its roses.

Twenty years after the Blitz, Bethnal Green also still wore its scars. Knox passed rows of old terraced houses, condemned but showing signs of occupation, collapsed buildings waiting to be cleared, and several low-rise blocks that had emerged from the wreckage of the war over the last decade. It was quiet now, but Knox remembered nights filled with people doubled over fires in the middle of streets and children with filthy faces tempting rats into traps so they could turn them into pets or a meal.

The war had been equal parts blessing and curse for Bethnal Green. The poverty of the years before the war had been grinding. It had killed countless people here. It had killed Knox's parents. After the war there was no way life could go back to how it had been. The East End had become too much of a symbol of London's tenacity and resilience to be left to fester and ruin. So, slowly but surely a new Bethnal Green was growing through its cracks and wounds.

The buildings might be changing, but the streets were still the same. He walked up Globe Road, then cut right onto Cyprus Street, one of the few old streets of terraced cottages that looked like it hadn't been touched by the twentieth century at all. It was a long straight street, uninterrupted on one side and with a small turning off it halfway along the other – the perfect place for Knox to reassure himself one last time that no one was shadowing him.

Knox was still running on adrenaline but after ten minutes watching the silent, empty street it finally started to wear off. He needed to find somewhere to spend the rest of the night, but before he did he walked the short distance to Sewardstone Road, where his grandmother's house had stood until it was knocked down five years ago.

Sewardstone Road had been a dirty, narrow street of tenement houses pressed up against the stagnant, filthy water of Regent's Canal. He could still smell the canal now, but the tightly packed old houses were gone, replaced by modern blocks of flats. Knox stopped for a moment outside the flat that now stood where he'd once lived in a tiny, two-room house with his grandmother. He remembered all the early mornings when he'd creep back in after a night's wandering the city, and the few times his grandmother had caught him before he'd reached his bed and spent hours screaming at him, out of anger, love, and fear of losing him like she'd lost his mother. Then he thought about how he'd now also lost the only two places he'd ever really called home.

He headed south back towards Roman Road. Next to Bethnal Green tube station he found the grandly and wholly inaccurately named City View Hotel. It was an old Victorian dosshouse that had been turned into the kind of place that rented rooms by the hour as well as by the night.

Knox woke up the night clerk, who was not happy about being disturbed, paid for a room until morning, and had the stairs pointed out to him. His room was at the very top of the building, and he might have been able to see the city through his high attic window, if the walls of a raised train track hadn't blocked the view.

He locked the door and wedged the back of the chair that served as a bedside table under the handle. Then he pulled off his jacket and trousers, balled the jacket up with the papers and passports under the bed, splashed his face, trousers and socks in the small sink, and lay down on the thin mattress. Even the sound of a freight train passing within ten feet of him, rattling the window and shaking the bed, didn't stop him from falling asleep almost instantly.

CHAPTER FORTY-THREE

Valera stood in the middle of Mikhailovsky Garden. In front of her the Moyka flowed lazily across the northern side of the park, feeding into the Neva, the great river that split Leningrad in half. To her right, the faded copper roof of Saint Michael's Castle was just visible above the trees that edged the park. To her left, the domes of the Church of the Saviour on the Spilled Blood rose high above her. It was late summer, and the air was pungent with the smell of city life and anticipation.

Valera remembered this day well. It was the day the German army had finally surrounded the city and the siege of Leningrad began.

She heard a droning noise in the distance, getting louder and closer. It wasn't a barge – there hadn't been any traffic on the river for days. It was the first wave of Luftwaffe arriving to bomb the city. Valera started running towards the Saviour on the Spilled Blood, hoping the band of trees between the church and the park would offer her some protection from the assault that was about to be unleashed.

But when she reached the trees she was suddenly no longer in Leningrad. She was in Povenets B, running towards the power plant and watching it explode in front of her. She saw the blast rip through the side of the plant and the school. She felt the first shockwave ripple past her, smashing windows and showering her with glass. Then a second, more powerful one smacked her in the chest like a hammer, throwing her backwards off her feet.

But instead of hitting the ground and feeling rubble stab her in the back, she found herself in a dark room, tied to a chair and gasping for breath. Her wrists were sore from the rope holding her in place, her head felt heavy, and her whole body was cramped, as if she'd been in the same position for hours. She didn't know what was real, what was memory, and what was neither. And she had no idea how many times she'd gone through this horrific cycle of torture.

Sometimes her mother was with her in Leningrad, sometimes it was the depths of winter and she was foraging Mikhailovsky Garden for food. Sometimes she could see Ledjo through his classroom window as she ran towards him, sometimes his lifeless body lay in the middle of the destroyed school, bruised, bloodied, and covered in dust. Sometimes she was alone in the dark room. Sometimes the figures in masks shouted at her in Russian and English. And sometimes they stayed in the shadows, throwing their words and ice-cold buckets of water at her.

The details changed, but the order was always the same: Leningrad, Povenets B, the dark room. And so were the words the masked figures repeated over and over: 'Tell us what you know.'

Even if Valera had wanted to tell them, she couldn't. She was completely lost in what was happening in her head. When the figures shouted at her, she shouted back, her voice cracking. And when they wrapped her in blankets and gently whispered their constant demand in soft voices, all she could do was mumble 'Mama' or 'Ledjo' before breaking down in desperate tears and falling back into the endless rhythm of memory and fantasy.

She didn't know when, but at some point the voices in the room changed. They stopped speaking as one and began fighting over each other to be heard. They came at her from every angle, getting louder and louder until the cacophony became too much and her mind took her back to Mikhailovsky Garden.

This time the trees were bare, the domes of the Saviour on the Spilled Blood were dull and cracked, and Valera was very heavily pregnant. She stood in the middle of the park, cradling her swollen belly. It didn't occur to her that this was wrong, that she didn't become pregnant with Ledjo until long after the siege. Her only thought was to protect her unborn child. She started walking east towards Saint Michael's Castle, and almost made it to the trees before the bombs started to fall.

Then she was in Povenets B again. The explosion at the power plant, the shattering glass, the feeling of hot dust on her skin. But instead of just being confronted with rubble or Ledjo's broken body, she saw a man standing in the ruins of the school, untouched by the destruction around him and reaching out to her. She'd never seen the man before, but she also had, in other, more peaceful fantasies. It was Ledjo, all grown up. She tried to run to him, pushing her legs harder and harder as she screamed his name. But no matter how fast she ran, she could never reach him.

And then, the dark room once more. She wanted to go back to Povenets B, back to Ledjo. She kept screaming. Her screams became a whimper, then a whisper, then silence. The masked figures were still there, surrounding her. But as she let her head fall and her body go limp against her restraints, the voices didn't start shouting at her. They shouted at each other. Voices fought for dominance, shifting from Russian to English and back again, until only two remained, battling it out.

Then a piercing crack ricocheted around the room and there was just one voice left, telling Valera everything was going to be okay. Now she fought with what little energy she had left to stay in the room and not fall back into more twisted memories. She felt the restraints on her wrists loosen, her body being lifted out of the chair, and a prick in her arm. She started to slip away again, not into a dream but into oblivion.

CHAPTER FORTY-FOUR

Dixon didn't enjoy feeling like he was being put on show. But it was part of the deal between NASA and the CIA that he would be on call for both whenever they needed him. This could mean going to seminars or meetings outside his field or, like this evening, finding himself padding out a room at a party.

He'd been summoned to Washington at short notice for what had been billed as a reception for all the great minds working to win the space race. The timing felt off to Dixon. Gus Grissom was scheduled to make the next Mercury launch in two days' time. Wouldn't it be more prudent to wait and celebrate after his mission was successful than to tempt fate before it? He'd asked Murphy that exact question when he'd called him that morning and told him to get up to DC. Murphy's response was that the event was the president's idea, and that attendance wasn't optional.

Dixon had spent yet another night banging his head against theoretical and real brick walls and was more than happy to take a break from the lab. But he resented that it involved a four-and-a-half-hour drive in bad traffic from Langley to Washington and, so far, an hour of awkward conversation with people he didn't know. Scientists, as a tribe, weren't good at small talk, and Dixon was no exception.

The reception was being held at the Phillips Collection on 21st Street, just north of Dupont Circle. Dixon had wondered briefly why if it had been the president's idea it wasn't taking place in the White House. Then he'd remembered that winning over the hearts of the nation had been a much easier job for Kennedy than ingratiating himself with Washington society, and he needed to make nice with the city's well-to-do.

The Phillips family were philanthropists and art lovers, and over the years had converted their sprawling 21st Street mansion into the city's finest private collection of modern art. The large rooms that Dixon moved through were hung with works by Renoir, Manet, and Pissarro. Taste and money seeped from the walls. The Phillips were exactly the kind of people Kennedy wanted to impress. Yet, so far there had been no sign of the man himself.

Ripples of excitement spread through the attendees whenever the mansion's front door opened, only to dissipate when yet another bemused scientist or society scion made their entrance.

Allen Dulles, the director of Central Intelligence, also appeared to be skipping the event. It was an open secret that Dulles and Kennedy didn't get on. In the eight years he'd been in charge of the CIA Dulles had overseen the American-backed coups in Guatemala and Iran, both of which had caused long-term damage to the country's reputation, as well as the U-2 programme and the Bay of Pigs invasion. Kennedy was looking for a reason to get rid of Dulles, and Dulles was keeping his head down. Dixon guessed that if Grissom's Mercury mission didn't go well, Dulles wouldn't want his name anywhere near it.

Finally, he saw someone he knew. Across the crowd, he spotted Murphy talking to an elderly dowager, festooned with mink and diamonds despite the heat and humidity. In summer Washington liked to remind people that it had been a real swamp long before it became a political one. With a brief nod, Murphy told Dixon that he'd seen him too and that he should stay put while he excused himself.

A moment later he was next to Dixon with two glasses of champagne in his hands.

'Quite the collection,' Murphy said, handing Dixon one of the glasses. Dixon was fairly sure he wasn't referring to the art. 'Did you know that lady's great-grandfather bought Louisiana?'

Dixon wasn't interested in making any more small talk, particularly with his boss.

'What's going on, Phinn?' he asked.

'We're drinking someone else's champagne, and giving ourselves pats on the back we don't deserve.'

Dixon realised that Murphy wasn't smoking. He

watched as his free hand kept reaching in and out of his trouser pocket, a force of habit and muscle memory.

'Is the president coming?'

'No. But you didn't hear that from me. Some senator started kicking up a stink about overdue federal funds a couple of hours ago and he's been sucked into it.'

'Well, I'll be leaving then.' Dixon handed his still-full champagne glass to a passing waiter. 'It's a long drive back to Langley.'

'Not so fast,' Murphy replied, picking Dixon's glass back up off the waiter's silver platter. 'You're not going back to the lab just yet.'

'I thought I had a deadline.'

'Yeah, well, something's come up.'

'Again, Phinn, what's going on?'

Murphy took a long swig of his champagne. 'We're taking a trip.'

'Where?'

'Some guy called Devereux in London wants to sell us something, and I need you to check he's not talking horseshit.'

'I didn't pack my passport.' Dixon meant it as a joke – even the CIA's beck and call had to have limits.

'Don't worry, we picked it up for you.'

Dixon finally took a sip of his champagne, accepting that he wouldn't be getting behind the wheel of his car any time soon. 'Did you at least put food out for the cat?'

'Of course we did. We're not savages.'

'How long until we go?'

Murphy finished his champagne and snatched two more glasses from a passing waiter. 'Tomorrow night. In the meantime, there's another reception in the morning it'd be good for you to show your face at, and a couple of senators it'd be worth meeting.'

That definitely sounded like a waste of Dixon's time. If they weren't flying until the next night he could still get a few more hours of work done and meet Murphy at the airport.

'Has the president suddenly stopped caring about what the Russians are up to?' he asked.

'Have you made any progress at all in the last week?' Murphy countered.

'No,' Dixon conceded.

'Then calm down,' Murphy said, taking another swig of champagne. 'What difference is a couple of days going to make?'

CHAPTER FORTY-FIVE

The final stretch up Parliament Hill was White's least favourite part of his Sunday-morning stroll with Stella. Even the Irish setter had started to tire of it in her advancing years. But it was the quickest way back to Hampstead and home after their walk around the heath.

White had hoped to avoid this Sunday's walk. With the OECD conference starting the next morning and almost every delegate already in the city, all hands were needed on deck at Leconfield House over the weekend. Except, apparently, White and his staff.

On Friday afternoon, word came down from the fifth floor that with Pipistrelle bugs now in place across the city, monitored by GCHQ and maintained by a rotating team of Watchers, there was no reason for the research and development department to lose out on their weekend along with the rest of MI5.

It had been Manning's first decree once he returned to Leconfield House after being made permanent director general, and White didn't like the message it sent. When Peterson came down to the basement to pass on the news he exploded at him, arguing that what Manning was suggesting was tantamount to dereliction of duty. This was not the time for anyone to be taking it easy.

'This is exactly when we need Atlas running Pipistrelle,' White said. 'We can't sit around waiting for GCHQ to tell us what they think we should know.'

Peterson didn't disagree with him, but he made it clear that while it might be unwise to be absent from Leconfield House at such a crucial time, it would be even less wise to turn down Manning's gift. 'And,' he'd said, 'if something comes up, we know where to find you.'

White had spent the whole of Friday evening and Saturday quietly seething while entertaining his wife's relatives, who were up from the country for the weekend – another task he'd hoped to avoid.

The early morning on the heath had cleared his head, but the hike up Parliament Hill was starting to inspire a fresh sense of irritation. It was solidified when he reached the top of the hill and found Knox sitting on the bench he always rested on to catch his breath.

'What the hell are you doing here?' White asked.

To add insult to injury, Stella happily wandered over to Knox and curled up at his feet.

'You're a creature of habit, Malcolm,' Knox replied. 'Same as the rest of us.'

'It's too early for amateur psychology,' White said, giving in to his legs' need for a break and sitting down next to Knox. 'What do you want?'

Knox looked out over the city. He could see east past St Paul's and west towards Battersea Power Station. All the way between, new buildings were changing the city's skyline, and cranes glinted as they turned in the sun. And in the middle of it all was Kemp House. Knox was sure he could see the top of the tower, smudged black, even from several miles away.

'How are things in Leconfield House?' he asked.

'I wouldn't know,' White replied, making no effort to hide the resentment in his voice.

'Well, let me tell you what's been going on in the outside world,' Knox said.

Knox had decided in Schiphol that Peterson had been right about one thing at least. He should have gone to White days ago. He was the only person Knox could talk to without risking exposing Pipistrelle's secrets because he already knew them all. There was always the chance that it was actually White who was behind everything, working with the Russians and using Manning, Peterson, and the two dead Italians as cover, but it was an extremely slim one. Knox was sure White believed in the Service, and he hoped that belief would outweigh whatever he might currently think of Knox and his own loyalty.

He relayed the events of the last seventy-two hours, starting with his visit to Dr Kaspar, then his discovery of Bianchi and Moretti's hidden research, and ending with the kidnapping of Valera in Stockholm, apparently by British forces.

When Knox had finished, he waited for White's response. And after a moment, White gave it.

'Nonsense,' White said.

'Excuse me?' Knox asked.

'Total poppycock.'

'It happened,' Knox assured him. 'I've got the bruises.'

'Oh, I'm sure you have,' White said, tempting Stella over to his side of the bench with a treat. 'But I'm also sure it's entirely within your capabilities to make all these things happen to you without it being part of some grand conspiracy. Where's the proof?'

Knox reached into his jacket pocket and pulled out the bundle of papers.

'I don't know if they found a way to reverse-engineer Pipistrelle, or just managed to replicate your genius by sheer chance,' he said. 'But these calculations aren't nonsense.'

White flicked through the papers. His face fell as he scanned the calculations.

'And these,' Knox continued, handing over the passports, 'are professional jobs. Only a few outfits that can create such convincing fakes. And we're one of them.'

White tested the passports, running his fingers along the covers and pages, checking the subtle security features most people had no idea were there. He had to admit Knox was right – they were near-perfect forgeries.

'I know you don't want to think about it,' Knox said. 'But what if this means Pipistrelle's already been blown?'

'It hasn't,' White replied. It was a knee-jerk, protective reaction.

'But what if it has? What if the Russians already have their own bugs in every embassy and hotel in the city? If they're as good as Pipistrelle we'd never find them.'

White hated scaremongering, and he had no interest in getting caught up in Knox's endless conspiracies about traitors and moles. But he couldn't ignore the passports he was still holding, or the Italians' equations that looked disturbingly close to his own.

'If they're really that good,' White admitted, 'we wouldn't even know they were there.'

'Until operations are compromised or assets are blown, and MI5 is landed with the blame.' Knox hoped playing on White's pride in the Service was the last push he needed.

'So,' White said, finally, 'what do we do?'

'Whatever we can,' Knox replied.

CHAPTER FORTY-SIX

The CIA archives under the US embassy were as quiet as ever, just a few other clerks on the weekend shift struggling with the amount of filing the run-up to the OECD conference had generated. None of them were surprised to see another of their ranks walking around the record stacks, and none of them paid Bennett enough attention to realise she wasn't there to file papers away but to hunt for them.

She began, as she always did, with Bianchi and Moretti's records. But when she spun the large wheel that opened the archive stacks and pulled them out of their hanging drawers the folders were empty. The last time she'd looked at them, barely forty-eight hours ago, they'd contained several months' worth of tracking reports and field observations. She checked the log sheet stapled to the front of the first folder. They hadn't already been moved to deep storage. They'd been checked out at midnight on Friday. Three letters were written next to the timestamp – COS. They stood for Chief of Station.

Bennett went to Irina Valera's folder next. It had

255

been filed in the stacks on Friday afternoon, then checked out, again in the dead of night, on behalf of the chief of station.

Michael Finney, London station chief for ten years, was one of the most senior figures in the entire CIA. He spent his time briefing senior members of the state department and the top level of government. So why was he suddenly interested in the Italians and Valera?

Before she gave up on the archives, she scoured the stacks for any information they had on General Medev. Eventually she found a reference to him in a mission report from a CIA asset in Moscow. It listed him as head of the KGB's scientific directorate. If that was true it explained why he'd been the one who had come after Valera. It also made him one hell of a sacrificial lamb.

Then she went to the other part of the embassy that was home to almost as much information as the archive – the canteen.

The canteen was on the next floor up – still underground but closer to the surface. It was busy with small groups of people from departments all over the embassy, huddled together up and down its rows of tables.

Bennett poured herself a cup of coffee from one of the giant pots that lined the canteen's long wall and were kept full and hot all hours of the day and night. She scanned the tables out of habit, looking for any junior field agents or embassy staff who were too young or too unimportant to worry about being discreet with their breaktime conversations.

She spotted two secretaries sitting close together on the far side of the room and casually made her way over to them. She sat down four seats away – far enough for them not to pay attention to her but close enough for her to hear every word they said. Both women were wearing the twinset, skirt, and pearls that most secretaries in the embassy defaulted to, and they both looked angry about being stuck at work on a Sunday in summer.

They were the kind of women who Bennett had been intensely jealous of when she'd first arrived in London, the kind of women who hadn't wanted anything to do with her. Now she looked down on them, because she knew that just because they were physically closer to the action, that didn't mean they had any idea about what was really going on.

'It's ridiculous, I told him,' the secretary on Bennett's side of the table said.

'I know,' the other one replied.

'The city's full. No room at the inn.'

'I know.'

'He shouldn't be surprised. Half the damn state department's flown in.'

'I know.'

'All I ask is enough notice to be able to do my job properly. A little decency, you know?'

'I know.'

'And for some scientist from NASA. What's he going to do? Launch a rocket off Tower Bridge?'

Bennett shot to her feet, shaking the table and spilling the dregs of her coffee onto its faded Formica surface. Both of the other women twisted round in surprise, then, realising who had caused the sudden commotion, turned back to each other, pretending they hadn't seen anything.

Bennett carried her cup over to one of the sinks. Then, once she was through the canteen's large double doors, she sprinted up the stairs to the embassy exit. The secretary was right. There was no reason for anyone from NASA to fly all the way to London for a conference on economic development – unless they weren't coming for the conference at all.

CHAPTER FORTY-SEVEN

Knox had one more stop to make before he
met Bennett.

He walked down the long eastern slope
of Parliament Hill, crossed the heath between the
wide, open boating lake and the tree-shrouded
men's bathing pond, and headed up into Highgate.

Highgate was one of London's old villages.
Like Montmartre, sitting above Paris, it had been
home to artists, writers, and politicians. It was an
enclave of people who had worked out how to
successfully combine creativity, power, and influence.

The Hollands' home was called Wytchen House,
but it was known both in and outside MI5 as 'the
cottage'. It was an ironic name as it was, by any
normal standards, a mansion. But it had a demure,
even humble air to it, set back from the road
behind a small, elegant garden and with most of
its bulk hidden behind high stone walls.

Knox knocked on the heavy oak front door, and
a few moments later Sarah opened it. She looked
like she hadn't slept since he'd last seen her in Guy's,
and she did little to hide her irritation at finding
Knox on her doorstep. But she still invited him in.

Knox had been to the Hollands' house countless times, but he always felt slightly strange when he stepped inside – like a child visiting his rich friend's parents.

Without a word Sarah walked into the drawing room, expecting Knox to follow her. She sat in a deep, high-backed chair in front of an empty fireplace. A pot of tea and an open hardback book were on a small table next to the chair.

Knox stopped in front of a chaise longue, set across from Sarah's chair on the other side of a large, intricately patterned rug.

'That's where I found him,' Sarah said, gesturing at the spot where Knox was standing.

Knox resisted the urge to leap to one side, and instead sat down on the chaise longue. It was overstuffed and he perched awkwardly on it. Sarah picked up the hardback – a sign that she didn't expect Knox to stay very long.

'What do you want, Richard?'

Knox cleared his throat and said, 'Did James ever tell you about my parents?'

She sighed. 'You really do think the world revolves around you, don't you?' Her voice was sharp. 'I don't care about you or your parents. I care about my husband.'

'How is he?' Knox asked.

'No change. They say that's a good thing, as if it could possibly be.' She checked her watch. 'I'm due there in an hour.'

260

'I just need five minutes,' Knox replied. 'It's about James.'

Knox watched Sarah check the temperature of the teapot with the back of her hand.

'Fine. Five minutes,' she said, marking her page and closing the book.

'It's about James,' he said again, 'but it starts with my parents. They were normal people. Normal for the East End. My father was a labourer, my mother took in sewing. They got by, until I came along and the economy went to hell. Work dried up. Sometimes there was no money. Sometimes there was no food.'

Knox knew Wytchen House had been in Sarah's family for over a hundred years. He wondered whether the hard times of the thirties had even touched her and the other residents of Highgate.

'They survived,' he continued, 'hanging on day after day, just like everyone else around them. But eventually things got too hard and people gave up. I don't mean they left. I mean they died. Starved, or got sick and couldn't get better. The East End had become a ghetto and people were being left to rot in it. It drove my parents mad.'

He paused for a moment, shifting his weight on the chaise longue. He knew he could end his story here and protect Sarah from the secret he and her husband had shared for so long. But he also knew he couldn't.

'There was an old builders' yard near our house,' he said. 'It had been shut up and forgotten about.

One day my father broke in, looking for tools or something he could sell. He found a locked box tucked away inside a cabinet. There were two sticks of dynamite inside.' He lowered his eyes to the rug in front of him. 'My parents weren't anarchists. They were desperate and stupid. They just wanted to get people's attention, make them see how bad things had got. They decided to blow a hole in the wall of a police station. But they didn't know how powerful the dynamite was. Or how quick the fuses would burn. Two policemen died in the explosion, along with my parents.'

He looked up, his eyes meeting Sarah's again. She hadn't moved. The hardback was still clutched in her lap.

'James knew about this?' she asked.

'The story was only in the papers for a few days, and they used my father's name, Campbell. Knox is my grandmother's name. But James still found it in the pre-war records. He knew the Service would never trust me if anyone else discovered what my parents had done. So he let my secret stay hidden.'

'What does this have to do with last Sunday night?' Sarah asked.

'It was the anniversary.'

Knox had learned not to hate his parents. But he still couldn't forgive them. Every year he marked their deaths and honoured the memories of the police officers they'd killed.

'And if you'd told the inquiry that,' Sarah said,

'they'd have found out everything and James would have been drummed out of the Service before he could defend himself.'

Knox nodded. The secret wasn't even Holland's, but he'd kept it. And the simple act of not exposing Knox would have damned him.

'And you'd become a scapegoat, blamed for the sins of your parents and anything else the Service felt like pinning on you.'

Knox nodded again. 'It would have been the end of both our careers. He's protected me for so long, I have to do the same for him.'

'Then what's changed now?'

Knox had come this far; there was no point holding anything else back. He told her about everything that had happened since she'd found Holland's body on the rug between them a week ago. He told her about Manning's rapid consolidation of power, about the sidelining of White at a time when he was most needed, and about the attacks on him in London and Stockholm.

Sarah was as shrewd as her husband at his best. She probed Knox, testing him to prove every connection and leap he'd made. And by the end of her grilling she agreed with Knox's conclusions: that Manning was most likely a Soviet agent and responsible for Holland's coma.

'That bastard,' she said. 'I want you to stop him. And I want him to pay.'

CHAPTER FORTY-EIGHT

Knox left Wytchen House and headed for Highgate tube station and the Northern Line back into town. But instead of changing onto the Central Line at Tottenham Court Road to meet Bennett, he made his way up to street level. He knew it was a risk to go back to Kemp House so soon after the fire, but he wanted to see just how much damage had been done, and if anything had managed to survive the inferno.

He took a circuitous route through Soho, dropping down Charing Cross Road and cutting along Old Compton Street before turning into Walker's Court at the southern end of Berwick Street.

Walker's Court was one of the small stretches of Soho that truly seemed to exist outside of time. Its narrow entrance off Brewer Street was framed by a windowed gallery that hung above the passage and connected the two buildings on either side. And it was lined with shops that looked like they belonged in a Dickens novel, and made their money selling the city's gentlemen provisions for the weekend.

There were always a couple of men loitering in the passage, building up the courage to go inside one of its emporiums. This afternoon was no different, and as Knox stepped under the gallery bridge he spotted two hanging around at the other end of the passage. Maybe they were nervous shoppers, maybe they were watching the entrance to Kemp House. Knox decided that either way it made sense to encourage them to move on.

'Good afternoon, gentlemen,' he said, doing his best impression of a plain-clothed police officer. 'Enjoying yourselves?'

Both men turned bright red and immediately started to back off. Knox waited until he saw them both disappear round the corner onto Wardour Street, then he crossed over to the entrance of Kemp House, glancing up at the charred streaks that crowned the building.

He took the lift up to the top floor and checked the corridor and stairwell before heading for his flat. The front door had been smashed in by the firefighters and replaced with a heavy tarpaulin sheet secured around the frame. Knox guessed this had been done by the police, who would have taken over from the fire brigade last night and who might now also be looking for him. Depending on who at the Met had been given the case, word of the fire might even have already made it to Leconfield House.

Every inch of the tarpaulin edge was fixed down, but it had a covered seal running up one side of it. As Knox pulled it open fresh air rushed into the flat and a burnt stench flowed out.

He stepped through the heavy sheeting and made his way inside. The air was still heavy with smoke particles and water vapour from the storm and the firefighters' hoses. There were more sheets across the blown-out windows – the place had been hermetically sealed.

The bedroom looked like it had survived the fire relatively unscathed. But the same couldn't be said for the main living area. The walls were black, the marble dining table stained and cracked from the heat, and the Eames lounger had been reduced to a pile of ash and a set of twisted legs.

Knox walked around the room, leaving damp black footprints in the small patches of floor not already covered in soot as he inspected the full extent of the damage. He recognised the shape of his kitchen, but like everything else it was now a dull, matt black. It felt like he was fumbling around in the dead of night.

There was no sign of what had caused the fire. The oven was badly burnt, but still intact – it hadn't exploded, and there were no scorch marks around it. The official line, as it always was in situations like this, would be that the fire had been caused by a gas leak. But the evidence in front of Knox proved that wasn't true.

The tarpaulin across the windows started to flutter. Knox assumed it was just wind blowing up the side of the building, and he decided to give the bedroom a more thorough check to see what he could salvage, even if it was just a change of clothes. But before he turned away from the oven something slammed into the back of his head, knocking him out and sending him falling, face-first onto the kitchen floor.

The fluttering sheets hadn't been caused by the wind but by someone else silently pulling apart the tarpaulin across the door and bringing more fresh air into the apartment.

The man had been waiting all night and day for someone to visit Knox's flat. After the fire brigade and police had left, he'd taken up his position on one of Kemp House's unoccupied lower floors. He'd spent all night peering through the small window in the door to the building's central stair-case. Then, when the lift was turned back on in the morning, he'd turned his attention to its display panel and waited for it to tell him someone was going up to the top floor. When it finally had, ten minutes ago, he'd made his way up the stairs and into Knox's flat.

He pulled a roll of thick duct tape from his pocket, and used it to bind the unconscious Knox's wrists and ankles before he dragged him into his bedroom and up onto the bed. He ran several long lengths of tape across Knox's chest and thighs, holding him in place. Then he cut off another strip to cover his mouth. His instructions weren't to kill Knox, just to make sure he couldn't leave or call for help. He didn't know if someone else was going to execute him or if he was just going to be left to die slowly and alone in the flat. And he didn't care – it wasn't his job or his problem.

He looked at the bruise that was starting to blossom across Knox's cheek and the bloody cut on his brow that was dirty with soot from the kitchen floor. Then he checked that all the pieces of tape were secure and, satisfied with his work, put the roll back in his pocket, stepped out of the flat, sealed the tarpaulin across the door back down, and called the lift.

CHAPTER FORTY-NINE

Bennett had discovered Speakers' Corner one Sunday four months ago.

Hyde Park was close enough to Grosvenor Square for a lunchtime stroll whenever she needed to get her head above ground. And it was on one such walk halfway through a weekend shift in the archives that she encountered a line of people in the north-east corner of the park raised up on chairs, stepladders and, in a couple of cases, actual soapboxes, waxing lyrical to anyone who would listen. This was Speakers' Corner, and it was a curious spectacle, both profoundly British and un-British at the same time. It worked as a kind of social pressure valve, letting the usually reserved people of London rant, vent, and rail about anything they wanted – within reason. The police monitored the speakers – particularly those who drew large crowds – but usually only intervened if their speeches crossed the line into profanity.

This Sunday a constant stream of orators offered benedictions, damnations, and prophecies to the passing crowds enjoying their afternoon in the park. Bennett had timed her arrival well. A couple of the speakers had just finished their speeches and their audiences were starting to move on. She had her pick of the benches and chose one that gave her clear lines of sight along the paths that converged on this part of the park.

A few moments later a man sat down on a bench two along from her. Like Bennett, he looked like someone who had been called into the office and was stealing a few hours of his Sunday back to enjoy the sun. He wore a light linen shirt and slacks, and carried a tightly stuffed document wallet. He was, Bennett had to admit, quite a good tail.

Bennett had realised she was half an hour early for her rendezvous with Knox as she'd raced out of the American embassy. So she'd taken her own meandering route to Hyde Park while she went over the implications of what she'd discovered about Finney and the sudden arrival in the city of a NASA scientist.

She'd first noticed the man following her when she'd paused in front of one of Selfridges' windows, then again when she made a loop of Portman Square, just north of the department store. He blended well with the general street traffic, but not well enough for Bennett to miss him passing her in the Marble Arch underpass or appearing two benches down from her in Speakers' Corner.

The CIA hadn't given her the skills to spot a tail. She'd acquired those herself in the Garden City library, reading novels like *The Thirty-Nine*

Steps and *The Secret Agent* over and over, soaking up everything they could teach her about spycraft. She'd put what she'd learned to use quickly, finally finding out where her brothers vanished to every day instead of working or looking after their mother. She'd followed them to a dried-up creek where they spent hours shooting at stunted bushes and sun-dazed lizards with an old revolver one of them had found somewhere. Then she'd made them teach her how to shoot it in exchange for keeping their secret.

The man made a good show of watching the world go by and listening to people talk about the end of civilisation and the healing power of Christ. But there was no escaping the fact that he and Bennett were the only people who had stayed on their benches and not moved on for several changes of speakers.

Knox was now late, but Bennett was less worried about that than she was about her tail following her to their backup meeting point in the Italian water gardens on the other side of the park. For all she knew, Knox was somewhere nearby, had also spotted the man shadowing her, and was purposefully keeping his distance.

She waited for the next natural shift in the crowd, chose her moment, and fell into step with a group of passing picnickers. Halfway down the eastern edge of the park she peeled off and crossed a wide, open section of ground. There were fewer people here, scattered and gingerly testing the grass to

271

see if it had dried out from last night's storm. She was exposed, but there was no other way to the Serpentine, the long lake that snaked across the park and led to the water gardens. She moved quickly, but not quickly enough – she hoped – to draw attention. It took her five minutes to reach a tree-lined section of path that gave her a little cover.

The Serpentine was choked with people. Families swarmed around deckchairs, couples promenaded along the lake edge, and groups of children chased swans. The surface of the lake was scattered with rowing boats.

Bennett crossed in front of a group of ladies pushing prams, all wearing dark dresses with starched collars. She glanced behind her and saw the man from Speakers' Corner emerging from the path to the lake. She started to move faster, weaving between more groups of people. She followed the edge of the lake as it curved northwards towards the water gardens, stopping for a moment under the old stone bridge that cut the lake in two.

She wondered who the man was. Was he KGB, out for retribution for Medev? An MI5 Watcher? Or had her snooping in Grosvenor Square finally caught the attention of someone in the CIA who wanted to know what she was up to?

When she couldn't see him on the bend of the path behind her, she decided she must have lost him, and continued along a quieter stretch of path, passing opposite the statue of Peter Pan that had appeared in the park as if by magic one night in 1912. Knox wasn't waiting for Bennett in the water gardens, but her tail was. He must have guessed where she was headed and cut across the park while she was on the lake path.

He was no longer playing the part of someone simply out for a stroll. He was standing in the middle of the water gardens, next to its large central fountain and surrounded by its ornamental lakes, scanning the faces of everyone around him.

When he saw Bennett he started to walk towards her, his eyes fixed on hers, and his hand reaching into his bulging document wallet. Bennett didn't know what he had hidden in there, but she didn't want to find out. He hadn't just been following her, he'd been stalking her – and now he was about to pounce. Bennett knew she wouldn't be able to outrun him if she tried to make a break for it across the park, and if she turned back the way she'd come she'd just end up confronting him somewhere secluded where she'd be considerably more vulnerable.

Luckily, she had another option – something he wouldn't be able to defend against. She walked straight towards him, closing the distance between them. Then, when he was about ten yards away from her, she started to scream.

'Help! Help!' she shouted. 'That man is following me!'

The man froze in place as heads turned first to Bennett and then to him.

'He's following me!' she screamed over and over again. Soon everyone in the water gardens was glaring at them.

'Leave her alone,' an old lady with a scarf over her head and a tiny dog at her feet called out.

'Clear off!' another added from a bench near the fountain.

The man realised he'd been outmanoeuvred. He slowly pulled his hand out of the document wallet and shot Bennett one last threatening look. She watched him march back across the gardens and down the far side of the Serpentine.

Two young men in bright suits who had been strolling through the gardens arm in arm with their short-skirted girlfriends walked over to her.

'You alright, miss?' one of the young men asked Bennett as the man disappeared in the distance.

'I sure am, mister,' she replied in her full Midwestern accent. 'Thank you kindly.'

Then she gave him a hug and ran away, leaving everyone in the water gardens to wonder if she'd really been in danger or was just some mad American.

Bennett left the park, crossed over Bayswater Road, and headed into Lancaster Gate tube station. She now assumed Knox had never made it to Speakers' Corner or the water gardens after all. She didn't know where he was, and she needed to find him.

CHAPTER FIFTY

Bennett took the Central Line from Lancaster Gate to Oxford Circus and, after checking that the man from the park hadn't followed her or handed her over to another tail, made her way to Kemp House.

She'd decided that Knox's flat was a good place to start her search for him. It wasn't until she reached the top floor of the building that she realised something was wrong. As soon as the lift door opened, the acrid smell of smoke hit her. It reminded her of her childhood and the never-ending task of keeping the kitchen fire burning through winter. The sight of the tarpaulin across the door brought her back to the present. She opened the seam, releasing even more old smoke into the corridor, and shouted Knox's name as she stepped into the flat and saw the destruction.

She found Knox strapped to the bed, smeared with dirt and blood. She rushed to his side and checked his breathing. It was shallow, but it was there. She shook his shoulders and shouted his name again, but he didn't wake up. She ran out into the kitchen, looking for something to cut him free, but only found the two sets of footprints that led into the open-plan area and the single set and long streak that led away from it. The drawers that lined the kitchen counter were all warped shut.

Bennett tried the bathroom next. Like the bedroom, it had survived mostly intact. She opened the mirrored cupboard that sat on the wall above the sink and found a small pair of scissors. Standing over the bed again, she opened them to make a single blade and slashed at the strips of duct tape holding Knox down. Then she cut the binding around his ankles and wrists. Finally, she ripped the tape off his mouth. She expected the pain of the glue tearing the skin off his lips would bring him round. It didn't.

Knox wouldn't wake up because he didn't want to. His mind was happy exactly where it was, dreaming that he was back at the Festival of Britain with Jack Williams.

It was late afternoon, a Friday. The sun was still high, the breeze off the Thames was just right, and Knox was drinking beer with his best friend. Soon they'd make a bet about who was going to buy the next round, Knox would lose, and Williams would make it up to him by taking him for dinner at a new restaurant he wanted to try. Then they'd inevitably end up at Bar Italia before stumbling back to wherever in Soho Knox was living at the time or taking a late train to Hertfordshire to spend the weekend recovering from their excesses. It was a perfect memory, and Knox's mind had no desire to give it up.

Unfortunately, Bennett had no idea how content Knox was. She was just scared that he was now stuck in a coma, just like Holland. There was one thing left she could try to wake him up. She slapped him hard across the face. Twice.

Slowly, and very unwillingly, Knox came to. He was confused to see Bennett in his bedroom staring down at him. Then, as he started to register the pain all over his face and the back of his head, his confusion turned to anger.

'Hello,' he said. His voice cracked. His throat was dry from inhaling the smoke-heavy air.

'What happened to you?' Bennett asked.

'I think I upset someone,' he replied, pulling himself up into a sitting position and delicately leaning his head against the wall.

'That makes two of us.'

He told her about seeing the aftermath of the fire last night, his visits to White and Sarah Holland, and the attack someone had sprung on him while he was checking the damage to his flat. Then Bennett told him about the man who had come after her in Hyde Park.

'It sounds like they really want us out of the way,' Knox replied when she was done.

'We might need to add another *they* to our list,' Bennett replied.

She told him about the missing records in the CIA archives, the file she'd found on Medev, and the conversation she'd overheard in the embassy canteen.

'I think it might not just be MI5 that's been compromised,' she said. 'Finney could have been turned too.'

Knox had spent years searching for signs of Soviet infiltration of British intelligence, and he was convinced he'd found them. But even he struggled to believe that the KGB could have turned the director general of MI5 and the CIA's chief in London. He thought for a moment, then asked, 'Why fly someone over from NASA?'

'You said why yourself. To find out what they can get from Valera before they hand her back.'

'Maybe.' A CIA station chief checking out files in the dead of night and the sudden appearance of a NASA scientist in the city were definitely strange, but they weren't the oddest things to happen over the last week.

'But, if Finney and Manning are both working for the KGB, then why circulate Valera's photo in the first place?' Knox asked. 'Why not bury it as soon as it came in?'

Bennett had thought about that too while she sat in Hyde Park.

'Anything that's held back has to be accounted for, eventually. They weren't expecting anyone to be looking for Valera, or even recognise her. It was low-level intelligence. Better to let it sit in plain sight and then quietly remove it. Then, once Valera's been put on a plane, or a sub, or buried in a shallow grave somewhere, they can just slip it back into the files.'

That, unfortunately, sounded entirely plausible to Knox. He felt along the edge of the bruise across his face, and along the line of his brow. He winced when his finger touched the gash and broke the thin scab that had started to form across it.

He had one last question for Bennett. 'What about Medev? Why kill a KGB directorate chief if that's who you're supposed to be working for?'

'I can't decide between two answers for that one,' Bennett replied.

'Which are?'

'First, they didn't know he was in play.'

'They didn't know one of the KGB's highest-ranking officers was involved?'

'I'm serious. How much does MI5 do that MI6 has no idea about? Getting the CIA and the FBI to cooperate on anything takes months of negotiation. The KGB is huge. Maybe there were two operations running at once.'

'And second?'

'He was a target too. Part of an internal KGB power struggle.'

Somehow Knox liked that idea even less than the notion that both Manning and Finney had been turned.

He pulled himself up off his bed and walked over to his wardrobe. He opened it, relieved to see both his clothes and the crate from Bianchi and Moretti's were still inside and in decent condition.

279

'What are you doing?' Bennett asked.

'I'm getting changed,' he replied. 'And then we're going to Leconfield House to have it out with Manning once and for all, before he can do any more damage.'

'That's great,' Bennett said. 'But Manning isn't at Leconfield House.'

'What?' Knox asked as he gave up trying to remove the duct tape from the front of his shirt and just pulled it over his head. He dropped the ruined shirt on the floor and took a clean one off a hanger.

'He'll be at the diplomatic reception in Portland Place. Along with Finney.'

Knox thought about Manning lapping up the attention of the great and powerful in Holland's place, all the while knowing he was about to preside over an intelligence disaster that Britain might never recover from.

'Well, then,' he said, 'we'll just have to crash his party.'

CHAPTER FIFTY-ONE

The distant blast of a car horn woke Valera. She had no idea where she was, just that she was no longer in the dark room, tied to a chair and surrounded by faceless, shouting figures. She didn't know how long she'd been asleep, but for the first time in a week she didn't feel completely exhausted. If it wasn't for the thick purple bruises on her wrists she might even have thought the dark room had just been a bad dream.

She was lying on top of a narrow, soft bed. Her clothes were dry and her shoes were still on her feet. She felt clean, really clean. There was no grit under her nails, no foul stench lingering in her hair.

She swung her legs off the bed – they were heavy, but they moved – and took in her new surroundings. The room was empty apart from the bed. The walls were bare, the floorboards exposed but varnished. There was a large sash window on one side of the room, and a door on the other. Valera slipped off the bed and stepped lightly round the room. She tested the door. It was locked. She peered through the window, looking for something that would reveal where she was, but all she could tell was that she was on the first floor of a house in the middle of a narrow street and, judging from the short shadows she could see on the few cars below her, it was the middle of the day.

She'd expected someone to come after her, but not the head of the KGB scientific directorate. And she definitely hadn't expected to watch a bullet pierce his skull and shower her in blood and brains.

She couldn't imagine the KGB killing one of their own so openly and brazenly, which meant someone else must now be holding her captive. The Swedes were the only people who knew anything close to the true extent of her breakthrough and what it was worth – not even the GRU or KGB knew how far her work had really progressed – but they already had her. She may not have served up all of her secrets on a plate, but she was cooperating with them.

She remembered the American woman and British man who, just like Medev, had appeared out of thin air in Skansen. Who were they? And who were they working for? For all she knew, they were another distraction, working with the people who kidnapped her, and right now she might just be enjoying a temporary reprieve before being thrown back into the dark room.

She tried to untangle the knots in her head. She could still see the broken domes of the Saviour on the Spilled Blood and the grown-up Ledjo reaching out to her when she closed her eyes. And she remembered the voices merging into two, then one, and the feeling of hands untying her and telling her everything was going to be alright. But could she be sure that had really happened?

Then she realised something more disturbing than everything she'd been through in the dark room. When she tried to picture the boat on the lake in her mind she couldn't see it. It hadn't changed, morphed into something new and unfamiliar. It wasn't buried in the mess of memories and nightmares that had taken over her mind. It was just gone, as if it had been ripped out of her. She was missing something else too. Ledjo's backpack.

Valera didn't know if she was being watched somehow or if her captors were on the other side of the locked door, waiting for her to bang or wail or completely break down. She couldn't cry even if she wanted to. She was too angry. She stood in the middle of the room, shaking with rage, until she couldn't hold it in any more and she let out a deep, guttural scream. The door didn't open. No one came to silence her, or comfort her, or drag her back to the dark room.

Now sure she was alone, she went back to the door, but instead of twisting the knob again, she kicked it, slamming her heel into it again and again until the panel it was embedded in fractured and the whole mechanism clattered onto the floorboards.

The door swung open and Valera peered out into the short landing on the other side of it, still half-expecting some unseen guard to jump on her. She ignored the other doors and other rooms on the first floor and ran for the stairs that would lead her down to the ground floor and out onto the street. But they didn't, because the bottom of the staircase was blocked by a huge slab of metal. It looked like a giant guillotine had sliced through the house, intended solely to block her way.

There was a door embedded in the thick metal, but no handle for Valera to turn or attack. She still kicked it, purely out of frustration, and heard a dull, deep echo on the other side.

She retreated upstairs. This time she went room to room in search of an escape route. At the back of the house were a small bathroom and kitchen, which, save for a quietly humming fridge, were as bare as the bedroom she'd woken up in. The only other room on the first floor, between the bedroom and bathroom, had been set up as a kind of living room. There were two chairs, a low table, and a large shelf full of well-worn books. They were all in English – the first real clue Valera had found about where she was.

The living room also had a large sash window. This one looked out onto a narrow, shaded yard. Valera shook the frame, trying to force it open, but it wouldn't shift. She hit the glass with her fist, but it didn't shatter. She even picked up one of the chairs and hurled it at the window. It fell onto the floorboards without leaving a scratch. She dragged it into the bedroom and tried to launch it out into the street, only succeeding in breaking one of the legs.

She was starting to feel claustrophobic, her deep tiredness beginning to creep back. She went back to the kitchen, still hunting for anything that might help her get out of this strange, empty house. She scoured the cupboards, but they were all bare. She tried the tap in the sink. A thin dribble of lukewarm water came out. It felt like she was back in her house in Povenets B.

She felt a familiar pang in her stomach and opened the fridge. Astonishingly, it wasn't empty. On the middle shelf was a small plate of sandwiches, half a loaf of bread, and a jar of jam. Valera inspected and then discarded the bread and sandwiches. She didn't trust them – the bread was too white and neat, the sandwiches filled with some kind of square-cut, processed meat. But she couldn't resist the jam jar. She picked it up, unscrewed the lid, and inhaled the rich, cloying smell of sugar and berries. Her sense of smell was dulled from the burning embers she'd breathed in as she'd searched the ruins of Ledjo's school but the pungent aroma was still almost enough to overwhelm her. Then she scooped a handful of the cold, sticky substance into her mouth.

The slick feeling on her tongue took Valera instantly back to her first spring in Povenets B, when the sun was starting to get hot and the days were getting longer. She had sat on the scrub in front of her bungalow, smearing jam made from Zukolev's private supply of raspberries that she'd kept over winter onto chunks of rye bread as Ledjo showed off his Young Pioneers neckerchief, which Valera had made for him the night before. He'd marched up and down as Valera clapped and laughed, chanting the Young Pioneers' motto, 'Be prepared!', over and over between bites of jam and bread.

Valera kept scooping jam into her mouth until the jar was empty. As the last of it slid past her tongue she came back to the present. She almost cried, remembering how proud Ledjo had been and that for a brief while she had been happy in Povenets B. She had no idea who was holding her, or what they had planned for her, but as she sucked her fingers clean she promised her son that she'd be prepared for whatever happened to her next.

CHAPTER FIFTY-TWO

The Royal Institute of British Architects had occupied 66 Portland Place since 1934. The building was a masterclass in Art Deco restraint. Its near-smooth stone-clad walls were adorned only by a few tall, slim bas-relief sculptures. Through the bronze double doors, a grand marble foyer stood in front of an equally impressive glass and polished chrome staircase, which led up to a large, double-height ballroom.

In a few hours' time a reception for the heads of state who had come to London would be held at Buckingham Palace. But the ambassadors, foreign and finance ministers who would actually be working during the OECD conference were being treated to the splendour of the RIBA headquarters for the afternoon. And so were their top spies.

Four Met officers stood outside the entrance, but when Knox and Bennett slipped down the narrow mews that led to the rear of Portland Place they didn't run into any more. There was just a set of steps leading down to a basement door with a lock that put up little resistance to Knox's shoulder.

They made their way through the bowels of the building, eventually finding a flight of stairs that took them up to a corridor just off the foyer. Knox glanced round the corner and out through the glass panels of the front door, checking that the policemen standing in front of the building weren't paying attention to what was going on inside it.

The reception was in full swing. The rumble of conversation and clinking of glasses coming from the first floor echoed around Knox and Bennett as they exchanged a long, silent look. Knox knew he was about to commit professional suicide in front of the leaders of the global intelligence community. He only hoped he'd do it in such a spectacular fashion that he'd bring Manning down with him. And they both knew that once they were on the grand staircase there'd be no turning back.

Eventually Bennett broke the silence, whispering, 'After you.'

On the first-floor landing they paused again. A string quartet played in the wraparound gallery above them, and waiters scurried around filling up trays with drinks and ferrying them through the tall doors that led through the glass wall of the ballroom. On the other side of the glass divide was a sea of old men in identical dark suits. Knox couldn't see Manning or Finney in the crowd and for a moment he wondered if they hadn't turned up after all. Then a waiter carrying a full tray forced the crowd to part round him and for a brief moment Knox saw Manning's tall frame, and Finney's shorter, broader one next to him, in the middle of the room. They were both wearing the same dark suits as everyone else – Manning's hung off him and Finney looked like he'd been stuffed into his. By chance, Manning glanced past the waiter as the crowd flowed around him and made eye contact with Knox. Confusion flashed across his face as he disappeared again behind a wave of suits.

'They're here,' Knox said to Bennett, and started towards the nearest door.

The sight of Manning where Holland should've been fanned the flames of anger that were already burning inside Knox. He kept his eyes fixed on the spot where Manning and Finney had been standing, which meant he didn't see another waiter walking towards the other side of the door. The waiter was only carrying a couple of empty glasses on his tray, but the sound of them crashing onto the ballroom's parquet floor as the swinging door knocked the tray out of his hands was enough to draw the attention of most of the people in the room. Knox didn't apologise for causing the crash. He'd wanted an audience for what was about to happen, and now he had one.

The sea parted once more as Knox and Bennett waded into the crowd, revealing Manning and Finney still standing where they had been a few moments before. Manning still looked baffled.

'Richard,' he said, 'what are you doing here?'

'Surprised to see me?' Knox replied.

'I'm surprised to see you looking like that.' The bruise across Knox's cheek looked even worse in the bright light of the ballroom. 'What's going on?' he asked.

'I could ask you the same question.'

'What are you talking about?'

'Murder, kidnapping, treason,' Knox said, loud enough for everyone around them to hear.

The crowd fell silent, every pair of eyes in the room suddenly focused on Knox and Manning.

'I don't know what you're talking about,' Manning said. 'But let's discuss whatever you think is happening somewhere more private.' He gave the room a reassuring smile.

'I'm happy right where I am,' Knox replied.

Manning snapped his head back to Knox, his smile gone. 'That wasn't a request.'

'I don't take orders from you,' Knox shot back.

Manning leaned in closer to Knox, lowering his voice. 'What's happened to you, man?'

'Your men happened to me.'

'My men? You're not making any sense.'

'Or maybe they were yours,' Knox said to Finney.

'Excuse me?' Finney replied, looking as confused as Manning had been when he'd first spotted Knox.

'You heard me,' Knox replied.

'That's enough,' Manning said to Knox. 'I won't have you embarrassing the Service like this.' Then he turned to Finney and said, 'If you'll excuse me, I'll deal with this and be back shortly.'

'No way,' Finney replied. 'I want to know what I've done. I'm coming with you.'

Manning glanced at the room and all the faces that were still turned towards them.

'Fine,' he said. Then he started to march towards the door.

Knox didn't want to lose his audience, but Manning wasn't giving him a choice. At least he now had a room full of witnesses who had seen him confront Manning. The crowd kept watching as Manning stepped around the waiter, who was still clearing up the broken glasses, and left the ballroom. Then they watched Knox and Bennett follow him, with Finney taking up the rear of the little procession. And they kept watching as the group crossed the landing and disappeared through a pair of large wooden doors on the other side of the staircase.

CHAPTER FIFTY-THREE

The four of them found themselves in an exhibition hall. If any of them had been paying attention they'd have noticed that they were surrounded by architectural models of new buildings planned for London. They'd walked into the future. There were scale reproductions of skyscrapers, bridges, and public spaces and, in the centre of the room, a rendering of the Barbican, the enormous brutalist complex planned for the hole in the city Knox had stumbled through the night before when he was being chased across the city by a ghost.

'Now, what the hell is going on, Richard?' Manning demanded once the doors had closed and he could hear the murmur of conversations starting up again behind them.

'Stop playing the fool. You know exactly what's going on,' Knox replied.

'I assure you I have no idea.'

Knox's anger intensified with every denial Manning made.

'Don't be so modest, Gordon. You've built an

impressive web. But you should have left me out of it.'

'This is nonsense,' Manning said. 'I offered you a chance to come back in. Gave you what should have been an easy job to do, then you disappear for two days and turn up looking like this.'

Manning moved further into the room, putting the replica of the Barbican between himself and Knox. He towered over the model, like a giant about to destroy a helpless village. He made a show of checking his watch. 'You've got five minutes to explain yourself.'

Manning hadn't mentioned Bianchi or Moretti or the details of the mission he'd given Knox. It was a basic precaution given Finney and Bennett's presence. Knox, however, no longer had any qualms about breaking operational security. In fact, now he was finally in front of Manning with no Peterson to come to his rescue, he was ready to throw every accusation he had at him in excruciating detail.

'You sent me off into the woods, and I found the one thing I wasn't supposed to. What was your plan? Quietly retrieve Bianchi and Moretti's real research when everything had died down, or were they just a distraction while you handed Pipistrelle over to the KGB?'

'What's Pipistrelle?' Finney asked, seizing on the word he hadn't heard before.

Manning chose to ignore the question.

'Those are not allegations to be made in public,' he replied coolly. Knox ignored the warning.

'Did you burn down my flat to destroy the Italians' papers?' Knox paused for a moment. 'Or was that because we saw what you did to Irina Valera?'

Manning's face didn't change at the sound of Valera's name – it stayed in the same combination of confusion and irritation. 'Should that mean something to me?' he asked.

'For God's sake, drop the act,' Knox replied. 'We know who she is, you know who she is.' He pointed to Finney. 'He knows who she is.'

'I do?' Finney replied.

'You've got her file on your desk,' Bennett replied, moving round an oblong, honeycomb skyscraper that was nearly as tall as her to stand next to Knox.

'Now, how in the hell would you know that?' Finney asked her, seeming suddenly suspicious of the woman he'd so far ignored.

'Because I pay attention to what's going on. And I recognise one of the world's most valuable intelligence assets when I see a picture of her.'

'That doesn't answer my question.'

'Sorry, boss.'

Finney's suspicion turned to realisation, then amusement. 'You're that nut-job secretary who thinks she should be an agent, aren't you?'

'I'm not a secretary,' Bennett replied. 'I'm a file clerk.'

'You're a little firecracker, I'll give you that.' He

turned to Manning. 'I'm not sure if I should laugh or apologise.'

'No need for you to do either,' replied Manning. 'The only person who should be apologising is Knox.'

'I'm not the one who ordered the abduction of a foreign national and the killing of a KGB directorate chief,' Knox replied, trying to land another couple of blows on Manning. 'Have your masters in the Lubyanka realised that was you yet? Or were you following their orders?'

Manning looked stunned. 'You've actually gone mad, haven't you?' he said.

'I was there. We were in Stockholm. We saw your men put a bullet through his head and kidnap Valera.'

Manning was silent for a long moment. He dropped his gaze down onto the model of the Barbican, but he wasn't really seeing it. He was thinking about what Knox had just said. His hands reached into his pockets, then he looked back up at Knox. 'What were you doing in another country?'

'I was taking a leaf out of your book,' he said.

'What on earth are you talking about?' Manning asked, his restraint wearing thin.

'Remember Singapore? Don't pretend Kuznetsov wasn't killed because of you,' Knox said. 'When did Russia turn you, anyway? Was that your big initiation, or were you already a good little mole by then?'

Now it was Manning who couldn't contain his anger. 'My mission to Singapore was a sanctioned

295

operation within British sovereign territory. I have no idea what you've got yourself into, but if you were involved in the death of a KGB agent on foreign soil then you'll have dragged MI5 into an international incident that could have disastrous consequences for the whole country.'

There was more emotion in this single outburst than Knox had ever seen from Manning. He was sure he was close to cracking.

'Christ, man,' Manning continued, 'we've got leaders from eighteen countries in the city. The Russians are begging for a reason to launch an ICBM at us.'

'And you'd probably tell them exactly where to aim the missile, wouldn't you?' Knox fired back immediately.

'This is insanity. Spouting wild accusations, running around with some mad secretary chasing conspiracies—'

'A secretary,' Finney cut in, 'who will be on the next plane back to the States.'

'I'm not a secretary,' Bennett snapped again. 'And will I be on the same plane back as the scientist you've got coming to question Valera?' She saw a flicker in Finney's eyes – she'd hit a nerve. 'There's no other reason for someone from NASA to be flown over here.'

'The whole of NATO is meeting in one place, Khrushchev's boasting he can take out any of our capitals with the push of a button, and you think there's no reason for one of our top scientists to fly in?' Finney asked. 'Maybe you're not as smart as you think you are,' he added.

'That still doesn't explain why you took Valera's photo from the archive,' Bennett said, suddenly on the defensive.

'I don't have to explain myself to you,' Finney said, his voice starting to rise. 'And I won't stand here and be called a traitor.'

Manning pulled one of his long, bony hands out of his pocket and held it up, a sign for everyone to calm down.

'I was happy for you to come back to Leconfield House, Richard,' he said to Knox. His voice was quiet. The only emotion in it now was disappointment. 'After an appropriate length of time. Or for you to leave if you decided you didn't want to stay without Holland. I even gave you something to do to stop yourself festering while you were suspended. But all this is unforgivable. There's no way you can come back in now. And I can't let you walk out of this room alone.'

'You can't stop me,' Knox sneered at him.

'I already have,' Manning replied.

He walked over to the big wooden doors and opened them. Three stony-faced Watchers stepped into the room. 'I told you you had five minutes to explain everything,' Manning continued. 'You chose to spend them damning yourself with insane fantasies.'

Knox suddenly realised he'd let himself be outmanoeuvred again. He should have known he was on borrowed time as soon as he left the ball-room. He had no idea who the Watchers were loyal to – Manning or the Service. For all he knew, they were the men who had attacked Valera, set fire to his apartment, and tried to take out Bennett in the middle of Hyde Park in broad daylight.

For a brief moment he thought about fighting his way out, but his body ached from everything he'd put it through and his energy was completely spent.

'You know,' he said, matching Manning's sombre tone, 'I thought I was paranoid too. Nothing made sense. None of what was happening seemed connected. Until I put you at the heart of all of it.' He started to move around the Barbican model, closing the distance between him and Manning. 'You were so keen to send me off to investigate Bianchi and Moretti, because you already knew exactly what had happened to them. You used them, then you killed them. But what does that have to do with a Russian scientist trying to defect? Nothing, except the amazing coincidence that she was working in exactly the same field as our dead Italians. And, of course, you.'

He glanced over at the Watchers. Now they didn't look like foot soldiers, ready to obey any order Manning might give them. They looked like they had no idea what they'd walked into the middle of.

'You've been the perfect asset,' Knox continued. 'Ready to sacrifice your men and leave them dead and disavowed just to prove how loyal you are.'

Manning's face still hadn't changed, but the Watchers' had. And they weren't looking at Knox like he might be crazy. They were looking at Manning like they weren't completely sure if he was their leader or their enemy.

'Tell me one thing,' he said, launching his final attack. 'Was getting rid of Holland the KGB's idea, or yours?'

Knox hoped Manning's mask would finally slip and he'd give himself away. But he just sighed, gave the Watchers a nod, and walked over to one of the floor-to-ceiling windows that lined the hall, both hands back in his jacket pockets.

With a reassuring look to Bennett, Knox let himself be led out of the room. When the door closed again behind Knox and the Watchers, she turned to Finney and steeled herself for her own battle.

'What are you going to do with me?' she asked. She was ready to lay out everything for anyone who would listen, here, in Grosvenor Square, or even Langley, to prove that she'd spotted what everyone else had missed – that the CIA had been compromised just as badly as MI5.

'Nothing,' Finney replied.

'What?' Bennett had expected a tirade to match Manning's, but there was no fire in Finney's eyes, no sign he was going to snatch at any of the bait she'd dangled in front of him.

'I don't deal with the clerical staff,' he said.

CHAPTER FIFTY-FOUR

Valera sat on the edge of the bed, waiting. She'd spent the last however many hours watching the colour of the sky slowly start to deepen. In Povenets B or Leningrad in July it would be as light as it was outside now until long into the night. Sunset in Stockholm would be late and brief too. But she suspected she wasn't in Sweden any more.

Five minutes ago she'd heard the heavy click of a lock and the deep groan of the large metal door being opened and closed. Then there were footsteps on the stairs and a prolonged sequence of shuffles and sounds from the other end of the house.

Now she heard more footsteps approaching the bedroom. She stood up. She wanted to face whoever had come to visit her on her feet. The steps stopped briefly outside the door, then with a gentle nudge it swung open to reveal a man in a grey suit carrying a tray with a teapot and two teacups.

'Ah, Miss Valera, you're awake,' Peterson said, a broad smile across his face. 'Wonderful.'

'Who are you?' she demanded. Her voice cracked as she spoke, and she realised she hadn't drunk anything since she'd devoured the pot of jam she'd found in the fridge as fast as if it had been ice-cold water, fresh from a mountain stream.

'I'm Devereux,' Peterson replied. 'It's a pleasure to meet you at last. How are you feeling?'

'Where am I?'

'You're safe. Don't worry, you're not back in Russia. You're in London.' Peterson gave the broken chair on the floor a brief, quizzical look, then put the tray down on the end of the bed. As he got closer to Valera, she instinctively backed away from him, ending up on the other side of the chair, pressed against the impenetrable window.

'Would you like some tea?' he asked.

Valera's mouth felt even drier at the mention of tea, but she stayed where she was.

'Who do you work for?' she asked.

'British intelligence,' Peterson replied, as he poured a cup of the hot, fragrant liquid. 'We like to keep tabs on everyone who makes it through the Curtain. We had a feeling the KGB might make a play for you in Stockholm, and when they did we thought it best to step in.' He poured a second cup. 'We weren't fast enough to stop them, but we followed the extraction team that kidnapped you to a warehouse on the outskirts of the city and made our move there. I'm sorry we couldn't get to you sooner, I know how brutal KGB interrogations can be.'

Valera thought back to Skansen. Her memory was still a little hazy and distorted, but she remembered Medev trying to persuade her to go back to Russia.

'The man who was killed. He said he was a KGB general.'

'KGB maybe, but not a general. He was a ploy to soften you up.'

'But they shot him in the head.'

'A mistake. Though you never know, the KGB isn't particularly concerned about collateral damage.'

'What about the others? The man and the woman.'

'You don't need to worry about them either.'

Peterson offered her a cup of tea. She reached out and took it from him, but she didn't drink it.

'I hope you like Earl Grey,' he said, sitting down on the edge of the bed.

He picked up his own cup and took a large gulp. Valera watched him swallow, then, reassured that she wasn't about to be poisoned, tried hers. She winced as the tea hit her tongue. It was hot and bitter, and tasted like it had been stewed for far too long.

Peterson smiled. 'I like it rather strong, I'm afraid. I could get you some sugar, or honey?'

'No,' Valera replied. 'This will be fine, thank you.'

She took another couple of sips, beginning to enjoy the feeling of the liquid soothing her dry throat. Her body relaxed, leaning against the window rather than pressing against it. 'So, Mr Devereux, what do you want from me?'

Peterson smiled again, and put his cup back on the tray. 'The British government wants you to be safe,' he said. 'And we are in a position to help make sure that's exactly what you are.'

'That is very generous of you.'

'Well, it's not an entirely altruistic act. We, of course, expect a quid pro quo.'

'Of course,' Valera replied.

'To be rather blunt, we need to know why the KGB was so eager to get you back. And, I'm afraid we need to know quickly.'

'So you can decide if I'm worth protecting?'

'To be even more blunt, yes.'

'And if I told you I don't know why they were after me? That I'm just a lowly comrade desperate to build a new life in the West?'

'Then I'd ask you not to waste my time.'

Valera took another sip of her tea. 'Am I free to leave here if I want?'

'Of course. You're not a prisoner.'

'Then why was the door locked?'

'For your protection.' Peterson topped up his cup. He raised the pot to Valera, but she shook her head. 'You had an awful lot of drugs pumping through your system. You needed time for them to wear off somewhere you couldn't hurt yourself. Now you're feeling better, you can do whatever you like.' He took a sip of tea. 'But the vultures are circling. It won't take the Russians long to work out where you've ended up. You can take your chances with them, or you can give me the information I need to convince the powers that be that we ought to keep them at bay.'

It was the same negotiation Valera had gone through over and over – her knowledge in exchange for her safety, and the implication that her life would be forfeit if she didn't cooperate. It might be more polite now, coming from a smiling man serving her tea rather than Zukolev looming over her or masked figures in a dark room, but it was still the age-old threat.

Her best, and only, option was to stall. 'I need time to think,' she said.

'Unfortunately neither of us has that luxury,' Peterson replied.

'Then take me to meet your scientists. I will talk to them about my work.'

It was another delaying tactic, but it was also a perfectly reasonable request. The Swedish security service had checked out her academic credentials before they even put her on a plane to Stockholm. She couldn't imagine a member of British intelligence not wanting to do the same thing.

The edge of Peterson's smile started to drop. 'There'll be time for all that, but right now I need to give my superiors something that demonstrates your willingness to work with us.'

Valera stood her ground. 'Tell your superiors I'll work with you once you guarantee my safety.'

Peterson's mouth twisted into a tight grimace. 'You're in no position to dictate terms here.'

'I am free to do what I want,' she said. 'Unless you were lying.'

Peterson slammed his cup back down onto the tray and shot off the bed. His body language changed as he stood upright. A deep line appeared across his forehead, his grimace turned into a scowl, and his shoulders became high and tight.

'I don't have time for this,' he said, glaring at Valera. His voice sounded like it had dropped an entire octave. 'Tell me what I need to know. Now.'

Strangely, his transformation didn't scare Valera. It calmed her. Now that Peterson had given up on his charade, she knew what kind of man she was dealing with – a man exactly like Zukolev.

'Why should I?' she asked.

'Because I've made several promises I need to see through. And if you can't help me then I have no reason to keep you alive.'

'What is it you've decided I know?'

'Don't play stupid with me. I know you're working on ways to control radio signals. That's what the KGB wants, and it's what everyone else in the world wants too. I could force you to give me your research, but I'm on a tight schedule. So you can either give it to me now, or you can die.'

Valera was now sure who her enemy was, that everything this man had said about her rescue from the dark room was a lie, and that he was

305

almost certainly the one who had put her there, yet she suddenly found her appetite for revenge fading. She might just have the strength left in her to hurt the man who called himself Devereux, but it wouldn't change everything the world had done to her. It had taken her parents and stolen her son. There was no way the scales could be balanced, so what was the point in trying? She could devote all her energy, waste her whole life, and only gain a fraction of the vengeance she deserved.

So, instead of fighting this man, she decided she would use him, give him just enough so she could get what she wanted.

'I am not going to give away my secrets,' she said, 'and you are not going to kill me.'

'I'm not?'

'We are going to work together.'

Peterson looked, and sounded, surprised by this sudden attempt to shift the power dynamic between them. 'We are?'

'Yes. We are going to be partners.'

Peterson let out a short laugh. 'Why would I do that?'

'Because I have something more valuable to sell than just a way to manipulate radio signals. You want to give people a way to eavesdrop on each other. I can give them something bigger. Something much bigger.'

'Why should I trust you?' he asked.

Valera walked over to the bed, put her cup down on the tray, then casually sat on the edge of the bed, exactly where Peterson had perched a few minutes earlier.

'You don't have to trust me,' she replied. 'I don't trust you. You just have to see what we both stand to gain. I have the product, you have the buyers. It makes sense for us to help each other get what we want.'

It took Peterson a moment to process the new possibilities Valera was presenting. He'd discovered too late that the research Bianchi and Moretti had given him was fake. He'd always planned to have them killed rather than let them walk away and sell their imitation Pipistrelle technology themselves. He'd never suspected that they'd double-cross him as well and leave him with a set of useless, meaningless equations. But he was, above everything else, a pragmatist, so he'd still been prepared to sell their bogus work to as many interested parties as possible, then disappear without a trace and with a very healthy balance in his bank account.

But he'd rather not have to spend the rest of his life looking over his shoulder. So when Knox told him he'd discovered the Italians' secret research he'd sent a couple of men after him for it. Unfortunately, they'd failed rather pathetically and he'd found himself back where Bianchi and Moretti had left him. Then Irina Valera had appeared, dropped into his lap like a *deus ex machina*, and now she might be giving him the chance to achieve something beyond even his wildest ambitions.

'What do you want?' he asked.

'Freedom,' she replied. 'Enough money to go wherever I want and be left alone.'

Peterson smiled, at her and to himself. He was happy to give her both, or at least the promise of them.

'I think I can help you with that.'

'Good,' Valera said, getting up from the bed. 'I'm hungry.'

'Well then,' Peterson said, picking up the tray and standing next to the open, broken door like a dutiful butler. 'After you.'

CHAPTER FIFTY-FIVE

No heads had turned in the ballroom as Knox was escorted down the grand staircase and out through the RIBA building's front doors to a waiting car that Manning had somehow summoned along with the Watchers.

He was driven straight to Leconfield House and taken directly from the subterranean car park to an interrogation cell on the third floor. Knox didn't know if it was intentional or just a coincidence that he was put in the same room that Sandra Horne had occupied while she'd been held at MI5 headquarters after the Calder Hall Ring was blown.

The cell also reminded Knox of the room in Holloway he'd visited Horne in. The walls were bare, a table and chairs sat in the middle, and a narrow shelf with a thin mattress on it ran the length of the back wall.

The guards left Knox with a large jug of water and a single glass. They didn't take his jacket, belt, or shoelaces. They either thought there was no risk of him killing himself or they didn't care if he did.

For the first hour of his incarceration Knox

indulged in the fantasy that the Watchers who had witnessed his tirade against Manning were repeating his accusations through the corridors of Leconfield House and were going to come and ask him to lead a rebellion against the director general at any moment. For the second hour he alternated between sitting at the table and pacing around the room, thinking about what White might have done with Bianchi and Moretti's passports and research. For the third hour he wondered if he'd been forgotten. Manning hadn't appeared to gloat, or sent Peterson to do it for him. No one had come to break him out, but no one had come to rough him up either.

At about nine thirty he finally lay down on the mattress. He felt dizzy for a moment and realised he couldn't remember the last time he'd eaten anything. He got up, poured himself a large glass of water, swallowed it in a single gulp, and returned to his bed.

He decided that whatever Manning had planned for him would wait until the morning, or maybe even after the conference was finished, and he'd dealt with Valera and whatever else he had planned over the next two days.

However, the longer Knox stared at the ceiling, the less he was able to shake a feeling that had been quietly taking root in his gut since Portland Place. Manning hadn't broken character the entire time Knox had been attacking him. His temper barely flared even when Knox accused him of being a traitor and personally responsible for multiple deaths.

As Knox relived the confrontation over and over in his mind, Manning only ever looked disappointed and hurt, like a gentleman whose honour was being unfairly smeared. Even when Knox was being marched off there was no little sneer or wink telling him he was right but had still lost.

It raised a worrying question. Did Manning's mask not slip because he was the greatest double agent in the history of espionage, or because there was no mask to begin with? Knox realised that he hadn't just thought Manning was the mole, he'd wanted him to be it. He'd wanted to tie all the loose threads of the man's career into a rope he could hang him from. But would anyone else do the same in Knox's place? Manning himself had said Knox had a personal interest in bringing him down. Maybe it was too personal.

Perhaps this was all just the final act in Manning's long rise to power, and Knox was simply a bit player, done with after strutting and fretting his hour on the stage. It was a sobering thought. But Knox wasn't ready to completely write himself out of the narrative just yet. He was still the hero of his own story, and if Manning wasn't his nemesis then someone else had to be.

CHAPTER FIFTY-SIX

At the same time Knox was lying on his back in Leconfield House trying to weave a new thread that would connect all the events of the last week and lead him to the person behind it all, Bennett was sitting in the front seat of a car that wasn't hers desperately trying to stay awake.

After Knox had left 66 Portland Place flanked by Watchers, Manning and Finney had returned to the reception, leaving Bennett alone in the exhibition gallery.

She spent five minutes processing the magnitude of what had just happened, and just how badly wrong things had gone. She decided there was no point returning to Grosvenor Square. In fact, she figured that chances were her security clearance had already been revoked. Instead, she left the RIBA building and walked up Portland Place to Regent's Park tube station. She briefly thought about returning to Brompton Cemetery, to pay one final visit to Pankhurst's grave, but decided against it. She'd come to London to prove she was just as smart and capable as any man in the CIA. Now she would be leaving in disgrace, written off as rash, emotional,

312

a liability – a prime example of why women shouldn't have ideas above their station. She wasn't sure Pankhurst's ghost would forgive her.

The boarding house Bennett called home was on Neville Street, ten minutes' walk from South Kensington tube station. The house, number nine, was three storeys tall, the first covered in white stucco and the second two exposed brick. Unlike the other houses in the street, which were in immaculate condition, the stucco and bricks of number nine were both crumbling. The black and white mosaic steps that led up to the front door were cracked, and the door itself hadn't been painted in a long time. The owner, Bennett learned shortly after moving in, had bought the house a long time ago, lived somewhere in the country, and rarely came into the city.

Bennett's room was on the first floor, facing onto the street, and it was cavernous. Once upon a time it had been a grand reception room. Bennett's single bed, wardrobe, and small table and chairs looked out of place pushed up next to its enormous, ornate fireplace. The room was draughty, but she didn't care. It was bigger than anywhere else she'd ever lived, and it was all hers. She'd found it, she paid for it, and she didn't have to share it.

Bennett's journey back to Neville Street had been full of self-pity. She hated the idea of giving up her life in London and going back to America. She didn't want to face her mother's attempts to hide her disappointment or her useless brothers' inevitable jokes, and she didn't want to end up working some meaningless secretarial job in New York or Chicago if she was lucky, or Garden City if she wasn't.

But when she reached her room, the home she'd made for herself, her pity transformed into anger. And fear. Seeing Medev killed and Valera kidnapped had shocked Bennett, but she'd told herself that she hadn't been a target – she'd just got caught up in the attack along with Knox. Now that Finney had effectively taken her out of the game her mind was starting to catch up with everything that had happened in such quick succession since Stockholm. The man in Hyde Park had been there purely because of her. He'd wanted to hurt her, maybe even kill her. She real- ised she'd been so consumed with proving herself that she'd put herself in real, mortal danger. But as much as that scared her it also persuaded her even more that she was right – something very wrong was happening in MI5, and Finney was up to something too.

There was no one waiting for her but an enve- lope bearing the seal of the American embassy had been slipped under her door. It contained a letter informing her that her cover position had been terminated with immediate effect. She care- fully slid the letter back into the envelope, then tore both of them in half.

She didn't know where her future was, but she now knew it wouldn't be in Neville Street. The embassy knew she lived there, which meant so did the CIA and so would anyone Finney might tell. She didn't want to be sent back to America, but she also didn't want to be kidnapped or killed and left to rot in her room. It was time to go. She started to pack.

She'd just finished sorting through her small pile of dirty clothes, wondering when and where she'd wash them, when she glanced out of the window and saw a man standing on the opposite side of the street looking up at her. He was middle-aged, with a shock of wiry blond hair, and his eyes were firmly fixed on her. They stared at each other for a moment before Bennett stepped back from the window.

She went back to her wardrobe, trying to ignore what had just happened, but she couldn't resist peeking back out into the street to see if the man was still there. He was.

Bennett was about to gesture at him to move on when he raised his hand and gave her a small wave. Not sure how else to respond, she waved back. Then he turned his hand and made a subtle beckoning motion, raising his other one too to show he wasn't hiding anything. Bennett was confused but intrigued.

She quickly searched her room for something she could use to defend herself in case this was a trick and the stranger waiting for her outside had been sent to finish the job the man in Hyde Park had failed to. The only things she could find were a small hardback edition of *Our Man in Havana* and her house keys. She left the book on her bed, bunched her keys in her fist, and headed downstairs.

Outside, the street lamps were starting to turn on. Bennett pulled her front door to and stepped down onto the pavement. But she didn't cross the road.

'Who are you?' she asked.

'I know a friend of yours,' White replied, trying not to shout. 'Richard Knox.'

'How do you know him?'

'We work together at Avalon Logistics.'

Bennett relaxed her fist slightly. Knox had told her about MI5's Avalon Logistics cover, and that she could trust anyone who used it.

White took the opportunity to cross over to her side of the street – he didn't want all the residents of Neville Street to hear what he was about to tell Bennett.

'Are you the famous Malcolm White?' she asked as he stepped between the parked cars in front of her.

'Apparently my reputation precedes me,' he replied. 'I had a rather troubling conversation with Richard this morning. He asked me to look into a few things, and let him know if I found anything odd. As he's somewhat indisposed at present, I thought it best to find you.'

'And you found something odd in Leconfield House?'

'Plenty of odd things have been happening there recently, but one in particular stood out.' He reached into his pocket, pulled out a small piece of paper, and handed it to Bennett. 'Two days ago a dormant MI5 safe house was reactivated. No staff were requisitioned, no operation attached to it, just the power switched back on. I thought you might want to take a look.'

Bennett looked at the address. It was a street somewhere in south London. Suddenly she had the chance to do more than just disappear or wait for whatever fate Finney or one of his lackeys wanted to inflict on her.

'I'll need a car if I'm going on a stake-out,' she said.

White pulled out a set of keys from his pocket. 'The green Anglia at the end of the street. And my home and private office numbers are on the back of the address if you find anything interesting there.'

Bennett took the keys. 'Can I at least give you a lift home?'

'No need,' he replied, starting to walk away. 'It's a lovely evening.'

Bennett watched him turn out of Neville Street, then she rushed back inside number nine and up to her room. She grabbed a jumper and the small packet of crackers she kept on the mantelpiece over the fireplace, then ran back out into the street.

White's Anglia was exactly where he said it would be, and half an hour later she pulled into Methley Street, a quiet row of small but well-kept terraces just north of the Oval cricket ground in Kennington.

317

CHAPTER FIFTY-SEVEN

Valera had spent the night alone. After Peterson had persuaded her to eat the tasteless sandwiches from the fridge, he'd explained that MI5 owned the building she'd woken up trapped in. He confirmed what Valera already suspected: the whole of the upstairs was soundproofed, the windows were reinforced, and the only way in or out was through the bulletproof door at the bottom of the staircase.

After she'd finished eating Peterson had asked her to tell him exactly what she was bringing to her side of their new business partnership. She spent ten minutes explaining the intricacies of spread-spectrum broadcasting, frequency degradation and code-division modulation until she realised he had no idea what she was talking about. So instead of trying to give him a crash course in advanced radio wave physics, she resorted to an analogy.

'If you are in a room full of people talking,' she said, 'how do you make yourself heard?'

'Shout over everyone else,' Peterson replied.

'But what if everyone else starts to shout as well?'

318

'Wait for them to stop.'

'Good. You've just described broadcasting at different pitches or sequences. There is also a third option.'

Peterson thought for a moment, then said, 'Different languages.'

Valera smiled. 'Excellent. Pitch, sequence, and frequency. If I was speaking Russian in a room full of people speaking English, another Russian person would be able to make out my voice and know what I was saying.'

'And no one else could.'

'Unless they also understood Russian, or were paying my Russian friend to tell them what they heard,' she replied. 'Now, imagine if this room we were in was very large, large enough to contain everyone in the world. Another Russian speaker nearby might hear me, but not one thousands of kilometres away or on the other side of the planet. What can I do to make sure that person can hear me?'

This time Peterson couldn't think of an answer.

'I build another room,' Valera said. 'One that only I have access to, but that has doors that open up all around the world.'

Peterson started to understand what Valera was describing. A secure, global communications network. Something like that really could change the world. Every spy agency on the planet would want to get their hands on it, and every major corporation as well. He could sell it to all of them, and finally escape his life spent serving two masters.

Like every branch of the civil service, MI5 offered its mid-ranking members job security and a reasonable salary. There was also excitement, power, and some discretionary riches to be had if you became a field agent or eventually rose to the very top of the Service. Peterson had wanted all three, but it had been made clear to him early on in his career that they weren't in his cards. He'd become tethered to Manning almost as soon as he'd joined MI5, and it was his lot to help Manning rise through the ranks, clinging to his coat-tails as he did.

Peterson might have let his resentment at the unsatisfying destiny he'd been handed lead him away from the Service, if a member of the MGB hadn't approached him in Brighton one day ten years ago.

Peterson had decided to spend a rare weekend off outside London, and had taken the train down to the south coast. He was sitting in a deckchair on the bluff of the pebble beach near the Palace Pier, struggling to eat an ice cream before the sun melted it or the wind off the Channel splattered it across his front, when a man pulled a chair over to his, sat down, and introduced himself.

It was a bold, blunt approach, but it worked. The MGB had guessed that Peterson would respond to being flattered and having his ego stroked, and they were right. They offered him the excitement, power, and money he wanted in exchange for becoming their asset inside MI5. And he leaped at the chance.

For almost as long as he'd served as Manning's sycophantic minion he'd also provided his Russian handlers with any information they'd requested from him. He'd even taken on the occasional mission for them, making or collecting the odd dead drop in and around London.

However, when he'd made the point that as he was becoming privy to more valuable information as Manning continued his unending ascent – and his risk of being caught was increasing – he should be paid more for what he was passing to Moscow, he was rebuffed. He pressed the point until he was told in very clear terms that it wasn't only MI5 that he needed to worry about exposing him. He stopped asking for more money. But he also began putting plans in place that would let him escape both Russian and British intelligence.

As soon as he found out about Operation Pipistrelle, he knew he'd found his way out. He'd tried for years to get his hands on one of the bugs, but White guarded them zealously. So he'd kept his ears and eyes open in case something similar came along, which was how he ended up meeting Bianchi and Moretti.

He knew he could sell the Italians' eavesdropping technology, and the OECD conference had given him the perfect market of paranoid governments and businesses. But now, with what Valera was offering, he could end up even richer than he'd hoped and, depending on what deals were done over the next couple of days, immeasurably powerful as well.

He'd briefly considered selling Valera's discovery – and Valera – back to the Russians. But he decided he didn't owe them such preferential treatment. Yes, his handler had asked him to look out for information about a defector passing through Finland, but it was he who found out who Valera really was, arranged for her to be extracted from Stockholm, and finally got her to confess just how valuable she could be.

Valera and Peterson had spent another hour going over her enhanced spread-spectrum code-division technology. By the time they were done Peterson had grasped enough of the basic principles to convincingly parrot them back to Valera.

As he left, he told her that someone would come by shortly with more provisions for her for the evening and a change of clothes for the morning. Half an hour later a man had delivered a fresh selection of bland sandwiches and a suit carrier, and she was now sitting in the living room, in a white shirt and plain black skirt and jacket, waiting for Peterson to return.

CHAPTER FIFTY-EIGHT

Bennett reached over to the passenger side of the car, opened the glovebox, rattled the tin of travel sweets inside, and shut the compartment again. She went through this little routine whenever one of the residents of Methley Street walked past the Anglia as they began their morning commute, because it made her look less conspicuous than if she was just sitting behind the wheel not going anywhere.

She'd managed to stay awake most of the night, only dropping off for a few minutes around three a.m. and again at five. After finishing her crackers an hour into her stake-out, she'd staved off hunger thanks to the travel sweets, which she'd found shortly after midnight and had dipped into every couple of hours. Despite her brief lapses, she was sure she hadn't missed anyone coming or going from the address White had given her.

Just as Bennett was starting to wonder if it might be time to try some more direct surveillance, like pulling a couple of wires out of the Anglia's engine and knocking on the safe house's front door for help, a large black Jaguar sedan shot down the street. She assumed it was someone running late for work, until it pulled to a sudden stop outside the safe house.

A man in a grey suit got out of the rear door nearest the pavement and Bennett instinctively sank down into the well of her seat as he walked up the steps, unlocked the front door, and stepped inside.

A minute later he re-emerged with Valera by his side in a dark suit. Bennett sank even lower as Valera paused at the top of the steps and scanned the street. She couldn't read the expression on her face – she didn't look exactly happy about following the man down into the waiting car, but she didn't look scared either.

Bennett let the sedan pull away, counted to ten, put the Anglia in gear, and started to follow them.

The Jaguar turned out of Methley Street and headed north. The driver had no idea who either of his passengers were. He'd been hired, along with the car, anonymously by Peterson and paid in cash. Peterson was always careful with the people who did his dirty work for him. He paid well, but never told them more than was absolutely necessary. And he never used the same person twice. The only time he'd broken this rule was when he'd sent the man who'd been guarding the Italians' flat to Stockholm because he hadn't had time to find anyone else to complete the strike team. But he'd ended up getting himself killed, so couldn't betray Peterson even if he'd wanted to.

Valera sat across from Peterson in the back of the sedan. She tried her best to look relaxed, but her body was rigid and her suit itched.

Peterson had an open briefcase perched on his knees. He held a manila folder in one hand while the other kept a vice-like grip on the handle of the case.

'We'll be at the Richmond in twenty minutes,' he said, without looking up from the documents he was studying. 'We'll get you settled in my suite for an hour, then we have two meetings this morning. After that, the car will take you back to the hotel, where you'll have lunch in the suite. I have another engagement I have to attend, but I'll be back around three in time for our afternoon appointments.'

Valera had already memorised their schedule, and knew what was expected of her. She was to dazzle Peterson's contacts with her genius, while he worked on extracting the best deal from them. She didn't know who she would be meeting, and Peterson had made it clear that she wouldn't find out until she was in the room with them. He may have been doing his best to exude an air of confidence, down to organising the ostentatious car and moving Valera to an expensive hotel, but his paranoia still showed through. Valera tried to sneak a look at the contents of his folder, but all she could see was the handle of a pistol resting under it in the briefcase.

'Then what?' she asked.

'Then,' he replied, closing the briefcase, 'it's back to the Richmond for dinner and an early night, and we do it all again in the morning.'

The Jaguar started to cross Westminster Bridge. Twenty seconds later, the Anglia did the same. Bennett followed Peterson and Valera over the bridge, past Big Ben and Parliament Square, and along the sides of St James's Park and Buckingham Palace, before turning east along Piccadilly and into Mayfair.

The little convoy travelled up Clarges Street, then Curzon Street, just a few hundred yards away from Leconfield House. It looped around Berkeley Square, then continued on along Conduit Street. After the junction with New Bond Street, the Jaguar slowed to a stop in the middle of the road, indicating right.

Bennett pulled in to the kerb fifty yards behind them on the other side of the junction, and watched as the car turned into the set-back entrance of a six-storey hotel. She got out of the Anglia and ran over the junction just in time to see Peterson and Valera walk inside, then she sprinted back to Berkeley Square, stepped into one of the bright red phone boxes that stood in a row at its northern end, and dialled White's office number.

CHAPTER FIFTY-NINE

The owners of the Richmond had started to worry that they'd made a terrible mistake. They'd bet that the super-wealthy were growing tired of the faded glories of hotels that had last been decorated at the height of the belle époque, and that there was money to be made by being the first to embrace a more modern aesthetic. So they'd spent a sizeable fortune stripping back and renovating the hotel, then filling it with one-of-a-kind pieces by designers like Arne Jacobsen and Eero Saarinen that blended forms and materials in radical, outlandish ways. Unfortunately it hadn't worked.

The hotel had featured in a couple of travel articles in the UK and America, and had even been used for a photoshoot for *Vogue*, but so far the rich had not flocked to the Richmond. There had been a steady stream of tourists coming to enjoy the novelty of the place, but there hadn't been a booking for any of its suites on the upper floors in over a month. The owners had wanted to get ahead of the times, but it seemed they'd gone a little too far a little too fast.

They were particularly concerned that they had no reservations for the OECD conference. Every other luxury hotel in Mayfair was fighting off booking requests, but the Richmond stood almost empty. The owners had no idea that Peterson had orchestrated this exact situation by removing the Richmond from the list of approved hotels MI5 had supplied to the conference's attendees. So they were extremely relieved when they finally received a booking for one of their most expensive suites for the entire week of the conference from a Mr Devereux.

They had no idea who Mr Devereux was or who he worked for, but they didn't care – he had money, and that was enough to make him important. Desperate to make a good impression, the front-of-house staff were told to cater to his every whim and accommodate all his peculiarities, such as checking in late on Sunday night, insisting no staff go up to the sixth floor or enter his suite without direct instruction from him, and bringing an unknown woman who he referred to unconvincingly as his niece into the hotel at nine o'clock on a Monday morning.

Peterson had chosen the Richmond out of convenience. It was close to both Leconfield House and Westminster Central Hall, where the majority of the OECD conference's official events would be held. The Central Hall had been picked to add a bit of weight and theatricality to the conference's proceedings. It had been the site of the first meeting of the inaugural General Assembly of the

United Nations in 1946, and the OECD hoped to borrow some of its historical significance.

The Richmond was also near all the other hotels – the Dorchester, Claridge's, Brown's and the like – that had been booked out by visiting dignitaries. And by keeping it off MI5's list Peterson could be sure he wouldn't bump into anyone he didn't plan on meeting, or worry about anyone listening in to his conversations. He'd even taken the precaution of having all Pipistrelle intelligence routed through GCHQ, so if any of his prospective buyers let slip about their meetings with him in their hotel rooms it would be too late by the time it got back to MI5.

And, just to be completely certain of his privacy, a month ago he'd taken a short-term lease on an empty office at the top of a building just off Dover Street, five minutes away. It was neutral, anonymous ground, and, importantly, it was untraceable – the company Peterson had used on the lease didn't exist.

Peterson and Valera walked across the hotel's sparse foyer, past the reception desk, which was a single, amorphous piece of dazzling white Lucite that seemed to grow out of the equally white floor, to its small bank of lifts.

They rode up to the sixth floor in silence, then Peterson led Valera to their suite at the end of a corridor that was lacquered black and lit only by small spotlights above each room's door.

The suite, in contrast to the hotel's monochrome

entrance and hallways, was a riotous rainbow of colour. The main space was dominated by two bright yellow leather sofas, facing each other across a low, angular onyx coffee table. Beyond them was a large, circular pedestal dining table made of the same white Lucite as the reception desk, surrounded by six intensely red moulded plastic chairs beneath an equally lurid orange pendant lamp hung above the table. Every wall was decorated differently – some in block colours, some in intricate, psychedelic wallpaper.

It was a sensory overload and Valera struggled to process it all. Peterson, already used to it after spending a night in the suite, walked over to the small oak desk next to the dining table, sat in its green leather tulip chair, opened his briefcase, and started reviewing the contents of his folder again.

Valera stood in front of the two sofas, turned a slow circle, and counted the doors in the suite. There were three: the one that led back out to the corridor, one for Peterson's room, and, she hoped, one for hers.

'Where can I freshen up?' she asked.

Peterson gestured behind him without looking up. 'The room on the left is yours,' he said. Then he checked his watch. 'We need to leave in fifty minutes.'

'I'll try to be done by then,' Valera replied, doing nothing to hide the sarcasm in her voice.

Peterson grunted in response, no longer paying attention to her.

CHAPTER SIXTY

Knox heard footsteps walking towards his cell. He had no idea how many hours he'd been languishing in the belly of Leconfield House but his stomach told him it was morning and he'd been there through the night. He hoped that whoever was coming to see him, and whatever they had planned to do to him, they were bringing him breakfast.

He swung his legs off the mattress and stood up as the door opened and White stepped into the room.

Before he could say anything, Knox said, 'It's Peterson, isn't it?'

White closed the door behind him and nodded.

Knox had spent the night going back over every event of the last week, every piece of evidence, and every supposition. He was still convinced there was a Russian mole, but it wasn't Manning. He'd made a list of everyone in MI5 who might have both reason to betray the Service and the access to information valuable enough to be worth something to the Russians. He went through the list again and again, and every time he came to the same conclusion. The mole had to be Peterson.

It wasn't just the most logical possibility. It was also, embarrassingly, the most simple one. Peterson had been the one who had overseen Knox's suspension, then orchestrated bringing him back in, both apparently under Manning's orders. He was the only person in MI5 apart from White who knew that Knox had found Bianchi and Moretti's secret papers. And, as Manning's right-hand man, he'd see any information shared by the CIA, which would have led him to Valera.

He'd played the part of the harried deputy perfectly, all the while using Knox's hatred of Manning to blind him to what was really going on.

'I went snooping, as you suggested,' White said. 'And discovered that Peterson had quietly activated a safe house in Kennington. He'd tried to hide the order, but not very well. There was no way I could come and talk to you last night after the stunt you pulled at RIBA, so I went to see your American friend. She's been keeping watch overnight.'

'What happened?' Knox asked.

'Five minutes ago she called me from a phone box in Berkeley Square to tell me that a man fitting Peterson's description arrived at the safe house this morning and left again with Miss Valera. They're now at the Richmond Hotel on Conduit Street.'

So Knox was right. Peterson had kidnapped

Valera under orders from the KGB, and he was going to use the conference as cover for getting her out of the country.

'He killed Bianchi and Moretti, and now he's going to hand her over to the Russians,' Knox replied. 'I need to stop him.'

'Yes, you do,' White replied.

'And you've come to break me out of jail?'

'Almost,' White said. 'Punch me.'

'Excuse me?'

'You can't send anyone else to help Bennett, and I can hardly despatch my engineers as cavalry. It has to be you. But you also can't just walk out of here.' He squared up to Knox. 'So punch me, make your daring escape, and I'll make sure you get a head start.'

'Are you sure?' he asked. There had been plenty of times Knox had wanted to give him a right hook, but this wasn't one of them.

'I wouldn't have said it if I wasn't. You're wasting time.'

'Fine,' Knox said. Then he shifted his weight, pulled his arm back, and slammed his fist into the side of White's face. White took a couple of stumbling steps backwards before stopping and righting himself. He felt a bubble of blood on the edge of his lower lip.

'That should do it,' he said.

'Sorry,' Knox replied, moving towards the door. 'And thank you.'

'One more thing,' White said, leaning one hand

on the table and caressing his jawbone with the other. 'I reviewed the calculations you gave me. They're crude and unsophisticated, but with a little refinement they'd work. If Peterson has them too, then Pipistrelle is blown.'

It took Knox less than ten minutes to get out of Leconfield House and run across Mayfair. The whole way he thought about what else Peterson might be handing over to the Russians along with Valera. He didn't have the papers Knox had discovered, but Knox had no idea what Peterson might have extracted from the Italians before killing them. Or what he might have taken from MI5. If he'd somehow managed to pass on information about Atlas, it would be an even bigger disaster than London being covered in undetectable listening devices, stealing all the West's secrets. With a supercomputer, Russian intelligence capabilities would take a massive, and terrifying, leap forward. No one and nowhere would be safe.

Knox slowed to a walk in Conduit Street, ignoring the burning of his scar and the dull ache that still covered his side. He found Bennett sitting in White's Anglia, staring so intently at the turn-in to the Richmond that he had to bang on the passenger-side window to get her attention.

'How was your night?' she asked, unlocking the door to let him in.

'Uncomfortable,' Knox replied.

'Ditto.'

334

Knox told Bennett that the man she'd seen with Valera was Nicholas Peterson, Manning's deputy.

'So Manning is still behind all this?'

'I don't think so,' Knox said. 'I think he's a patsy. Peterson is the mole and he used Manning to deflect attention as he burrowed deeper into MI5.'

She filled him in on the details of the morning that White hadn't had time to pass on, and told him that she hadn't seen Peterson or Valera leave the hotel, or the black Jaguar come back.

'Unless they slipped out when I was on the phone to White, they're still in there.'

'So we just need to walk in and ask which room the MI5 traitor and kidnapped Russian defector are staying in,' Knox said

'We only need to get past the front desk,' she replied. 'And I've got a plan for that.' She pointed at a small newspaper kiosk down New Bond Street that had a rack of London maps hanging off its awning. 'We're just a couple of tourists coming back from our morning stroll.'

'That might work for you, but it wouldn't explain this,' Knox replied, gesturing at the bruise across his face that was still an intense, deep purple. 'I've also got an idea, though.'

CHAPTER SIXTY-ONE

They got out of the car and crossed the junction to the Richmond, pausing just before the turn-in.

'Give me a minute, then follow me in,' Knox said.

Then he ran round the corner, through the hotel's front doors, and straight up to the reception desk.

'Sorry, excuse me. Hello,' he said to the young man at the desk between panting breaths. 'Oh God,' he continued, his eyes darting across the foyer and back to the receptionist again. 'He's going to kill me.'

'Can I help, sir?' the receptionist asked, covering his confusion with professional courtesy.

'My boss, is he already here?' Knox spun round, facing away from the desk. 'A man, about ten years older than me, grey suit?' He turned back to the receptionist. 'I can't believe I didn't get here first. This is it. I'm done.'

'I'm sorry,' the receptionist replied, 'but I can't give out any information about our guests. Or possible guests.'

'Just tell me,' Knox said, a pleading edge in his voice, 'did he look angry?'

The receptionist looked at Knox's desperate eyes, and the bruise across his cheek, and very slightly shook his head.

'Oh, thank God,' Knox said. 'Maybe I can still fix this.' He started to move away from the desk to the bank of lifts. 'Fifth floor, right?' he called back to the receptionist.

'Sixth,' he replied, instinctively.

'Of course,' Knox said, pantomiming smacking the side of his head and wincing at the pain it caused in his cheek.

As the lift doors closed behind Knox, a woman walked through the hotel doors, drawing the receptionist's gaze away from the lifts. Halfway across the foyer she turned towards the receptionist, raised up a folded A-to-Z of the city, and said, 'Lovely morning out there,' in a broad American accent.

'Yes, madam,' he replied, immediately forgetting her as he went back to reviewing the morning's depressingly short list of departures and arrivals.

Bennett reached the bank of lifts in time to see the display above the one Knox had taken stop at the sixth floor. She called the next lift, rode it up to the fourth floor, then took the stairs the rest of the way.

By the time she reached the sixth floor Knox had already made it most of the way down the corridor, moving silently from door to door listening for any movement inside.

There was only one room left, at the very end of the corridor.

Bennett tiptoed over to Knox and they both pressed their ears against the last door. At first they heard nothing, then what sounded like another door somewhere inside the room being opened.

Knox stepped away from the door, and then opened another across from it, revealing a cleaning trolley. He moved it under the spotlight next to Bennett, pressed his back against the wall, and gestured for Bennett to do the same.

'Be ready as soon as the handle moves,' Knox whispered. Then he knocked on the door.

Inside the suite, Valera, who had just come back out from her room, instinctively walked towards the sound of knocking.

'Just a minute,' Peterson said, getting up from the desk. 'I'll take care of this.'

Valera was fully aware that it wasn't gallantry or manners that prompted Peterson to move past her. It was fear of his new business partner making a run for it, and irritation at being disturbed against his strict instructions.

He looked through the fisheye lens and saw the trolley. He considered ignoring it, but instead turned the handle, ready to give the chambermaid who had disturbed him a piece of his mind. But before he could open his mouth the door was flung open and he was shoved backwards by Knox and Bennett forcing their way inside.

At the sudden appearance of the two people she'd last seen in Stockholm Valera dashed back inside her bedroom. Peterson stumbled over his feet away from Knox and Bennett and, as Valera locked her door behind her, finally lost his balance and toppled over, skidding across the onyx coffee table and falling off the far side of it.

'What the hell are you doing here?' he demanded as he pulled himself back up using the arm of the sofa nearest the desk.

'Surprised to see me?' Knox said. 'You need to hire some better muscle, Nicholas.'

'I don't have time to indulge you this morning, Richard,' Peterson said, falling seamlessly into the role of harassed underling and covering his shock that Knox wasn't slowly asphyxiating in his flat, as he edged towards the desk and his open briefcase. 'I've got too much to do for Manning.'

'For Russia, you mean,' Knox countered, moving closer to Peterson between the sofa and coffee table.

'You really are an idiot,' Peterson said. He reached into the briefcase, pulled out the pistol – a Beretta 70 – and levelled it at Knox. 'A complete, bloody idiot.'

The balance of power had suddenly shifted, but Knox didn't flinch. Even with the gun it was still two against one.

'Stand down. It's over,' he said.

Peterson just laughed at him, letting all his pretences finally drop away.

'Let Valera go,' Bennett said, stepping away from Knox, splitting Peterson's target.

'She's here entirely of her own accord,' Peterson replied.

'I don't believe you.'

'I don't care,' he replied. Then he shot her.

CHAPTER SIXTY-TWO

The gunshot was so loud it made Valera dive for cover. She thought the bullet must have smashed through the door to her bedroom, but it hadn't. The door was still in one piece, still locked, keeping her safe but also stuck.

Valera had already checked the room for possible escape routes. Now she checked again. The bedroom window opened, but only a crack and out into thin air. There was another window in the en-suite bathroom. It might have led to a ledge but it was far too small for her to fit through.

There was nowhere for her to go. All she could do was stay where she was, listen to the crashes and shouts coming from the other side of the door, and hope they stayed there.

Out in the suite, Bennett crumpled to the floor. Her hands reached for the red blossom of blood already spreading across her torso. She knew what it felt like to fire a gun, and she'd read about what it was like to take a bullet, but her books hadn't prepared her for the sudden flood of adrenaline that made her feel boiling hot and freezing cold all at once.

She tried to control her breathing and stop herself from hyperventilating. She pressed her hand against her side. The front and back of her shirt were both wet with blood, and she could feel the tears where the bullet had ripped through the fabric on its way in and out of her body. She knew she needed to put pressure on the wounds if she was going to stop herself bleeding out, so she clumsily shuffled backwards until she could rest against the wall and prop herself up against it, adding an extra smear of deep red to its vibrant print.

Peterson stared at the Beretta, frozen in surprise that he'd actually pulled the trigger. He'd fantasised about firing a gun but he'd never actually done it, not even at the MI5 practice range.

Knox, faced with either helping Bennett or stopping Peterson doing any more damage, took advantage of Peterson's paralysis and lunged at him over the side of the sofa. They both hit the hard edge of the dining table as Knox tried to wrestle the gun out of Peterson's hand. But Peterson's grip was surprisingly strong and Knox had to settle for slamming his wrist against the table until the gun tumbled out of his grasp and disappeared under the sofa next to Bennett. Unfortunately she was in no position to reach out and grab it.

Peterson shoved Knox off him, almost sending him tumbling back over the side of the sofa, then moved around the dining table, putting it between them.

'So you finally worked out what's going on,' he said, his voice pure condescension.

'You killed Bianchi and Moretti,' Knox said. 'Sold out Pipistrelle to the Russians, and now you're delivering Valera to them.'

'Oh dear,' Peterson replied. 'Only one out of three. What on earth did Holland see in you all these years? It can't have been your powers of deduction.'

Knox faked a leap round the right-hand side of the table, forcing Peterson back towards the desk and away from the sofa the gun was under.

'Why did you do it?' Knox demanded. 'Wasn't being Manning's lapdog enough?'

'That's rich, coming from Holland's favourite pet,' Peterson replied.

'I'm no one's pet,' he shot back.

'Holland handed you everything you've ever wanted on a plate. You're the golden child who doesn't have to follow the rules.' Peterson took another step round towards the desk, mirroring every step Knox made towards him. 'I'm just taking the advantages I wasn't given.'

'You're a traitor,' Knox said.

'And you're a hypocrite,' Peterson spat at him. 'You play the part of the poor child from the East End but you live in a penthouse on top of a block of council flats, just to remind everyone how much better than them you are.'

Knox couldn't control himself any more. He

hurled himself at Peterson. But Peterson was ready for him. He sidestepped out of the way and let Knox crash straight into the desk.

'A predictable hypocrite.'

Knox, doubled over on the desk, took a second to compose and quickly berate himself for underestimating Peterson. He guessed Peterson expected him to come back up swinging. So instead he let out a groan, slumped down to his side, and used the tulip chair to steady himself. Then, when he did stand back up, he brought Peterson's briefcase with him, throwing it at his head.

Peterson jerked out of its way, catching his foot on the corner of the coffee table and falling onto it again, this time smashing through the onyx and crashing onto the floor.

'At least I'm not betraying my country so the KGB can spy on the whole world,' Knox said, as he stepped over Peterson and started raining punches down on him.

Instead of trying to protect himself Peterson started to laugh again. 'A predictable, small-minded hypocrite,' he said between blows.

Knox was so confused by Peterson's reaction to the battering he was taking that he didn't notice his hands reaching out under him, searching across the smashed shards of onyx.

'Are you here to defend Dear Old Blighty?' Peterson asked. 'Britannia's long dead. This is just a sad little island trapped in a fantasy of self-importance.'

'Is that the line Moscow sold you?'

Peterson's laughter finally ran out. 'Oh Richard, this isn't about anything as trivial as ideology,' he said. His voice was quiet, mournful, like he was explaining to a child that their dog had run away and wasn't coming back. Then he suddenly sat up, and slashed at Knox's leg with a razor-sharp onyx shard. 'This is business.'

The pain knocked Knox off balance and he fell onto a sofa. As he did, Peterson sprang to his feet and plunged the shard into his thigh.

'The future isn't anything as small as politics or patriotism,' Peterson said. 'It's about private enterprise. Finding something to sell and selling it to the highest bidder.'

'And damn everyone else to a life of fear and oppression,' Knox said through gritted teeth.

'Maybe. Maybe they'll fall into line like scared sheep. Or maybe they'll finally realise all the promises of rewards for good behaviour are just lies to keep them in their place.'

It all finally, crashingly, hit Knox. He hadn't been hunting the long machinations of a regime but the petty opportunism of someone caught up in them.

'You're a real hero of the revolution,' Knox said, mustering some sarcasm.

'I don't really care what happens,' Peterson said, leaning over Knox and driving the onyx shard deeper into his leg. 'The only thing I need everyone to do, including you, is stay out of my way.'

'Sorry about that,' Knox said, between groans.

'I tried to warn you, but you wouldn't take the hint. I thought you might when I burned down your flat, but you really are quite stupid.'

'Was Holland in your way too?'

'Well, I don't have anything against him personally, but I couldn't have him sniffing round, asking questions. And he wasn't the only one who knew about your dirty little parental secret.'

Peterson stepped out of the remnants of the table and towards the sofa on top of the Beretta, keeping his eyes firmly fixed on Knox.

'My Russian friends were happy to help me arrange his unfortunate medical problem.' Peterson kneeled down and reached under the sofa, this time wrapping his fist around the barrel of the Beretta. 'They'll be less than thrilled when they realise it's only got them a halfwit as a new DG, but they tend to take a long view at the Lubyanka, so it won't be a total disappointment.'

Knox couldn't move. The pain in his leg was too intense. But he needed to stall Peterson, keep him talking. 'Aren't you worried about them coming after you?' Knox asked.

'They can try. But by tomorrow I'll be untouchable.' Peterson stood up, levelling the gun at Knox. 'Now, I'm afraid I've got a schedule to keep.'

In the split second it took Peterson to steady himself before shooting, Knox pulled the shard from his thigh and lunged at Peterson, driving the onyx into his stomach as he shoved the gun away from him with his other hand. Peterson's finger

346

pulled the trigger, sending a bullet into the carpet as he doubled over. Then Knox pulled the make-shift dagger out of Peterson's side and plunged it into his neck.

Peterson tried to say something as he fell to the floor, but whatever it was just came out as a bloody gurgle. He landed first on his knees, then on his side. By the time his head hit the suite's deep-pile carpet he was dead.

Knox stumbled over to Bennett. She didn't look good. Her shoulders had dropped, her hands had fallen into her lap, and her eyes were half closed. Her breathing was shallow. He pressed his hands against the large red stains on her side. The fresh pressure brought her round, and she stared at him. A thin smile curled her mouth.

'Looks like we got there in the end,' she said in a whisper.

'Who said anything about the end?' Knox replied, matching her smile.

He heard the click of a lock. The door to Valera's bedroom opened and she cautiously stepped out. She looked down at Knox and Bennett, then walked slowly over to where Peterson's body lay.

'Is he dead?' she asked.

'Yes,' Knox replied. 'You're safe now.'

Valera looked at the folder that was still on the desk, then at Peterson again.

'Who are you?'

'MI5.'

Knox could tell Valera's mind was racing to understand what was happening.

'So was he,' she said, after a pause. She nudged the Beretta out of Peterson's mortis grip with her foot. 'What will happen now?' she asked.

'I don't know,' Knox said, turning back to Bennett to check that she hadn't passed out again. 'But there's plenty of time to work that out.'

'No,' Valera said, her voice suddenly very hard, 'there isn't.'

Knox twisted round just in time to see her lean down, pick up the Beretta, and shoot him in the chest.

As Knox slumped down next to Bennett, a fresh blood bloom staining his front, Valera dropped the gun next to Peterson, picked up the folder, and walked out of the suite.

CHAPTER SIXTY-THREE

Knox knew where he was before he opened his eyes. He recognised the quiet hum punctured by distant footsteps and beeps, the smell of bleach masking other odours, and the rough cotton sheet tucked tightly under his arms. He forced his eyelids apart. It felt like a long time since they'd closed as he slid down the wall of Peterson's hotel suite, blood seeping from his chest and thigh.

It took a moment for him to focus, taking in first the general, fuzzy details of the private hospital room he was in and then, more clearly, the two people sitting in wheelchairs at the end of his bed.

'Hello, sir,' Knox said to Holland.

'Ah, the sleeper awakes,' Holland replied.

'It's about time,' Bennett added.

'I told you it wasn't the end,' Knox said, trying, and failing, to shift his weight. He didn't know how long he'd been in this bed, propped up on pillows and pinned in place, but he guessed it had been a while.

'That was before you got yourself shot,' Bennett replied.

'True. How long have I been out?'

'Two days,' Holland answered. 'You spent most of Monday in surgery. The doctors decided to keep you sedated for twenty-four hours to make sure you didn't undo any of their hard work straight away. They thought you might come round yesterday, but they had to make do with me instead.'

'Sounds like a reasonable trade. What did I miss?' Knox asked.

'Rather a lot, as it happens.'

Holland recounted the events of the last two days, starting with the chaos that MI5 had been quietly plunged into when the police informed them what and who a team of paramedics had been called to the Richmond for on Monday morning.

Peterson was pronounced dead at the scene, but Knox and Bennett, who were still clinging onto life, were rushed to Guy's for emergency surgery. Bennett was out of the operating theatre relatively quickly once her surgeon established that the bullet that had pierced her side had missed her vital organs. She was stitched up, given a blood transfusion, and sent to recovery.

Knox, however, took considerably longer to stabilise. The bullet Valera had shot into his chest had ricocheted off one of his ribs and come to a stop with its tip lodged in the wall of his left ventricle. It took his surgeon several hours to safely remove the bullet, repair the lining of his heart, assess the damage to his rib, and then take a look at his thigh. Luckily, the rib was cracked but not shattered, and the onyx shard had created a clean wound in his leg without slicing any important tendons. After enough rest and some light physiotherapy, the surgeons predicted Knox should make a full recovery.

Knox looked at his wrists, realising there were no handcuffs or straps on them. 'How are the police treating Peterson's death?' he asked.

'As an internal MI5 matter,' Holland replied. 'Thanks, in large part, to Miss Bennett.'

'I wasn't totally out of it,' Bennett said. 'I heard everything Peterson confessed, and told everyone I could as soon as I came round.' She smiled at both men. 'By Tuesday morning people were lining up to listen to me.'

'Including myself,' Holland said. 'Whatever drug I'd been slipped finally wore off and I woke up at four in the morning on Tuesday, with no idea where I was or what was going on.'

'That sounds like one hell of a sedative,' Knox said.

'We know the KGB have been inducing comas and staging fake deaths for years, but we haven't heard of any cases of it lasting over a week. I may have set a record.'

'I'll bet White will want to run some tests on you.'

'He's already tried,' Holland replied, a touch of irritation creeping into his voice. 'But I have no desire to continue being someone's guinea pig.'

Thinking about White reminded Knox of the other fear that had been driving him on. 'Is Pipistrelle secure?' he asked.

Holland nodded. 'Now the conference delegates are leaving, the retrieval teams are clearing out our bugs. So far none of them have found anything to suggest the Russians – or anyone else – were listening in too. They've also disavowed Peterson.'

'Hardly a surprise. What about Manning?'

'He's going to quietly stand down in a week or so, once I've been given the all-clear. He'll probably be pensioned off with an OBE.'

It had been very quickly agreed to keep Holland's miraculous recovery and Manning's departure quiet until after the conference had ended to avoid any awkward questions. The last thing MI5 needed was to make public not only that it had been penetrated by the KGB, but also that their mole had ended up with unfettered access to all the Service's intelligence and the complete trust of its freshly installed director general.

'So you're still DG?' Knox asked.

'Can you think of a reason I shouldn't be?' Holland replied.

'No, sir,' Knox replied, relieved that their shared secret was still safe. 'What about me?'

'You have Peterson's mess to clear up once you're discharged.'

Another wave of relief washed over Knox. In a few days he'd be back in Leconfield House, working with Holland again. Investigating Peterson's crimes after his punishment had been dispensed wasn't the usual way justice was served, but he could live with it.

'I could use some help,' Knox said to Bennett. 'If you're available.'

'My fate is still being decided,' she replied.

'I've already told Finney she has a job waiting for her at Leconfield House if he doesn't give her one.'

'He should,' Knox said. 'She was right about everything.'

'You'll make me blush if you talk like that,' Bennett said. 'And I was wrong about plenty.'

'Miss Bennett has more than proven her worth,' Holland said. 'No one else even had any idea who Irina Valera was. People should have paid attention to what she was saying a lot sooner.'

'Speaking of Valera . . .' Knox said.

'She was on a plane to DC by lunch on Monday,' Bennett said. 'That I was right about,' she added, smirking.

'Shame.' Knox's voice took on a sharp tone. 'I'd have liked to have continued our conversation.'

'Don't be too hard on her,' Bennett said.

'She shot me in the heart,' Knox replied.

'She was the one who told the receptionist at the Richmond to call the emergency services,' Bennett replied, smiling again. 'Technically, she saved your life.'

JULY 1962

JULY 1962

CHAPTER SIXTY-FOUR

Mission control was buzzing with nervous energy. Dixon watched scientists and engineers rush between huge banks of whirring computers and the blinking control panels and screens they fed a constant stream of information to. Everyone around him was busy with some crucial job, but he knew he was basically just there to pad out the room.

It was almost a year to the day since he'd found himself sitting in a room in central London, straight off a red-eye from Washington, with little idea about why he'd just spent the night crossing the Atlantic.

Murphy had refused to tell him who he was supposed to be meeting despite him asking on the flight, in the taxi into the city, and as they'd climbed the several flights of narrow stairs that led up from the anonymous black-lacquered door just off Dover Street in Mayfair to their mysterious appointment. There had been no one waiting to greet them. Murphy had produced a key to unlock the door on the street, then another one for the room at the top of the building.

357

It turned out Dixon had travelled three and a half thousand miles to meet a lady called Irina Valera. She'd arrived twenty minutes after they had. When she stepped into the room by herself, Murphy, for the first time, didn't seem entirely in control of the situation.

'Where's Devereux?' Murphy asked Valera, using Peterson's alias.

'He is no longer part of this arrangement,' she replied. She didn't offer any further explanation.

Murphy became even more confused when it became apparent that the woman who'd come to meet them wasn't there to sell them some new type of clandestine listening technology, but something several orders of magnitude more valuable.

Valera described her breakthrough using the same analogy of her room that stretched around the world, at which point Dixon realised she might be the answer to most, if not all, of his problems. He asked her a string of technical questions and could tell from their short conversation that Valera was on the level – and that she was in a rush to do a deal.

Once he'd given his nod to Murphy, she laid down her terms. Her spread-spectrum code-division technology in exchange for a home in America, a job, and protection.

'If we go back to the States and this thing checks out, we'll give you a green card and all the work you can handle,' Murphy said. 'And if it doesn't, we'll go our separate ways on good terms.'

He was playing it cool, but now that he understood the full scope of what Valera was offering, Dixon could tell Murphy would have said anything to get her on a plane.

When they did get back to America, they realised just how valuable Valera was, and the impact of the events surrounding her escape from the Soviet Union. An entire *naukograd* had been put out of commission, and the KGB scientific directorate had lost its chief. The CIA had been handed a major advantage and it didn't intend to squander it.

Dixon and Valera had made a good team, working together to bring her lab work to life in the real world, and slowly getting to know each other.

They'd spent months developing and refining Valera's discovery into a fully fledged Earth-to-orbit communications system, secretly testing it in Corona satellite after satellite. They'd even included a version of it in John Glenn's *Mercury-Atlas 6* capsule when he finally became the first American to orbit the Earth in *Friendship 7* six months ago.

Dixon had led the celebrations when the communications system took over control of *Friendship 7* as Glenn briefly lost contact with ground control over his standard radio during his descent back to Earth. The official story was that Glenn had triumphantly piloted the *Mercury* capsule all the way to its splashdown site by himself, but as far as Dixon was concerned, his electronic co-pilot had been the real hero.

Suddenly Kennedy's twin dreams of putting a man on the moon and advancing America's intelligence-gathering capabilities so fast and so far that no one else would be able to catch them both seemed achievable. Dixon could relax at last after two years of constant stress. But his downtime didn't last long. The president and the CIA were still waiting for him to come up with a way to hunt the Vietcong, from space. And Valera, as Murphy had promised, was offered all the research projects she could handle.

Dixon had always been astonished by Valera's seemingly limitless capacity for work. She was always the first in the lab in the morning and the last to leave at night. When he'd finally persuaded her to take a little break of her own and celebrate everything she'd achieved he understood why.

She told him about her years in Povenets B, growing up in Leningrad, and everything in her life that had been taken away from her, including her son. She talked about the old dream of her and Ledjo floating in a small boat on a calm lake, which she hoped would return every night when she fell asleep, but still hadn't. And about the single physical memento she had – Ledjo's small backpack – that had been lost when she'd been snatched from Stockholm. Her work was the only thing she had left.

It took a few weeks of phone calls, but Dixon managed to find the backpack. It had been given to the Swedish security service by the Hotel Reisen and filed away in evidence storage. They had no use for it now Valera was a long way from their jurisdiction and were more than happy to send it on. It was a small gesture, but Dixon was glad to see Valera produce a thin, brief smile when he returned it to her.

Now, she was about to unveil her latest world-changing piece of technology and Dixon was, as ever, behind in his work and chasing an elusive breakthrough. Half of him wanted to be back in his lab, but the other half didn't want to miss out on what was about to happen.

So, he stood at the back of the room, waiting for Murphy to show up, and watching Valera move anxiously from panel to panel, surrounded by a cadre of assistants, checking every readout and making adjustment after adjustment to be sure everything would work perfectly when the big moment arrived.

Dixon hoped she felt some pride about everything she'd achieved since she'd come to America. But she didn't.

Valera had felt something like relief when she reached Washington and wasn't immediately arrested, but she had quickly realised that the United States wasn't so different from the Soviet Union. She was still watched, still suspected, and still controlled. She was in the so-called land of the free, but she wasn't. She'd been put to work at Langley straight away and even now she was called in for questioning whenever the CIA wanted to go over her life story again or check some new piece of intelligence about somewhere or something in Russia she'd never heard of.

At least most of the people she worked with respected her and tended to leave her alone. But there were still stares whenever she walked into a canteen or was seen outside the NASA compound. And some of her supposed colleagues were less than thankful when she was called in to solve an impossible problem that had stumped them for months.

She knew she owed the CIA for getting her out of the KGB's reach, and she owed Dixon for giving her work that actually challenged her and for giving her back her only physical memory of her son. But she also knew she couldn't work for them forever, being allowed to stray gradually further and further from her lab but always kept on an invisible leash.

Valera had been generous, giving NASA and the CIA as much of her brain as they could handle. But she was close to paying off her side of the bargain she'd struck in London with Dixon and Murphy. In fact, she'd decided that after her next major success, which might be mere minutes away, she'd wait for the celebratory party Americans were so fond of throwing to reach its height, then quietly slip out, put a jumper and some biscuits in her small backpack, disappear

362

into the great American wilderness, and go find a lake somewhere to sail a boat on.

So, she was anxious as she moved from panel to panel, followed by her assigned acolytes, but not for the reasons Dixon imagined.

CHAPTER SIXTY-FIVE

Knox walked through the front door of Leconfield House with absolutely no attention or fanfare, which was exactly how he liked it. For the first month after the Peterson affair and Holland's return, whenever he arrived at MI5 headquarters he'd always encounter someone who wanted to congratulate him or apologise for believing the rumours and character assassinations that had been spread about him during his suspension. Now, a year later, things had settled down and it was back to business as normal.

MI5 had covered the cost of restoring Knox's flat, and his extended stay at Duke's Hotel on St James's Place. When he'd stepped back into his flat again for the first time after everything had been repaired, he remembered Peterson calling him a hypocrite for using his connections to buy it in the first place. After three weeks of building work he decided the least he could do was introduce himself to the other residents who were starting to fill up the building, if only to say sorry for the inconvenience he'd put them through.

Knox had also been given his own office on the fifth floor of Leconfield House again, next to Holland's and one that had been put aside for White but which he never used, preferring to stay down in the depths of the building with his engineers.

With Operation Pipistrelle still secure, White had vigorously campaigned for an expansion of its scope and use. He also insisted that primary control be brought in-house to MI5 from GCHQ and Atlas turned back on. After balancing the ever-growing need for better-quality intelligence with the increased potential for a breach that more Pipistrelle bugs in the field could cause, Holland cautiously agreed to both.

Holland had also faced repeated questions from Michael Finney about Pipistrelle. He had scolded Knox for revealing the name of one of MI5's most important secrets to the CIA, but he also enjoyed seeing Finney squirm, aware that British intelligence had some sort of trick up their sleeve he knew nothing about.

The two men who had attacked Knox in Strand station and the man who had tried to assault Bennett in Hyde Park had been picked up by the police shortly after their identikit descriptions had been drawn and circulated. They'd all identified Peterson when they were shown his photograph. But none of them admitted to knocking Knox out in Kemp House, or being part of the masked team that had kidnapped Valera in Stockholm.

Knox's first job once he'd been discharged from hospital was to work out just how badly Peterson had compromised MI5 over the years. The answer was, it seemed, mercifully little.

The Service had been very lucky. Knox combed through all of MI5's most important operations over the last decade, as well as intelligence supplied by MI6 about Russia's activities over the same period. He couldn't find any major strategic decision or tactical move by the Soviet Union or operational problem that could be attributed to a KGB mole at the heart of British intelligence. In fact, it had taken getting access to Peterson's bank accounts to establish when he'd started working for the Russians.

As Peterson had made clear to Knox as he stood over him in the suite in the Richmond, he wasn't an ideological traitor. His relationship with the KGB had been strictly based on remuneration, and they'd paid him very well over the years for very little return. Peterson hadn't left a record of exactly what he'd passed on to Russia, but by cross-referencing the timings of his second salary Knox was confident in his conclusion that the KGB had either ignored or chosen not to act on whatever information Peterson had given them.

The only loose end that still worried Knox was the ghost of Cecil Court. Even after she'd been sentenced, Sandra Horne had refused to confirm if it had been Peterson who had been helping the Calder Hall Ring. Knox couldn't tell if she was trying desperately to hold on to one last sliver of power, or if she was bluffing and actually had no idea who the mysterious contact had been. Holland was happy to leave this particular thread dangling so it could be pulled on in the future if needed.

After Knox had completed his report and compiled a list of ongoing operations that should be closely monitored just in case the KGB knew about them, Holland insisted that he take a holiday.

Knox decided to go back to Sweden. He flew to Stockholm, and spent a couple of days exploring the city and, inevitably, having some conversations with the Swedish security service. Their representative was a very tall, straight-talking man called Alve. Knox liked him immediately.

Alve filled in some of the details about Valera's long, hard journey from Russia to Sweden, and Knox reassured Alve that sending illicit extraction teams into foreign capitals was not standard MI5 procedure. Learning more about Valera and her life gave Knox a greater appreciation for what she'd gone through, but he still wasn't sure he'd ever forgive her for shooting him.

He then spent another week driving a rented Saab along the southern Swedish coast, on Alve's recommendation. A fortnight after he'd returned to London several crates of teak furniture and Scandinavian art arrived at Kemp House.

Since the new year, most of Knox's time had been taken up with monitoring the Committee of 100, the direct-action wing of the Campaign for

Nuclear Disarmament. It had spent 1961 committing increasingly bold acts of civil disobedience, staging protests across London and at military bases all over the country. But the wheels were now starting to come off, and Knox was in charge of making sure they didn't cause any damage when they did. MI5 had braced itself for a long summer of watching the Committee implode. But, after the CND's annual Easter march, things had gone quiet. It turned out the Committee and the CND were both almost broke.

Knox's last few months had been fairly subdued, consisting mainly of reviewing reports, catching up on training, and waiting for the events of the previous summer to come back and haunt him.

It had taken Finney two weeks to arrange for Bennett to be accepted into CIA field agent training and be sent back to America. Given the events around the OECD conference he couldn't deny that she was talented, but she also needed some of her rougher edges smoothed, and ideally somewhere far away from him. He didn't enjoy being accused of treason by his junior staff.

'Are you sure it's what you want?' Knox had asked when she told him. 'You're still more than welcome at Leconfield House.'

'I will miss this city,' she'd replied. 'But I hate to walk away from a challenge. Especially one I made for myself,' she added with a smirk.

On her last day in London, Knox had taken her to Bar Italia. After they'd both finished their espressos, she pulled two photographs out of her bag and slid them over the counter.

'Who are we after now?' he asked.

'A going-away present,' she replied, smiling.

'I think I'm supposed to get you one, not the other way round.'

She split the two photographs, revealing both faces, and pointed at them in turn. 'That's Patrick Dixon, the NASA scientist, and that's Phinneus Murphy, his CIA liaison.'

After saying goodbye to Bennett, Knox had taken the photos straight to Leconfield House. A single phone call by Holland to MI6 had established Dixon's role in the Corona spy satellite programme, and a conversation with White had revealed why the Americans had been so suddenly interested in Valera. Knox was fascinated and terrified by what he'd learned about both. Pipistrelle and Atlas paled in comparison to the potential of Corona, and Valera might just be the greatest intelligence asset ever to slip through MI5's fingers. It was some consolation that she was now in the hands of an ally, but not much.

For the last year, people at the top of MI5 and MI6 had been anxiously speculating about what Valera and the CIA might cook up together. Now, at long last, Knox thought, they were about to find out.

CHAPTER SIXTY-SIX

Knox crossed the secretarial pool on his way to the lifts. For once, discipline had completely broken down and no one minded at all. Desks had been cleared and a small television set in a wooden box had been set up in the middle of the room. A large group of people were already huddled around it. Knox checked his watch. He still had three minutes – plenty of time to reach Holland's office.

Five floors up he found another group of people gathered in front of a considerably bigger television screen. The director general's private sanctum was normally reserved for one-on-one meetings, but today the heads of all MI5's various departments swarmed it en masse. Holland didn't like this, which explained his hectoring of White, who was still adjusting the television as Knox made his way to the space that had been left for him next to Holland.

'Perhaps we should adjourn downstairs,' Holland said as he rubbed his glasses with a small square of chamois.

White ignored the thinly veiled criticism and

continued tinkering with the set. A moment later the static on the screen cleared, revealing a baseball game in mid-play. Jokes rippled round the room. Had so much effort gone into the first-ever live transatlantic broadcast just to subject Europe to America's bastardised version of cricket?

After a full minute of play and accompanying witticisms, the screen switched to reveal Richard Dimbleby, the BBC journalist, in crisp black and white. He explained that most of the historic broadcast between America and Europe that was about to begin would be taken up by President Kennedy's weekly press conference, transmitted live outside America for the first time.

'But, before that remarkable event,' he said in his clipped, received-pronunciation voice, 'viewers on both sides of the Atlantic will be given a glimpse inside the control room that is in charge of transmitting the president's words to the *Telstar 1* satellite, which is travelling high above the ocean in its orbit as I speak, and which will in turn relay the broadcast signal to antenna stations in Goonhilly Downs in Cornwall and Pleumeur-Bodou in France.'

Telstar 1 had been launched on top of a Thor-Delta rocket from Cape Canaveral ten days earlier. It was the result of a joint initiative that involved AT&T, Bell Labs and NASA in America, the Post Office in Britain, and its French equivalent, PTT. It was a revolutionary piece of technology, and the kind of potent statement that many in the West were keen to make about the power of cooperation between governments and private industry.

At the heart of the satellite was a unique transponder that could capture and retransmit television and phone signals from one point on the planet to another. It took two and a half hours for *Telstar 1* to orbit the planet, and for twenty minutes of every cycle it came within range of the American and European antenna stations. For that short window it could relay real-time signals between the two continents.

The camera began to pan across the control room in Cape Canaveral. Walter Cronkite, the CBS journalist who had taken over presenting duties from Dimbleby when the live feed switched to America, listed some of the more notable members of the NASA team who were appearing on screen.

'There we can see John Robinson Pierce, the leader of the project,' Cronkite said in his sonorous, southern drawl, as a tall, thin man in heavy glasses stalked across the frame, flanked by people carrying clipboards.

Then the camera settled on two more middle-aged men talking to each other. 'And I believe that's James M. Early, the man who designed the satellite's transistors and solar panels, and Rudy Kompfner, the physicist who invented the travelling wave tube amplifier on which *Telstar 1*'s advanced transponder is based.'

Several of the people watching in Holland's office

started to lose interest and chat among themselves. They wanted to see Kennedy, not a bunch of technicians. Knox, White, and Holland, however, kept their attention firmly on the screen.

Holland was watching out for any high-ranking officials the camera might catch. White was soaking up as much information as he could from the control boards the camera drifted over – he wondered how much of the technological spectacle was for show, a flickering metal curtain hiding a hundred invisible mathematicians frantically crunching numbers. And Knox was looking for one person in particular. Then for one brief moment he saw her.

Irina Valera. The woman who had almost killed him twelve months ago was standing at the back of the room, staring up at something Knox couldn't see. She looked calm. Her face was unreadable – if she felt anything about what was happening in front of her, she wasn't showing it. A phantom pang of pain shot through his chest.

Knox also recognised the man standing next to Valera. It was Dixon, the head of the Corona project and one of the two men who had persuaded Valera to get on a plane to America a year ago. He thought about Bennett, and if she was watching the broadcast somewhere, maybe crammed into a room as full as Holland's office with her fellow trainee CIA field agents.

The camera only lingered on Valera and Dixon for a few seconds before it cut away again, this time to the White House and an empty dais bearing the presidential seal and flanked by American flags. The big moment had finally come. Kennedy walked into shot and Holland's office fell silent again.

He took to the stage and immediately began his address, his speech punctuated with his trademark 'err's and pauses.

'I understand that part of today's press conference is being relayed by the *Telstar* communications satellite to viewers across the Atlantic,' he said. 'And this is another indication of the extraordinary world in which we live.' Mocked-up footage of the satellite spinning in space then came on the screen. 'The satellite must be high enough to carry messages from both sides of the world, which is of course a very essential requirement for peace,' he continued, as the camera switched back to him. 'And I think this understanding which will inevitably come from these speedier communications is bound to increase the well-being and security of all people, here and those across the oceans.'

It was a casual, relaxed performance but the words had been very carefully chosen, and Kennedy's message was clear.

He went on to talk about the price of the American dollar, which had been a rumbling news story across Europe for the last few weeks. However, Knox didn't hear any of that. He was too busy thinking about the president's opening remarks and the presence of Irina Valera at the heart of the Telstar project.

Telstar had been pitched as the newest triumph of innovation driven by America's dual belief in itself and limitless budgets. But as far as Knox was concerned, that's not what Telstar was at all. It was a public relations exercise, a dazzling piece of propaganda beamed directly into millions of households up and down Britain, and even more across Europe and America. He wondered what Khrushchev would have said if he was the one behind the podium, being broadcast to the world.

Telstar was something for the public to be wowed by and for governments and intelligence agencies to pay close attention to. It was also a cover. Kennedy's comments about international security and seeing Valera at Cape Canaveral had given it away. Even with an unlimited budget there was no way the US would have invested millions in breaching the atmospheric barrier for a relay satellite that worked for less than three hours a day.

Knox was willing to bet that the next generation of Corona satellites was already in orbit, sending everything they spotted straight to the watchful eyes of the CIA. Some people in Holland's office would probably think that was a good thing. Knox wasn't so sure.

At the end of the broadcast the collected department heads started to chat again, alternating between how impressed or underwhelmed they were seeing America's greatest living orator speak live for the first time. Knox, White, and Holland, who had all paid closer attention to what the president had actually said, remained silent.

After a few minutes, Holland sat down at his expansive and fastidiously clear desk, signalling that it was time for everyone to get out.

'Did you notice?' Knox asked Holland after everyone except he and White had left.

'We shouldn't be too surprised,' Holland responded. 'And now at least we know for certain.'

'What can we do?'

'We can do nothing.' Holland turned to White. 'Though it might perhaps be time to bring Six in on Pipistrelle and see what they come up with.'

White didn't look thrilled at the prospect, but he had also caught sight of Valera and could read between Kennedy's lines.

'Are you sure that's wise?' he asked.

'Total secrecy appears to be a luxury we can no longer afford,' Holland replied. 'And neither is paranoia. We have to trust someone, and it may as well be our own.'

'I'm sure the Americans would never dream of pointing one of their satellites at us,' Knox said. 'But it would be nice to get a little warning if they did.'

'Quite,' Holland responded.

'I'll arrange a meeting,' White said. Then he took his leave, followed almost immediately by Knox.

The conversations continued out in the hallway, but Knox didn't join in with them. Instead, he headed straight to his office.

He shut the door behind him, sat down, and briefly cast his eyes over the reports that had been left on his desk for him to review. He thought again about Bennett, about discovering her in his kitchen, and the vision of a whole planet living under total surveillance that had scared her so much. He'd humoured her to begin with, then he started to share her concerns. Now he had the uncomfortable feeling that he'd just witnessed them take a very large step towards becoming reality.

He wanted to know if Bennett felt more terrified now, or relieved that at least it was her own government bringing her darkest fears to life. He also wanted to know if Valera was pleased with what she'd helped unleash on the world. But those were questions he couldn't ask either of them.

Knox got up, removed a bottle of ten-year-old Ardbeg single malt whisky and a crystal glass from the low teak cabinet that ran the length of his office, and poured himself a drink. Then he stood at his window as the whisky sat untouched on his desk, looked out over the roofs of the city, and wondered if someone high above was looking down on him.

AUTHOR'S NOTE

The Cold War science and technology in *Red Corona* may seem fantastical, but it's all real. Or at least based in fact.

The sixties was an intense period of innovation in this arena, driven in equal parts by ambition and paranoia. For several years the Corona programme was the apex of global surveillance, complete with parachutes and giant hooks. And ever-more-sophisticated listening devices were constantly being created by intelligence agencies all over the world, though Pipistrelle and Atlas brings a few major developments in that sphere forward by a few years.

But it wasn't just the West that was coming up with new ways to spy on people from the stars or through walls. For most of the sixties, the USSR led the space race. Russia even had their own version of Corona called Zenit (codenamed Kosmos), which was only decommissioned in 1994. The Soviet *naukograd* system of closed cities is also well-documented, and both Kupriyanovich's mobile phone and the BIOS-3 sealed ecosystem were real.

There's no proof of any connection between the Corona programme and the Telstar communications satellite. But, as they were developed so close to each other, and represented a step-change evolution of the same technology, it's compelling to speculate that there might have been a link.